Southern Literary Studies
Louis D. Rubin, Jr., Editor

Yeoman Versus Cavalier

Yeoman Versus Cavalier

*The Old Southwest's
Fictional Road to Rebellion*

Ritchie Devon Watson, Jr.

Louisiana State University Press
Baton Rouge and London

Designer: Laura Roubique Gleason
Typeface: Trump Mediaeval
Typesetter: Precision Typographers
Printer and binder: Thomson-Shore, Inc.

Library of Congress Cataloging-in-Publication Data
Watson, Ritchie Devon.
    Yeoman versus cavalier : the old southwest's fictional road to
  rebellion / Ritchie Devon Watson, Jr.
      p.   cm.
    Includes bibliographical references and index.
    ISBN 0-8071-1829-X (alk. paper)   ISBN 0-8071-2525-3 (pbk)
    1. American fiction—Southwest, Old—History and criticism.
  2. Southern States—History—Civil War, 1861–1865—Literature and
  the war.   3. Aristocracy (Social class) in literature.   4. Frontier
  and pioneer life in literature.   5. Plantation life in literature.
  6. Southwest, Old, in literature.   7. Southern States—Civilization.
  8. Myth in literature.   I. Title.
  PS261.W36   1993
  813′.309976—dc20   93-14001
                                                            CIP

The paper in this book meets the guidelines for permanence and durability of the
Committee on Production Guidelines for Book Longevity of the Council on Library
Resources. ∞

For Sue, Susan, and Jane Forbes

Contents

ix

Yeoman Versus Cavalier

Introduction

The Abiding Power of the Cavalier Myth

In 1934 *So Red the Rose*—Stark Young's fictional account of life in antebellum Natchez, Mississippi—appeared in bookstores throughout the country. Though the popularity of Young's novel was soon eclipsed by Margaret Mitchell's phenomenally successful *Gone with the Wind* (1936), *So Red the Rose* was considered at the time a serious work by a critically respected writer who was closely associated with the South's twentieth-century literary renaissance. Today what will likely strike a reader about Young's novel is the extraordinarily reactionary view it takes of the Deep South's violent and blood-dimmed past. No critic in 1934 would have lumped Young with those mediocre, backward-looking southern writers of the previous century, whose quaint, propagandistic, rhetorical approach to their native region has been brilliantly indicted by Allen Tate.[1] Yet if one strips away the sophisticated veneer of *So Red the Rose*, one encounters a shallowly romantic, artificially embellished, highly clichéd treatment of the antebellum South emotionally kin to works by John Esten Cooke and Thomas Nelson Page.

The precious romantic tone of *So Red the Rose* is evident from the novel's opening pages. Young describes the aristocratic Bedford and McGehee families, who live in plantation mansions on the outskirts of Natchez. The Bedford house is named Portobello in honor of the Virginia original owned by the Bedfords' Old Dominion ancestors, the Randolphs. One approaches it along an avenue, where light strikes "here and there on the statues with their marble pedestals,

1. See Allen Tate, "A Southern Mode of the Imagination," in Tate, *Collected Essays* (Denver, 1959), 554–68.

1

and on the walks with their green borders." The plantation facade is graced with double galleries and intricately fluted columns, balanced by one-story wings "with little columned porches set deep into the garden." The effect of the house, the narrator observes, is "that of a retreat, a lovely and secret place, strangely formal and domestic at the same time, extravagant but never beyond taste, the product of romantic feeling and thought."[2] One is inclined to believe that the romantic feeling displayed here is the secondhand romanticism of Young himself. At any rate one can hardly escape the notion implicit in this opening description that Portobello represents some kind of inward-dwelling rural Eden—an Eden that, as the novel unfolds, will be wrenched into the present and destroyed by the ravaging forces of Yankee materialism.

In *So Red the Rose* the exterior architectural splendors of Natchez mansions are matched by the elegance, the sophistication, and the impeccable genealogies of the Mississippians who dwell within them. At a soirée the reader is introduced to a matron named Miss Percy, who was lady-in-waiting at the French court of Louis Philippe (14). Lining the wall of Portobello's entry hall are portraits of Virginian ancestors, visual records of family trees that extend back to George Washington and Thomas Jefferson (5–6, 48). Even Natchez punch has a pedigree. As one highborn hostess casually explains, "The recipe was given by the valet of Pius VII to Napoleon's valet, Constant, who gave it to my grandfather's Old Philo, in Paris" (11).

Rustication on the edge of the frontier has not dulled the intellectual and cultural brilliance of Young's Natchez aristocrats. These planters and their ladies are acquainted with writers as varied as Condorcet, Adam Smith, and La Rochefoucauld (61, 147). The Bedford plantation contains a library of nearly ten thousand books (56). Almost all of the author's southern ladies play the piano and possess pure and exquisite singing voices. In an orgy of well-bred name dropping, one plantation matron compliments another's daughter: " 'Child, before we know it you'll be wafted away and standing on that bridge of Canaletto's.' She waved her sandalwood fan toward the painting on the wall near them. 'But I'm sure she'd rather be our Carlo

---

2. Stark Young, *So Red the Rose* (New York, 1934), 5, hereinafter cited in the text by page number only.

Dolci, with the eyes,' " her mother replies, delicately suggesting the extent of the family's art holdings (138).

Young's antebellum Eden is not soiled by the intrusions of poor people, laborers, or small farmers. Brief reference is made to "piney wood whites," "squatters," and the "scum" of Natchez-under-the-hill. But we are assured that neither "the rough frontier nor the human dregs of the river, concerned the town of Natchez itself nor the society of the great plantation houses" (8). Such labor as we see is performed by docile, happy, and willing slaves. Each child at Portobello has his own darky for a playmate, and the plantation rings with their songs and their laughter.

Alas, amidst this perfect society lurks a Yankee serpent who takes the form of a governess on the Bedford plantation. This woman is a grim-faced, excessively moral character who, as the narrator supercilously observes, "had an aggravated sense of responsibility that dulled her, as if some final judiciality had been assigned her for life" (55). Naturally the darkies neither like nor trust this northern do-gooder, and her pointed questions regarding the morality of slavery are good-naturedly dismissed by Mr. Bedford as "New England puritan old-maid idealism" (61). Other planters, however, are less sanguine and more realistic about the threat northerners pose to the southern way of life. As one of these gentlemen observes, Yankees profess the dangerous notion that a person must judge everything for himself, that one average opinion is as good as another. In aristocratic Mississippi such ideas are anathema; never mind the irony that similar notions have been proposed by a Virginian and fellow southerner—Thomas Jefferson. Jefferson, the planter contends, "has always seemed to me confused about these things" (132). In Young's novel, Jefferson is fine enough as a genealogical source. It is simply the man's philosophy that is not to be trusted.

When the South's paradisiacal social order is inevitably threatened by Yankee aggression, her aristocratic sons willingly go off to fight for her. Young makes clear, however, that they are not fighting for slavery, but for community and blood. One of the planters expresses the idea succinctly: "You stick to your blood, son; there's a certain fierceness in blood that can bind you up with a long community of life" (151). In spite of the fact that Natchez's noble sons battle tenaciously and bravely, the South they are fighting for is inevitably destroyed.

If Yankee women are portrayed in *So Red the Rose* as sour, narrow-minded religious fanatics, northern soldiers come across even more abominably, descending on Natchez like barbarous Vandals. Montrose, the seat of the McGehee family, is sacked by drunken black troops. Its fine dining room table is splintered for kindling. Its thousands of books, its original Audubons, its Holy Family of Parmigiano, are all burned along with the mansion. In the event that readers may have missed the point, Young puts it into the mouth of none other than General William T. Sherman himself. The infamous Yankee general enters the novel long enough to admit ruefully to an aggrieved planter: "As a matter of fact, I'm ashamed of my army for the amount of plundering and stealing" (305).

After Appomattox the surviving sons of Natchez's aristocracy return in defeat to a city controlled by carpetbaggers—people, we are informed, who "brought in a spirit of assertion, ruthless methods and greedy purposes that was new, strange, and ominous" (383). Although a more cynical reader might wonder what could be more greedy or ruthless than the institution of chattel slavery, Young asserts that it is the North that brings to Mississippi the alien notion that society is founded on "competition without social principles" (386).

And how will the Old South deal with the brutal challenges of the future? Young does not provide a clear or unequivocal answer in *So Red the Rose*. On one hand the author seems to accept the inevitability of the South's defeat and of social change. The mother of one of the returning warriors realizes pragmatically that her son will not be a planter like his father but will demonstrate his talent for leadership "at railroad companies or enterprises that'll be starting up" (400). Yet Young suggests that in these new endeavors the South can learn nothing from the greedy and ruthlessly competitive North. Though it is hard for the reader to imagine how railroads and factories can be successfully operated on the principles of plantation paternalism described in *So Red the Rose*, Young seems convinced that any virtues that the New South may come to possess will be inextricably bound to the virtues of the Old South.

It is perhaps not surprising that most southerners of the 1930s were blind to the transparently revanchist tone of *So Red the Rose*, though one may be surprised by the self-proclaimed pioneer of southern realism, Ellen Glasgow, lavishly praising the book for its "unerring" social penetration. However, what does come as a shock is the way northern reviewers enthusiastically accepted its vision of the antebellum South. One critic rapturously described the novel as "a glass through which one sees the Old South radiantly alive." Another observed that in reading *So Red the Rose* one was meeting and learning to love "some exquisitely sensitive and brave people who lived in the twilight of a serene and gracious civilization." Writing in the New York *Times*, J. Donald Adams compared Young's planter-aristocrats to the great "landed families of Imperial Russia." He rhapsodized, "If you would understand what was best in the Old South, its attitude toward life, the things that its men and women felt were worth living for and dying for, you will find them here, glowing with that same vitality which was theirs in life." Amidst this profuse critical praise, one astute Yankee, the young Mary McCarthy, took Young to task for abandoning his job of creating real characters for the "more routine job of pleading their cause" and for writing not a historical novel but a "poem of glorification." She concluded, "The total effect of *So Red the Rose* is that of a dream—long, luscious, and finally cloying."[3]

McCarthy's critical caveat aside, the success in this century of books like *So Red the Rose* demonstrates the enduring imaginative appeal of the aristocratic South of legend. If one doubts the power of this moonlight-and-magnolia vision, one has only to look at the commercial success of the large number of plantation romances that have come after *So Red the Rose*—most notable among these being *Gone with the Wind*. Indeed, romanticized treatments of the antebellum South so dominate the literary marketplace that if one is not careful he may overlook the occasional attempts by southern fiction writers to treat their region's antebellum past with historical accuracy. One work that achieves considerable success as a southern historical novel is Jesse Hill Ford's *The Raider* (1975).

The protagonist of Ford's novel is Elias McCutcheon, a pioneer who pushes west in the late 1830s into the wilderness of northwest

3. Ellen Glasgow, Review of Stark Young's *So Red the Rose*, in *New York Herald Tribune Books*, July 22, 1934, p. 1; J. A. Toomey, Review of Young's *So Red the Rose*, in *America*, August 25, 1934, p. 474; R. D. Skinner, Review of Young's *So Red the Rose*, in *Commonweal*, August 17, 1934, p. 392; J. Donald Adams, Review of Young's *So Red the Rose*, in *New York Times Book Review*, August 5, 1934, p. 1; Mary McCarthy, Review of Young's *So Red the Rose*, in *Nation*, August 8, 1934, p. 167.

Tennessee. Staking his claim to virgin land, earning hard cash by trapping and selling furs, McCutcheon initially resides in the hollow of a huge sycamore. Yet as he clears his land and sows his crops of cotton and corn, he soon moves into a log cabin and quickly replaces his mud chimney with stone. Through unremitting toil McCutcheon ultimately succeeds in developing one of the largest plantations in his county; and his house with brick chimneys and white columns is the visual symbol of his success.

The Raider is certainly not a plantation novel in the tradition of *So Red the Rose*. Ford never lets his readers forget the rough, semifrontier nature of his protagonist and of his protagonist's culture. McCutcheon and his sons remain throughout their lives essentially "backwoodsmen."[4] The rough-hewn planter's "lady" is a common-law wife, a woman given to him by the Indians who raised her from infancy. Though McCutcheon owns a modest number of slaves, he is surrounded by smaller farmers who possess few slaves or, more commonly, no slaves at all. The McCutcheon plantation boasts a formal dining room, but the master's family commonly eat their meals in the kitchen with the servants. The civilization that McCutcheon and his sons carry toward Civil War is a "veneer" (199) that imperfectly masks humble pioneer origins.

Yet even though Ford's vision of antebellum Tennessee is a downright and earthy one, the author understands the peculiar social ideal that sets his southern pioneer apart from pioneers north of the Ohio and west of the Mississippi. From the very beginning, when McCutcheon calls his claim Oakleigh, he is consumed by a dream: "*The plantation, a bold dream*" (60). This dream requires slaves, a white-columned mansion, and sons who fight duels in the manner of Andrew Jackson (202–203). It is a dream that must be preserved—by secession and armed conflict if necessary.

The destruction of Oakleigh amidst the conflagration of the Civil War sends the elderly McCutcheon to spend his final years in the cabin he had built when he first cleared his land. This circular pattern seems less an exercise in *Gone with the Wind* nostalgia than a wry commentary on the intrinsic worth of the protagonist's youthful

---

4. Jesse Hill Ford, *The Raider* (Boston, 1975), 198, hereinafter cited in the text by page number only.

plantation dream. Still, the dream, no matter how suspect or bogus it may be, dominates and structures the lives of McCutcheon and his sons, and even the lives of the small farmers who willingly fight alongside them to preserve it.

As we have seen, a sentimental novel like *So Red the Rose* can badly muddy historical waters. By contrast, good historical fiction can probe the inner dynamics of a society and generate an understanding of it that anticipates or confirms the most original ideas of social historians or scholars of literary or intellectual history. In the case of *The Raider* the evolution of Elias McCutcheon from pioneer to planter mirrors remarkably a profound mythic shift that took place in the interior South during the opening decades of the nineteenth century and that Henry Nash Smith has described in an essay entitled "The South and the Myth of the Garden." Smith points out that when the frontier first pushed beyond the Alleghenies the entire Mississippi Valley from the Great Lakes to the Gulf of Mexico embraced the yeoman ideal "as a rationale of agricultural settlement."[5] Jefferson's stalwart and independent farmer was the mythic figure that gave most dynamic expression to and most compelling justification for the expanding western frontier; and this potent symbol of rural democracy was embraced by settlers in both midwestern and southern territories. By 1830, however, residents of the newly settled states of the Old Southwest—Kentucky, Tennessee, Alabama, Mississippi, Louisiana, and Arkansas—had initiated a profound imaginative movement away from the frontier myths that had linked them firmly to midwesterners.[6]

This turning away from the yeoman ideal was accompanied by a turning toward the figure of the planter-aristocrat, as Ford's Elias McCutcheon set before himself the dream of being a planter. McCutcheon knew that his goal could not be attained by the sweat of a single yeoman's brow. Slaves were necessary to realize such wealth and power. Unfortunately for ambitious men like McCutcheon, slavery was an institution subjected to mounting moral opprobrium outside areas where it naturally flourished. Stephen A. Smith has recently ob-

5. Henry Nash Smith, "The South and the Myth of the Garden," in *Myth and Southern History*, ed. Patrick Gerster and Nicholas Cords (Chicago, 1974), 122.

6. I define "Old Southwest" in its broadest sense. See E. Merton Coulter, "Southwest, Old," in *Dictionary of American History* (Rev. ed.; New York, 1976), VI, 356.

served that as the nineteenth century progressed, the South became increasingly frustrated by its failure to defend its position on slavery, either morally or politically. Wherever slavery had taken hold, from the manicured lawns of James River estates to the recently constructed plantation houses of western Tennessee, a siege mentality began to manifest itself; and men below the Mason-Dixon Line began to develop a distinct group consciousness. "The collective mind of the South was ripe for the development of a group culture and was in need of a shared mythology to explain and defend itself."[7]

But what unifying mythic figure could southerners rally themselves around? In the Old Southwest, where the large majority of men were small farmers a mere one or two generations removed from the frontier, that unifying cultural icon might have been the yeoman, celebrated earlier in the century. Yet, as Henry Nash Smith contends and as my analysis of the region's antebellum fiction will make abundantly clear, residents of the interior South spurned the yeoman and gave their imaginative allegiance to the figure of the aristocratic planter or Cavalier. The dream of Elias McCutcheon became the dream of most southern farmers.

Charles S. Sydnor believes that the institution of slavery forced the South to face the conflict between values associated with the great plantation and values associated with the Declaration of Independence and the Bill of Rights—values inextricably linked with our nation's yeoman tradition. Heeding the siren song of the plantation, residents of the Old Southwest joined cultural and intellectual forces with the more established plantation societies of the eastern seaboard and, in doing so, chose implicitly to disown their yeoman heritage. "Compelled to make a choice," Sydnor writes, "they denied the accuracy and validity of the Revolutionary doctrines; and Jefferson, the personification of democratic idealism, they repudiated as a theoretical and dangerous visionary."[8]

The Southwest's repudiation of the nation's dominant ideals was a repudiation of myths as well as political doctrines. As my study of the region's literature will show, its people obstinately chose to unify

7. Stephen A. Smith, *Myth, Media, and the Southern Mind* (Fayetteville, Ark., 1985), 12.

8. Charles S. Sydnor, *The Development of Southern Sectionalism, 1819–1848* (Baton Rouge, 1948), 334.

themselves around the iconic figure of the Cavalier, not around what would seem to have been a more natural and realistic cultural hero, the yeoman. This mythic shift in the antebellum Southwest from yeoman to Cavalier would have fateful consequences for the region. The events of 1861 as well as Young's romantic novel of 1934 bear common witness to the accuracy of George Brown Tindall's observation that sometimes "a myth itself becomes one of the realities of history, significantly influencing the course of human action, for good or ill."[9]

The texts analyzed in the following chapters are not, by and large, important because of their inherent literary value. In fact most of these works are clichéd, formulaic, and conventional in the worst senses of these words. But while they do not demand critical attention for their belletristic merits, they remain significant today because of the light they shed on the newly evolving culture of the Old Southwest. Robert Darnton has observed that "individual expression takes place within a general idiom. . . . We learn to classify sensations and make sense of things by thinking within a framework provided by our culture." The antebellum literature of the Old Southwest tells us much about the social idioms and the particular cultural framework that was rapidly evolving in the Deep South between 1810 and 1860. Examination of these early antebellum works will, I hope, serve to ratify Stephen Greenblatt's dictum regarding the relationship between literature and culture. "If an exploration of a particular culture will lead to a heightened understanding of a work of literature produced within that culture," he observes, "so too a careful reading of a work of literature will lead to a heightened understanding of the culture within which it was produced."[10]

9. George Brown Tindall, "Mythology: A New Frontier in Southern History," in *Myth and Southern History*, ed. Gerster and Cords, 2.

10. Robert Darnton, *The Great Cat Massacre and Other Episodes in French Cultural History* (New York, 1984), 6; Stephen Greenblatt, "Culture," in *Critical Terms for Literary Study*, ed. Frank Lentricchia and Thomas McLaughlin (Chicago, 1990), 227.

One

Andrew Jackson and the Clash of Yeoman and Cavalier Ideals

It is difficult for Americans living in the 1990s to imagine that there has not always been a clear and distinct sectional entity known as "the South"—a region that might conservatively be described as beginning on the eastern seaboard with the Commonwealth of Virginia and extending south and west through the states of Arkansas and Louisiana into eastern Texas. Yet Charles Sydnor reminds us that in the early decades of the nineteenth century no clearly articulated southern regional identity had yet evolved in this country. "The South"—solid or otherwise—simply did not exist. States we today describe as border states—Virginia, Maryland, Kentucky, Tennessee—"had much in common with the North." Cotton states like Alabama, Mississippi, and Arkansas, which are now associated with quintessentially southern cultural attitudes, exhibited in the formative years of their settlement "preoccupations and characteristics that were distinctly Western." In fact, Sydnor concludes, it is probably "anachronistic to speak of Southerners at the beginning of the year 1819."[1]

There is indeed considerable historical evidence to suggest that all settlements west of the Appalachians in the great valley of the Mississippi River—whether they were in Ohio or Illinois, in Tennessee or Mississippi—were considered part of a vast region known simply as "the West." These new territories were neither southern nor northern, but from the beginning of the Republic, Americans living in the

1. Sydnor, *The Development of Southern Sectionalism*, 32.

Northeast expressed their concern that these newly settled areas would eventually consolidate their interests with the southern seaboard states, tipping the political balance of power away from the Hudson and toward the Mississippi. As early as 1786 New Englanders strongly supported an agreement with Spain in which America would have promised not to use the Mississippi River for commercial purposes for at least twenty-five or thirty years. The effect of this arrangement would have been to stifle the growth of trans-Appalachian settlements and, in the words of James Monroe, "throw the weight of population eastward and keep it there."[2]

Over forty years later in his description of the "National Character of the Western People," Timothy Flint included not only the residents of Ohio and Indiana but also those of Kentucky, Tennessee, Missouri, Alabama, Arkansas, and Louisiana. These people were linked by a strongly independent spirit. "The rough, sturdy and simple habits of the backwoods men," he wrote, "living in that plenty, which depends only on God and nature, and being the preponderating cast of character in the western country, have laid the stamina of independent thought and feeling deep in the breasts of this people."[3] Flint acknowledged the existence of slavery in southern areas of this farflung backwoods empire. However, in 1828 he did not view this peculiar institution as creating a profound gulf between a place like Ohio and a place like Louisiana. For Flint, Indiana was western and Mississippi was western. Both states were firmly bound by the genius of the region, which he perceived in Jeffersonian terms as that of the stalwart yeoman farmer.

Eleven years after Flint's description, Frenchman Michael Chevalier continued to view the West as a single cultural entity, and he shared the conviction of earlier observers that it was destined to bear most deeply the spiritual imprint of the seaboard South. "If the Union lasts and the West continues to form a united mass from the falls of Niagara to New Orleans," he predicted, "this third type of the West, which is growing and aspires to rule over the others, will take a great deal from the Virginian and very little from the Yankee." The ten-

2. Stanislaus M. Hamilton, ed., *The Writings of James Monroe* (7 vols.; 1889–1903; rpr. New York, 1969), I, 150.

3. Timothy Flint, *A Condensed Geography and History of the Western States; or, The Mississippi Valley* (2 vols.; Cincinnati, 1828), I, 207.

dency to assume the commonality of western and southern interests was as persistent as it was pervasive. In 1846 William Gilpin of Pennsylvania described the movement of the American frontier as a southern movement. "The progeny of Jamestown," Gilpin observed, "has given to the Union twelve great agricultural states." He included, among Jamestown's progeny, Ohio, Indiana, Illinois, and Iowa, along with southern and border states. Indeed, as Henry Nash Smith has noted, Gilpin had reason to describe the settlement of the frontier as a southern undertaking. Those men most familiarly associated with western exploration—Boone, Lewis and Clark, Fremont—were, after all, southerners.[4]

The cataclysmic events of the Civil War have obscured in our present century the fact that, for at least half of the decades prior to the war, all states lying beyond the Appalachians were thought to share a unified western consciousness. Even stranger to Americans living today would be the commonly accepted assumption that the roots of this new western culture were southern. This conviction that western interests would ultimately merge with those of the South helps explain New England's staunch opposition to the Louisiana Purchase of 1803, to the War of 1812, and to the Mexican War of 1846.

★   ★   ★

If any single man might be described as embodying the stalwart, independent, and triumphantly surging spirit of the West, that man would be Andrew Jackson. And if any one event might be viewed as symbolizing the ascendancy of the western yeoman, that event would be Jackson's stunning victory over the British in 1815 at the legendary Battle of New Orleans. Though contemporary historians may offer their caveats concerning the contributions of the American frontiersman toward Jackson's astonishing military success, John William Ward convincingly demonstrates that from the earliest days following the battle up to the present, the victory has been interpreted not only as the individual triumph of Jackson and the con-

4. Michael Chevalier, *Society, Manners, and Politics in the United States: Letters on North America*, ed. John William Ward (1839; rpr. Garden City, N.Y., 1961), 108; William Gilpin quoted in Henry Nash Smith, *Virgin Land: The American West as Symbol and Myth* (1950; rpr. Cambridge, Mass., 1982), 145–46.

firmation of his status as an American hero but also as the triumph of the American yeoman with whom he was associated.[5]

In 1815 George M. Troup, a congressman from Georgia, stood before the House of Representatives to deliver a speech celebrating "the yeomanry of the country." Drawing upon the Caesarean rhetoric of ancient Rome, Troup pronounced America's accomplishment at New Orleans in these terms: "I came, I saw, I conquered, says the American Husbandman, fresh from his plough."[6] Jackson's victory was thus inextricably linked in the popular imagination with the puissance of the virtuous American yeoman, a class of men for whom the general served as symbol.

From the day that Jackson's star first blazed through American skies, the phenomenal progress of this popular and controversial figure was viewed as a western phenomenon. Jackson's frontier pedigree was confirmed when he visited Washington in 1824, soon after losing the presidential election to Massachusetts' John Quincy Adams in the House of Representatives. At a White House reception given by outgoing president James Monroe, Jackson met and greeted the victorious Adams warmly, an effusive greeting to which the reserved Adams could barely bring himself to respond. According to one observer, "the crowd felt the chill and began murmuring about how extraordinary it was to see a frontiersman, Indian fighter, and simple soldier so gracious and congenial, while the experienced diplomat, eastern gentleman, and Harvard graduate appeared stiff and rigid and unfeeling."[7]

Viewing the historic encounter between Jackson and Adams from the perspective of the twentieth century, it is interesting to note that the observer interpreted it not as a confrontation between northern and southern traditions but rather as a meeting that underlined the contrast between hearty and expansive western manners and haughty and reserved eastern manners. This sense of Jackson as the type of the pioneer yeoman is confirmed by a study of the voting patterns that led to his election as president in 1828 and again in 1832. In both elections Jackson drew as much, if not more, of his support from

5. John William Ward, *Andrew Jackson: Symbol for an Age* (New York, 1955), 27.
6. *Ibid.*, 7–8.
7. Robert V. Remini, *Andrew Jackson and the Course of American Freedom, 1822–1832* (New York, 1981), 97.

the trans-Allegheny states as he did from the states of the seaboard South.[8]

David Hackett Fischer's recently published *Albion's Seed: Four British Folkways in America* links Jackson's political style with the folkways of an American backcountry that was settled primarily by emigrants from northern Britain and Ireland and that transcends northern and southern territorial boundaries. Fischer sees these western folkways illustrated in Jackson's political career, which was characterized by "intensely personal leadership, charismatic appeals to his followers, demands for extreme personal loyalty, and a violent antipathy against all who disagreed with him." Fischer's analysis of voting patterns supports his association of Jackson with a backcountry ethos. Rejected in New England as well as in the Delaware Valley, Jackson swept not only the Mississippi Valley and the highland South, but also central and western Pennsylvania—all areas with high concentrations of Scottish and Scotch-Irish settlers.[9]

The American nation almost inevitably has come to understand Jackson as a westerner, a representative of the frontier-yeoman class who, in the words of biographer Robert Remini, symbolized both the nation's "democratic spirit and its driving and greedy ambition." Yet if this popular mythic view of Jackson as pioneer yeoman seems altogether natural, it is nonetheless a view that cannot begin to encompass all the complexities and contradictions of Jackson's personality. More specifically, Jackson-as-yeoman does not fully accommodate Jackson's own understanding of himself, especially his lifelong insistence that he be regarded by others as a gentleman. In consistently drawing on the gentlemanly tradition as a means of defining himself, Jackson was drawing from what Fischer calls a Cavalier folkway, one very different from the backwoods folkways with which he is more popularly associated.[10]

An examination of his life and career reveals that even though Jackson viewed himself at times as a yeoman, and indeed was able to con-

8. *Ibid.*, 390.

9. David Hackett Fischer, *Albion's Seed: Four British Folkways in America* (New York, 1989), 849.

10. Robert V. Remini, *Andrew Jackson and the Course of American Democracy, 1833–1845* (New York, 1984), 7, and *Andrew Jackson and the Course of American Empire, 1767–1821* (New York, 1977), 31; Fischer, *Albion's Seed*, 412–16.

vert this image into potent political symbolism, he also viewed himself in a more fundamental sense as a gentleman. Remini's biography stresses the fact that Jackson consistently and carefully maintained a noble bearing. With the kind of awe inevitable in an easterner who had snobbishly expected to see a bumpkin, one observer at his inaugural ceremony marveled at the new president's "grace and 'composed dignity' which I never saw surpassed." Indeed, Jackson rarely revealed to his public his more relaxed country mode. James Buchanan told the story of coming to the White House early one morning and finding the president lounging about in rough work clothes, smoking a corncob pipe. Horrified by this appearance, Buchanan reminded Jackson that he was shortly scheduled to meet a certain "Lady E from England." When this aristocratic personage arrived soon thereafter, she was presented to a faultlessly arrayed chief executive, who entertained her "with such grace and courtesy that she declared she had never met a more elegant gentleman in all her travels."[11]

If it is clear that Jackson regarded himself as a gentleman, it is equally obvious that in defining the gentlemanly concept, he drew from the Cavalier tradition of the seaboard South. Coming to the Tennessee territory in 1788 as a twenty-one-year-old fledgling lawyer, Jackson entered the village of Jonesboro with two horses and a pack of dogs. He quickly purchased a female slave to attend him, and racing horses to help establish his reputation among his neighbors. Within a short period of time he had fought his first duel.[12] Jackson's activities during his early months in Tennessee indicate that he sought to set himself up as a southern gentleman of the old school. If Virginia and Carolina gentlemen gamed and raced horses, so would the aspiring young gentleman from Tennessee.

Jackson sought diligently to possess two essentials without which no southern gentleman could exist. One of these essentials was personal honor, a quality that, according to the Cavalier code, was vouchsafed by a community of like-minded men. By the end of the eighteenth century the Cavalier code was increasingly prone to mandate the duel as the instrument through which the essential quality of honor might be maintained unsullied, and Jackson embraced the ritual of the

11. Remini, *Andrew Jackson and the Course of American Freedom*, 176, and *Andrew Jackson and the Course of American Democracy*, 397.

12. Remini, *Andrew Jackson and the Course of American Empire*, 37–38.

code duello with gusto.[13] The letter of challenge he sent on the eve of his first armed confrontation is revealing. "My charector [sic] you have injured," he complained, "and further you have Insulted me in the presence of a court and larg audianc [sic]. I therefore call upon you as a gentleman to give me satisfaction for the same."[14] The spelling may be barbarous, though it is phonetic, and the syntax may be labored; but the tone of the letter is so haughty and inflexible that it might easily have been written by a blue-blooded Virginia Cavalier demanding satisfaction at an oak-shrouded dueling ground along the River James.

In one of his most famous duels, his encounter with Charles Dickinson, Old Hickory exhibited qualities of fortitude, coolness, and dauntless courage that even Rhett Butler would have admired. Armed with pistols at twenty-four feet, Jackson allowed Dickinson to shoot first. Though he took a bullet near his heart, he barely flinched. Instead he calmly raised and fired his own pistol, killing Dickinson instantly. Then he walked from the field without revealing to Dickinson's friends that he was seriously wounded. For the remainder of his life he carried a bullet lodged too close to his heart to be removed. Yet neither then nor later did he ever reveal a moment's weakness, fear, or regret. When one of his seconds cried out in horror that his shoe was full of blood, Jackson replied calmly, "I believe he has pinked me a little."[15]

Almost as indispensable to the southern Cavalier as maintaining his honor was attaining land and slaves to support the lifestyle of the gentleman. Jackson was equally assiduous in both endeavors. From his earliest days in Tennessee the ambitious young lawyer curried the favor of territorial governor William Blount and avidly accumulated land. He also set about buying the slaves to tend his ever-expanding property. In 1794 he owned 10 slaves and by 1820 he owned 44. At the time of his election to the White House his plantation held 95 slaves. At the end of his life 150 slaves were in his possession, a number that easily qualified him as a large slaveowner.[16]

Of course, Jackson was more than a planter. In establishing himself in Tennessee he became, in the words of Remini, "lawyer, land

13. See Ritchie D. Watson, Jr., *The Cavalier in Virginia Fiction* (Baton Rouge, 1985), 3–5, 110–11.

14. Remini, *Andrew Jackson and the Course of American Empire*, 38.

15. *Ibid.*, 142–43.

16. *Ibid.*, 133.

speculator, government official, and storekeeper."[17] In fact Jackson demonstrated many of the same entrepreneurial skills that had characterized the founders of Tidewater Virginia's great plantation oligarchy, skills that are thoroughly American and that transcend specific regional identification.[18] But along with his standard American acquisitiveness Jackson embraced other values—such as the code duello, the possession of slaves, and the plantation system—that had become integral to the particular culture of the seaboard South. These were values that would seem less and less naturally American as the nineteenth century progressed.

The popular myth of Jackson-as-yeoman was therefore rather far removed from reality by the time he came to Washington as president. Indeed, his political opponents remained continually amazed, outraged, and frustrated by his easy ability to assume the mantle of the simple yeoman. "The comparison of the occupation of our hardy yeomanry to that of a man whose plantation is worked by slaves and superintended by an overseer," acidly observed one of his enemies, "is almost too ridiculous to be seriously noticed." How could someone claim himself to be a man of the people when he ordered hand-painted French wallpaper for the hallway of his plantation mansion, the Hermitage, as well as thousands of dollars' worth of cut glass for his personal use? Yet this same man insisted on calling his elegant plantation his "farm"; and, to the utter dismay of his opponents, he got away with it.[19]

Given the bitter aftermath of the Civil War, it is not perhaps surprising that as Jackson's life receded further into a haze of myth, southerners tended to abandon Jackson-as-yeoman in favor of the more flattering image of Jackson-as-Cavalier. It is, however, rather more surprising to find a confirmed midwesterner and loyal Hoosier, novelist Meredith Nicholson, worshiping at Old Hickory's aristocratic shrine. The opening page of Nicholson's *The Cavalier of Tennessee*, published in 1928, presents the reader with "Andrew Jackson, Esquire." In the course of his narrative, Nicholson delineates a powerful hero, a man "marked for leadership" who, in Fischer's backcoun-

---

17. *Ibid.*, 88.

18. See Watson, *The Cavalier in Virginia Fiction*, 51–58.

19. Ward, *Andrew Jackson: Symbol for an Age*, 42–43; Remini, *Andrew Jackson and the Course of American Empire*, 144.

try tradition, demands "unquestioning obedience."[20] Yet, the author insists, behind Jackson's rough exterior there abides a frankness and a courtesy "suggesting that under his hunting-shirt he might wear the armor of some knightly ancestor" (28). Thus Nicholson begins a relentlessly developed motif in which he associates his hero with the chivalric, Cavalier tradition.

Nicholson even performs reconstructive surgery on the somewhat dubious reputation of Jackson's wife, Rachel. Her parents, he assures the reader, "had known ease and comfort in . . . Virginia." In fact, the Donelsons had numbered among their friends "the Washingtons and others of the gentry of the Old Dominion" (31). What family could better qualify to serve as the fictional gentry of Nicholson's newly settled Tennessee than a family associated with the gentry of Virginia, the spiritual birthplace of the Cavalier ideal? Even Jackson's love for Rachel is invested with a high, aristocratic tone. It is associated with Jackson's impulse of "chivalry," an impulse ignited by "the brutality of an unappreciative husband" (57). Jackson carries this innately chivalric temperament east, where he presents himself to a senator in Philadelphia "like a perfect gentle knight to the manner born" (194).

Nicholson's chapter titles illustrate as vividly as the novel's contents the thorough manner in which the author develops his hero's knightly, Cavalier qualities: "The Cavalier in Love"; "The Cavalier Travels Again"; "New Honor for the Cavalier"; "The Cavalier Is Homesick"; "The Cavalier in Fighting Humor"; "The Colonel at the Hermitage"; "The Cavalier Fights a Duel"; "The Cavalier Meets Lady Malderode"; "The Cavalier Is Indignant" (9). By the end of the book, one wonders how anyone could ever have imagined Jackson to have been a rough frontiersman.

In his antebellum romance novel, *The Cavaliers of Virginia*, William Alexander Caruthers had made his artistocratic characters of the Order of the First Families of Virginia (FFV) the leaders of America's westward movement.[21] Nearly one hundred years later Nicholson also molds his chivalric hero into a spokesman for the foreordained expansion of the United States. "This whole continent must

---

20. Meredith Nicholson, *The Cavalier of Tennessee* (Indianapolis, 1928), 18, hereinafter cited in the text by page number only.

21. See Watson, *The Cavalier in Virginia Fiction*, 115–16.

be ours," Jackson announces. "France and Spain must be got rid of to the south; the British must be driven from the northern border" (86). The Battle of New Orleans, which serves as the novel's climax, is therefore viewed as a historic moment in the nation's inevitable sweep to the Pacific. Refusing to address the contradictions and complexities associated with linking an aristocratic value system with the expanding frontier, Nicholson insists, as did antebellum southern novelists before him, on casting the Cavalier Jackson, not the yeoman Jackson, into the role of champion of the nation's manifest destiny.

After reading sources as varied as Remini's biography and Nicholson's romantic novel, one remains with a vexing question: Who was Andrew Jackson? Was he a rugged frontiersman and man of the people; or was he a southern gentleman with expensive tastes, a fine regard for personal honor, and a devotion to the accumulation of land and slaves? Perhaps the most satisfactory answer to this question is that Jackson was both men. He wore the mantle of yeoman easily because, in one sense, he was a yeoman. Part of his nature must have accepted this definition wholeheartedly. But another part of Jackson affirmed just as wholeheartedly the idea that he was a gentleman, fashioned in the mold of the original gentlemen of Virginia and the Carolinas. Jackson might have been the people's candidate, whose motley legions swarmed through the White House after his inauguration. But he was also a type of Cavalier whose manners were as impressive as any that a great English lady had ever encountered.

John Ward believes that Jackson completely embodies the spirit of his age, which he interprets as the spirit of unchecked individualism.[22] However, Ward's understanding of Jackson's symbolic significance accommodates only one of his personae—the persona of Jackson-as-yeoman. In truth Jackson's life was more grandly paradoxical than Ward realizes; in it Old Hickory displayed characteristics that were both typically American—in the sense that the frontier is thought to epitomize the American character—and uniquely southern. Embodying as he did the spirit of both the newly settled West and the older seaboard South, Jackson can ultimately be understood as a symbol of his region, as well as a symbol of his nation. Like the Old

---

22. Ward, *Andrew Jackson: Symbol for an Age*, 210.

Southwest that spawned him, he carried within his nature the conflicting spiritual claims of the yeoman and the Cavalier ideals, claims that exerted themselves on the entire region between 1815 and 1860.

Though at his death in 1846 Jackson might be said to have cannily balanced the competing spiritual claims of log cabin and plantation mansion, the Old Southwest, whose cultural conflicts he embodied, would not ultimately be as successful in sustaining this mythic synthesis. The struggle between Cavalier and yeoman ideals so vividly illustrated in the life of Andrew Jackson would eventually be resolved in favor of the Cavalier ideal, pulling the states of the Old Southwest away from an ideological identification with those states lying north of the Ohio and west of the Mississippi and toward an ideological identification with the established plantation societies of the coastal South.

★ ★ ★

In 1830 Senator Thomas Hart Benton of Missouri, lifelong champion of western interests, delivered a speech warning his audience of the dangers of the West's abandoning its commercial ties with New Orleans in favor of links to the Northeast. Reminding his listeners of New England's long-expressed hostility to America's westward expansion, he argued that commerce flooding toward the Hudson constituted "an injury to the people of the west." He also posed an important question for his fellow westerners: "Who are our defenders?" His answer to this question was that the West's supporters were to be found in "the states south of the Potomac."[23] Benton's admonitions indicate that as early as 1830 the merging of western with southern economic interests was beginning to seem less and less a certainty.

Seventeen years after Benton's speech the South continued to lay claim to the commercial allegiance of the northern Mississippi and the Ohio River valleys. The influential *De Bow's Review*, published in New Orleans, linked the future of the Crescent City firmly with that of the burgeoning West: "Westward is the tide of progress," it boasted, "and it is rolling onward like the triumphant Roman chariot, bearing the eagle of the republic or the empire, victorious ever in its steady but

---

23. Thomas Hart Benton, *Speech of Mr. Benton, of Missouri, in Reply to Mr. Webster: The Resolution Offered by Mr. Foot, Relative to the Public Lands, Being Under Consideration* (Washington, 1830), 53–54, 65, 73.

bloodless advances." The tone of this article is manifestly confident. But an essay appearing a few months earlier in the same publication suggests that southerners were using such affirmative rhetoric to mask the serious misgivings they entertained concerning the much-trumpeted commercial and cultural alliance between South and West. This alliance was threatened, as the author of the second *De Bow's Review* article frankly acknowledged, by the proliferation of canal and rail links between the Northwest and the Northeast. To combat competition from the North, the writer argued, New Orleans needed more warehouses and the Mississippi River needed improved navigation. "It is not to be questioned . . . that much . . . commerce, is now already, and a great deal more will be taken from New Orleans to the northern Atlantic seaboard, by way of the numerous Canals and Railroads, already in existence, and others that may follow after."[24]

What the South probably did not fully comprehend in 1847 was that the economic identification of the Northwest with the Northeast, against which the *De Bow's Review* was warning its readers, had been growing inexorably stronger for several decades prior to the 1840s. James McPherson marks 1815 as a watershed year in the trans-Appalachian region. After this date economic development intensified much more rapidly in states north of the Ohio than in southern states. "By the 1840s," McPherson observes, "the tonnage transported over the Great Lakes–Erie Canal route exceeded tonnage on the Mississippi; by the 1850s, tonnage on the east–west water and rail routes was more than twice the north–south river volume. This reorientation of trade patterns strengthened interregional ties among the free states—a development that would help weld them together against the South in the secession crisis of 1861."[25]

By 1860 the South had lost its economic war with the East for possession of the western market. As a consequence of this commercial defeat the region was forced during the 1850s to undergo a remarkable about-face concerning the desirability of western expansion. Shortly before the outbreak of the Civil War, in 1860, Senator Louis

24. "Progress of the Great West in Population, Agriculture, Arts and Commerce," *De Bow's Review*, IV (September, 1847), 31; "New Orleans, Her Commerce and Her Duties," *De Bow's Review*, III (January, 1847), 41.

25. James M. McPherson, *Ordeal by Fire: The Civil War and Reconstruction* (New York, 1982), 8.

T. Wigfall of Texas delivered a states' rights speech in the finest John C. Calhoun tradition in which he contemptuously rejected the notion that some sort of "blatherskiting Americanism" was destined to spread from sea to shining sea. "There is," Wigfall declared, "no such people as the people of the United States." The single unifying principle of American society was, in the senator's opinion, the principle of state sovereignty. There was, moreover, no compelling need for the admission of new western states into the Union. The Constitution consisted of a compact between sovereign states, but this compact had certainly never been established "with a view of colonizing and extending the area of freedom and that sort of thing."[26]

The Texas senator's speech, given just thirteen years after the *De Bow's Review* had celebrated the movement west, indicates the astonishing rapidity with which all the South, including the states of the Old Southwest, had regressed into an attitude of defensiveness and sectional paranoia. From the earliest trans-Appalachian settlements Dixie had confidently asserted its spiritual kinship with the West. The triumph of Jacksonian politics had seemed to confirm this South-West cultural axis. Yet within the space of two short decades southerners were forced to abandon their claim to states north of Kentucky and west of Missouri and Arkansas. By 1860 the South's championing of manifest destiny had come to seem suicidal to political leaders like Wigfall. Instead, with a kind of desperation, southerners were forced to resort to half-baked and reactionary political ideas to defend their region from the threat of an expanding nation. Neither Jackson nor the essayist for the *De Bow's Review* could have imagined what a profound political reorientation the South would be forced to undergo between 1850 and 1860.

The South's failure to hold its claim to the Northwest was thus partially the result of its failure to compete economically with the Northeast. But, as Henry Nash Smith has astutely observed, Dixie's defeat was as much ideological as it was economic. As the nation moved irresistibly closer to civil war, the South was more and more inclined to see plantation agriculture and the institution of chattel slavery as the essential and identifying elements of the southern way

---

26. Louis T. Wigfall, "Senate Speech," *Congressional Globe*, 36th Cong., 1st Sess., 1303–1304.

of life. But the plantation, in Smith's words, "could not compete with the myth of the garden of the world as a projection of American experience in the West." The image of the lordly aristocrat surveying his domain from the Greek-columned porch of his plantation mansion was bound to be an alien image to a farmer from the Indiana corn belt or the Iowa wheat belt. Dixie thus "had no imaginative weapons to supplement [its] geographical and economic arguments for maintaining the Mississippi Valley under the hegemony of the South."[27]

Rollin Osterweis essentially confirms Smith's hypothesis regarding the South's loss of the West. He recognizes that western frontier regions from Minnesota to Louisiana exhibited many common cultural characteristics. Yet, as he points out, "the basic conditioners of Southernism—slavery and the plantation system—tended gradually to differentiate [the Northwest from the Southwest] all through the antebellum years. The romantic patterns in both sections included flamboyant folklore and emotional religious revivals; but the Southern pattern was distinctive in its cult of chivalry and related manifestations."[28] This southern pattern managed to hold in areas south of the Ohio, but it could not hold in lands to the north. There the Northeast's victory was both economic and cultural. The "Great Northwest" would give its allegiance to the broadly American yeoman figure, not to the more narrowly parochial Cavalier.

★ ★ ★

During the opening decades of the nineteenth century the states of the Old Southwest had shared many social characteristics with the newly settled states north of the Ohio. Both areas were marked, in the words of Smith, by "rapidity of change, crudity, bustle, heterogeneity," and both were committed to the ideal of the pioneering yeoman farmer, whose virtues were thought to have been preeminently displayed on the battlefield at New Orleans. Yet by the 1850s the Southwest had come to share with the seaboard South an active hostility to the very yeoman ideal that had constituted the rationale for the region's original settlement.[29] The Southwest turned away from

27. Smith, *Virgin Land*, 151.
28. Rollin G. Osterweis, *Romanticism and Nationalism in the Old South* (New Haven, 1949), 186.
29. Smith, *Virgin Land*, 152, 145.

the memory of the hardy pioneers who had blazed their paths through the wilderness. The region ultimately could not resist the siren call of the plantation and of the Cavalier ethos. It hardly seemed to matter that this Cavalier ethos was superimposed upon a raw and recently settled land just decades removed from the frontier.

The denial of the Southwest's humble pioneer beginnings and the preference for an aristocratic Cavalier design is visually represented by the impressive columned facade of Jackson's Hermitage. It is both deliciously ironic and thoroughly appropriate to learn that Old Hickory so admired the grandeur of Greek columns that he added a false front to the more modest original facade of his house in order to accommodate "columns big enough for the desired effect."[30] The front of Jackson's Hermitage is a fake, bearing no architectural relationship to the rest of the house. The grand portico is like a stage setting, a properly dramatic backdrop for Jackson-as-Cavalier. The thousands of similar columned facades that sprouted throughout the Southwest between 1830 and 1860 testify to the magnetic appeal of the plantation to the imagination of the region. Jackson's aristocratic design would become the pattern for the Old Southwest.

30. Remini, *Andrew Jackson and the Course of American Democracy*, 189.

Two

Frontier Egalitarianism and the Plantation Ethos

During the first half of the nineteenth century the Old Southwest moved away from its imaginative identification with the yeoman ideal and adopted instead the ethos of the Cavalier tradition. This profound shift in mythic focus begs a historical question: What sort of environment did the region provide for the nourishing of the Cavalier myth? Was the antebellum Southwest in reality a land of numerous and widespread plantations, inhabited by sophisticated planter-aristocrats and refined southern belles?

One of the earliest histories of Alabama, Alexander B. Meek's *Romantic Passages in Southwestern History,* provides scant support for the notion that the Southwest—at least in the early decades of its settlement—was significantly aristocratic in its social tone. Those who settled Alabama were, in the author's words, "industrious and practical" people. They were hospitable, independent-minded men who lived together as equals. In such a simple egalitarian environment there could be "nothing like aristocracy in society." The great mass of early Alabama's population, Meek observed, were "not dwellers in our towns and villages." They were not "planters who rule over large numbers of slaves." They were "humble and industrious" farmers, "reaping, according to the primal ordinance, the fruits and treasures of the earth."[1] Meek's rhetoric echoes the phrases that Timothy Flint had employed a few decades earlier to describe the

1. Alexander Beaufort Meek, *Romantic Passages in Southwestern History* (2d ed.; New York, 1857), 51, 52, 57–58.

character of western settlers, and it seems to draw with equal force on the Jeffersonian principle of the noble yeoman.

In a region settled by simple, hard-working farmers one would not have expected to encounter rigid social divisions. Indeed, early travelers to the Southwest were impressed with the fluid social structure they found there. Even the relatively well-established city of New Orleans partook of this flexible social atmosphere. In the 1830s Joseph Holt Ingraham, a native of Maine, admired the society of the Crescent City, with its "constant influx of strangers." He discerned no "exclusive *clique* or aristocracy" with its concomitantly ossified social structure, such as was present in the city of Boston.[2]

Striking upriver by steamboat to Baton Rouge and beyond, Ingraham encountered on board "black legs," or "sporting gentlemen" (gamblers), as well as Mississippi planters "wearing their clothes in a careless, half sailor-like, half gentleman-like air, dashed with a small touch of the farmer" (II, 10–11). The farther from New Orleans Ingraham traveled, the more amorphous society became. In the river town of Natchez he rubbed shoulders with drunken Indians and "rough, rude, honest-looking" Mississippi yeomen who assumed a "'cheek by jowl' familiarity" with their slaves (II, 26).

Natchez was a rapidly improving town that harbored the founders of what would soon be a wealthy planter class. But Ingraham observed that the town's dwellings often matched neither the manners nor the fortunes of the would-be Cavaliers who dwelled within. "Many of the wealthiest planters," he wrote, were lodged "wretchedly" in the original log cabins they had built on first arriving in Mississippi, so that a "gorgeous Brussels carpet" might often be seen "laid over a rough-planked floor" (II, 51). Below the residences of Natchez hill, along the river bottom, one found oneself amidst a mélange of whores, thieves, free Negroes, slaves selling their produce, and boatmen—all, to Ingraham's utter consternation, going about their respective businesses on Sunday morning (II, 54–61).

Once Ingraham struck away from Natchez into the interior of the state, he left behind all traces of plantation society. Here was a land of small farmers—ignorant and often illiterate men with little or no for-

---

2. Joseph Holt Ingraham, *The Southwest, by a Yankee* (2 vols.; 1835; rpr. New York, 1968), I, 115–16, hereinafter cited in the text by volume and page number only.

mal religious instruction and a "total absence of courtesy." These farmers, he observed, bent their wills to no man. A gentleman must needs do battle with them for the right-of-way on public roads. But in a kinder mood Ingraham allowed that the state's small landowners generally worked hard in their fields. He was convinced that, with the help of public education and regular religious instruction, they were capable of marked social improvement (II, 171–72). Though far less sympathetic in his assessment of the small farmer than Meek, Ingraham essentially supports the Alabama historian's view of a Southwest dominated by the yeoman class.

Probably the most detailed and insightful period analysis of southwestern society has been provided by Daniel Hundley in *Social Relations in Our Southern States*, published in 1860 just before the Civil War. Although Hundley acknowledged that the South could boast of a significant number of aristocratic planters, he believed that the North's tendency to focus its attention as well as its opprobrium on these plantation owners had resulted in its ignoring three other classes of southerners, each far more numerous than the planter class.

The class that constituted "the greater proportion of [the South's] citizens" was the middle class, composed of merchants, teachers, doctors, artisans, and, more numerously, farmers.[3] These farmers were largely descended from "sturdy Saxon" stock and were neither so polished nor so physically graceful as the Cavalier planters. Though fond of simple food and simple pleasures, the southern middle class farmer was not averse to hard work. Indeed, he could sometimes be found laboring in the fields alongside his slaves (81, 84, 85). Hundley believed that the agrarian middle class of the southern states bore favorable comparison with "the more well-to-do and intelligent farmers of New England" (91). Though this class was, as a rule, indifferently educated and provincial in manners and speech, its members might mingle socially either with the planters just above them in the social order or the yeomen just below, according to the individual level of refinement and inclination (95).

Beneath the rural middle class was the yeoman class, which was

3. Daniel R. Hundley, *Social Relations in Our Southern States* (New York, 1860), 77, hereinafter cited in the text by page number only.

almost as large. Though this group usually owned no slaves, it was quite distinct from the poor white class just beneath it. Southern yeomen were independent, brave, and hospitable farmers, noted for their acute marksmanship. In manners, speech, and household surroundings much like the middle class, they were worthy in every way of comparison with the small farmers of the North or West (193, 199, 201). Hundley observed that this group was "unanimously proslavery in sentiment," though it was nonslaveholding (219).

The fourth and lowest of Hundley's southern social divisions was the class of poor whites. Descendants of pauper and convict emigrants, poor whites had remained on the debased social level of their ancestors. They were an angular, lean, and bony race—illiterate, lazy, with little or no property. Combining primitive "hard-shell" religiosity with heavy drinking, and squatting on land until they were eventually pushed west by the influx of more industrious and successful farmers, these wretched people were proslavery "from downright envy and hatred of the black man" (226, 273).

Hundley's description of southern social classes is significant in many ways. One of his work's most interesting aspects is its acknowledgment of the existence of poor whites, a class that most southerners of the period simply pretended did not exist. Yet even though Hundley's book describes both aristocratic planters and shiftless, landless poor whites, its primary purpose is to document the fundamentally middle class–yeoman texture of antebellum southern society. Since the only significant difference between middle class farmers and yeoman farmers, in Hundley's view, was the possession of slaves, the picture he paints is of a region dominantly populated by social classes that derive their values from the yeoman tradition.

Twentieth-century historical investigation has largely confirmed Hundley's description of a diverse southern social structure dominated by a broadly based middle class. Howard Floan notes that out of approximately eight million white farmers living in the South in 1860 fewer than four hundred thousand owned slaves, and only 4 percent of these slaveholders had more than one hundred. Clement Eaton presents statistics that also demonstrate the South to have been most typically a land of small farms, not of great plantations. In 1860 two thirds of Tennessee's farms were less than 200 acres in size.

Two thirds of those in Louisiana were less than 100 acres large. In Mississippi 52 percent of the state's farmers owned no slaves, and three-quarters of the white population were nonslaveholders.[4]

Historical studies of the economies and social structures of individual states of the Old Southwest confirm the more broadly focused studies of Floan and Eaton. Thomas P. Abernethy sketches an antebellum Alabama dominated by small farmers. Even the majority of slaveowning planters, he observes, were men of modest circumstances. "The frontier conditions which threw men upon their own resources and promoted rapid changes in station; the relatively narrow extent of cotton producing areas and the consequent proximity of planting and farming districts; the moderate estates of the planters and the lack of exclusive society outside the largest towns; the relatively small number of planters as compared with farmers,—all these conditions made Alabama a state where democracy was the rule in spite of slavery." To the north of Alabama, Blanche Clark describes a Tennessee dominated by a "group of middle-class and yeoman farmers, slaveholders and nonslaveholders, who achieved much the same economic status when owning the same amount of acreage." Clark contends that social distinctions in Tennessee were "based on economic status, rather than on the fact that one group owned slaves." In the flexible social order of antebellum Tennessee, slaveowners and nonslaveowners of comparable wealth mingled freely.[5]

Both early descriptions of the Old Southwest and later historical analyses thus confirm Eaton's observation concerning the lifestyle of the typical southern farmer. "The great majority of Southerners," he writes, "lived very much like the subsistence farmers north of the Ohio River and in the Middle Atlantic states."[6] The porch of a farmer's shotgun cabin was a more accurate visual symbol of the antebellum southern way of life than the columned piazza of a plantation mansion.

---

4. Howard Russell Floan, *The South in Northern Eyes* (Austin, 1958), viii; Clement Eaton, *A History of the Old South: The Emergence of a Reluctant Nation* (3d ed.; New York, 1975), 270, 273.

5. Thomas Perkins Abernethy, *The Formative Period in Alabama, 1815–1828* (Montgomery, Ala., 1922), 138; Blanche H. Clark, *The Tennessee Yeomen, 1840–1860* (1942; rpr. New York, 1971), 20.

6. Eaton, *A History of the Old South,* 414.

The dominance of the yeoman class in the antebellum Southwest was reflected in the region's vigorous and open political systems. Though indulgers in *Gone with the Wind* nostalgia may prefer to imagine the Deep South as a land ruled by Wilkeses and O'Haras, southern historians as early as the turn of the twentieth century were taking pains to emphasize that the planter class had never completely controlled southern politics. Even the relatively unreconstructed chronicler of the lower South, William Garrott Brown, reminded his readers in 1902 that governors and legislators had been chosen in the region from a variety of social ranks. In this political scene, Brown observed, "many prominent men were distinctly of the self-made type."[7]

In his *History of the Old South*, Eaton points out that the 1830s flood of Jacksonian democracy swept away the original conservative constitutions of states like Tennessee and Mississippi—constitutions that had restricted suffrage and mandated high property qualifications for holding state office. By 1850 no southwestern state retained property qualifications for holding state office and all of these states had embraced the principle of manhood suffrage. Through the first six decades of the nineteenth century, progressive forces steadily broadened the base of democracy in the South, producing a vigorous two-party system marked by citizen participation comparable to that in the North.[8]

In a region like the Old Southwest, filled with relatively new settlers and composed principally of small landowners who were often poor and rudely educated, democracy not infrequently was associated with excesses of corruption and demagoguery. Charles Gayarré's novel *The School for Politics* provides a dramatic glimpse of the free-wheeling political style of antebellum Louisiana. Gayarré describes a state in which candidates attract drunken mobs of supporters, votes are routinely bought and sold, and citizens place bets on the outcomes of elections. As one enterprising and cynical voter declares: "This is a free country. . . . Election days are holidays—privileged time for getting drunk—earning an honest penny—indulging in some

7. William Garrott Brown, *The Lower South in American History* (1902; rpr. New York, 1969), 44.

8. Eaton, *A History of the Old South*, 323–26; Fletcher M. Green, "Democracy in the Old South," *Journal of Southern History*, XII (1946), 3–23.

little pot-luck speculations, and raising the committee of ways and means for household purposes."[9]

In Gayarré's view Louisiana politics makes life miserable for any man who considers himself a gentleman of principle. One aristocratic politico describes with distaste the manner in which he must stoop to the quotidian when running for elections. One is forced, in his words, to "shake hands with every low fellow you meet—the dirtier the better; dress shabbily—affect vulgarity—learn to swear as big and loud as possible—tap every man affectionately on the shoulder—get drunk once a week—conspicuously, mind you . . . spout against tyrants, aristocrats, and the rich—above all talk eternally of the poor oppressed people and of their rights." The path to victory is easily trod. "Drop entirely the garb, the manners, and the feelings of a gentleman," he counsels, "and you may have the chance of a triumphant election" (120). A recently arrived emigrant from Virginia with the aristocratically redolent name of John Washington Randolph observes with disgust the Louisiana governor's election and ponders: "Has it come to this? Are free men to be bought like hogs in the market? Well! Well! What will that cost?" The victorious candidate matter-of-factly responds, "As a round sum, you may put down the whole expense as $25,000" (119).

As the bitterly disillusioned voice of Gayarré's aristocratic politician suggests, life could be hard on wellborn settlers from the coastal South in the roughly egalitarian milieu of the Old Southwest; and Louisiana was not the only state that gave a rude reception to wellborn inheritors of an established plantation tradition. Years after embarking on the arduous journey from Tidewater Virginia to central Mississippi, Susan Dabney Smedes remained vexed by the refusal of the Dabneys' new yeoman neighbors to accept their properly subservient place in the traditional social order as it was conceived in the Old Dominion. "The plainer classes in Virginia," she imperiously noted, "like those in England, from where they were descended, recognized the difference between themselves and the higher classes, and did not aspire to social equality. But in Mississippi the tone was

---

9. Charles Gayarré, *The School for Politics: A Dramatic Novel* (New York, 1854), 80, hereinafter cited in the text by page number only.

different. They resented anything like superiority in breeding."[10] A perceptive reader of Smedes's text would have little trouble understanding what there was about her and her family that put their Mississippi neighbors off. Smedes, however, remained genuinely perplexed as she reflected that it had taken years in this new land for her family to be accepted by the community. In both its social and political tone, Mississippi, as the Dabneys were forced to learn, was far, far removed from Tidewater Virginia.

★ ★ ★

In 1841 the citizens of Opelousas, Louisiana, urgently petitioned the secretary of war to establish a military outpost in their area "because of the outrages committed by Indians and white outlaws in the vicinity." One year later Governor Yell of Arkansas pronounced himself seriously concerned by the "numerous outrages" of Indians on his state's western border.[11] These two incidents vividly accent the fact that in the middle decades of the nineteenth century the Old Southwest remained not only a rural region composed largely of small farms but also a raw society still permeated in widespread areas by a quasi-frontier atmosphere.

How could frontier conditions have endured in a society that enjoyed comparing itself to classical Athens and that boasted of the symbiosis of its planter class gentility and its peculiar institution of slavery? In *The Cotton Kingdom*, published on the verge of the Civil War, Frederick Law Olmsted blasted the cherished southern notion that slavery had produced a high tone of social sophistication. At the same time he offered an explanation for the puzzling and stubborn persistence of a frontier ambiance in states south of the Ohio River. In Olmsted's view slavery had fostered not a more refined and sophisticated society but a more violent and primitive one. "The whole South," he wrote, "is maintained in a frontier condition by the system which is apologized for on the ground that it favors good breeding."[12]

10. Susan Dabney Smedes, *Memorials of a Southern Planter*, ed. Fletcher M. Green (1887; rpr. New York, 1965), 53.

11. John Hope Franklin, *The Militant South, 1800–1861* (Cambridge, Mass., 1956), 29, 30.

12. Frederick Law Olmsted, *The Cotton Kingdom: A Traveller's Observations on Cotton and Slavery in the American Slave States* (1861; rpr. New York, 1953), 554.

Whether or not slavery was the chief cause of the Southwest's lingering frontier character, there is no doubt that well into the nineteenth century the region was a rough and dangerous land. It certainly represented a hostile environment for men molded by a Cavalier ethos. Joseph Glover Baldwin's *The Flush Times of Alabama and Mississippi* describes in sharp detail the unhappy fates of those "eminently social and hospitable" Virginia gentlemen who made their way to the new states of the Southwest in search of fame and fortune.[13]

These newly arrived Virginians—whom Baldwin described as uniformly "well-mannered, honorable, spirited, and careful of reputation" (79)—were drawn west from the Old Dominion, just as Baldwin himself was, by the lure of the wealth to be obtained in a region where credit was limitless and "state banks were issuing their bills by the sheet" (83). In the rapidly developing, semifrontier states of Alabama and Mississippi, prices for farmland and village lots rose "like smoke" (83). The times produced a fevered speculative climate in which "larceny grew not only respectable, but genteel" (85). Emigrants from the Old Dominion plunged unwittingly into a nouveau riche society of "vulgarity—ignorance—fussy and arrogant pretension" in which "men dropped down into their places as from the clouds" (88–89). When the overheated and unregulated southwest real estate boom went inevitably bust, the naïve Virginian, who "knew nothing of the elaborate machinery of ingenious chicane—such as feigning bankruptcy—fraudulent conveyances—making over to his wife—running property," sank into genteel ruin. This bankrupt Cavalier, Baldwin ironically observed, had the bitter consolation of knowing that, though he had "involved himself like a fool, he [had] suffered himself to be sold out like a gentleman" (94).

It is unfortunate that Baldwin's high-minded Cavaliers were not privy to the valuable counsel of James Dixon, a vicious slave dealer in Thomas Bangs Thorpe's novel *The Master's House.* Dixon advises a young Virginian about to set out for the Southwest that being a success in the new country depends largely on the initial impression one makes:

13. Joseph Glover Baldwin, *The Flush Times of Alabama and Mississippi: A Series of Sketches* (Americus, Ga., 1853), 79, hereinafter cited in the text by page number only.

If you can flare up, and make a figure, you'll do—but if you just go quietly to work at some honest business, selling niggers or dry goods, or teaching a school, or getting up railroads, the people will set you down as lacking spirit. The very best way is to get up a duel and kill somebody, but if you can't do that, there's other openings 'most as good; credit—if rode fast and made a short heat of, will carry a fellow through until he can marry rich, or something of that sort—but everything depends on the way you cavort around—talk about state rights, and Southern independence—next to hard cash, splurging will get you ahead.[14]

Baldwin's satiric description of 1830s Alabama and Mississippi exposes a lawless and crude society overlaid with a thin veneer of newly acquired and often ill-gotten wealth. Two decades later outside observers still remarked on the pervasive crudity they encountered in traveling through the Deep South. Olmsted sneered at the pretensions of the wealthy planters who assumed for themselves "a special social respectability and superiority." These men, he caustically observed, were "distinguished for all those qualities which our satirists and dramatists are accustomed to assume to be the especial property of the newly rich of the Fifth Avenue." In fact, Olmsted found the would-be aristocracy of the Old Southwest "far more generally and ridiculously" pretentious than "the would-be fashionable people of New York."[15]

For Olmsted the hollow pretensions of the region's newly established planter class were reflected in the discrepancy between the often impressive facades of their plantation mansions and the scant evidence of culture one found inside these mansions. He visited one substantial planter's house that contained no library, only "a few books and papers, mostly Baptist publications," strewn carelessly across a handsome parlor table. Another "unusually promising plantation" displayed all the exterior signs of opulence, including the requisite massive white Greek columns. Yet inside Olmsted found rooms "meagerly furnished . . . not nearly as well as the most common New England farm-house. I saw no books and no decorations. The interior wood-work was unpainted." On the veranda the sixteen-

14. Thomas Bangs Thorpe, *The Master's House: A Tale of Southern Life* (New York, 1854), 266, hereinafter cited in the text by page number only.

15. Olmsted, *The Cotton Kingdom*, 563.

year-old son of the master of the manor entertained Olmsted. "No prince royal could have had more assured and nonchalant dignity," he remarked. "Yet a Northern stable-boy or apprentice, of his age, would seldom be found as ignorant." Olmsted would have heartily concurred with the twentieth-century historian Ulrich Bonnell Phillips, who observed that on a southern plantation "Caesar and Cicero were more often the names of Negroes in the yard than of authors on the shelves."[16]

Another northern traveler, De Puy Van Buren, observed that Mississippi in the 1850s exhibited a remarkably unfinished appearance. Van Buren spent some time on a relatively large plantation worked by thirty slaves. The master's house was reasonably commodious, measuring thirty by sixty feet; but it was built of oak logs. The planter was, at the time of the writer's visit, striving to bring his house more into accord with his status as a substantial slave owner by finishing his log mansion "inside and out, like a frame building." It seemed remarkable to Van Buren that, with the rare exception of an occasional planter's house, all buildings in Mississippi were built of logs. There also seemed to be no barns, grist mills, or bridges, and few saw mills. Though less censorious and markedly less condescending than Olmsted, Van Buren modestly but frankly concluded that life in Mississippi was "surely rather primitive."[17]

Living conditions grew even more primitive when one crossed the Mississippi River into Arkansas. Arriving in 1840s Little Rock, traveler George Featherstonhaugh was accosted by state legislators, who asked him for a loan so that they could engage in some honest gambling at cards. Though they promised that they would pay him back as soon as they had received their per diem legislative wages, Featherstonhaugh politely refused their entreaties. Whereupon they "proposed to play on tick [on credit], sat up almost the whole night smoking, spitting, drinking, swearing and gambling." At about five in the morning two of these esteemed representatives threw off their clothes and climbed into bed with the narrator. A short stay in Little Rock convinced Featherstonhaugh that "with some honourable ex-

16. *Ibid.*, 366, 365; Ulrich Bonnell Phillips, *Life and Labor in the Old South* (Boston, 1929), 110.

17. A. De Puy Van Buren, *Jottings of a Year's Sojourn in the South* (Battle Creek, Mich., 1859), 82, 85.

ceptions perhaps there never [was] such another population assembled—broken tradesmen, refugees from justice, travelling gamblers, and some younger bucks and bloods, who, never having had the advantage of good examples for imitation, had set up a standard of manners consisting of everything that was extravagantly and outrageously bad."[18]

The coarse texture of life in the Old Southwest remained evident to outside observers even as the region prepared to enter the Civil War. The English newspaper correspondent William Russell, visiting Jackson, Mississippi, in 1861, wrote that the capital city was "in the usual style of the 'cities' which spring up in the course of a few years amid the stumps of half-cleared fields in the wilderness—wooden houses, stores kept by Germans, French, Irish, Italians; a large hotel swarming with people, with a noisy billiard-room and a noisier bar." The residences of Jackson sported "portentious and pretentious white porticoes, and pillars of all the Grecian orders." Church steeples of the city, striving for a properly impressive aesthetic effect, tended to be too large for the "feeble bodies beneath." The result was what Russell rather contemptuously dismissed as "hydrocephalic architecture."[19]

Russell observed that violence and dueling dominated life in Mississippi. Again and again he listened to stories about "how such a man shot another, and was afterward stabbed by a third; how this fellow and his friends hunted down, in broad day, and murdered one obnoxious to them." Such stories convinced Russell that, though property was quite safe, "its proprietor [was] in imminent danger, were it only from stray bullets, when he [turned] a corner."[20]

Of course, southerners have always held the opinions of outside observers of their region, and particularly of Yankee observers, to be deeply suspect. It is indeed possible that the reflections of Olmsted

18. George W. Featherstonhaugh, "Rough Settlers in Arkansas," in *The Leaven of Democracy: The Growth of the Democratic Spirit in the Time of Jackson,* ed. Clement Eaton (New York, 1963), 320, 318.

19. William Howard Russell, *Pictures of Southern Life, Social, Political, and Military* (New York, 1861), 116.

20. *Ibid.* For a full description of the pervasiveness of violence in the Old Southwest and a discussion of its connection to the cult of personal honor, see Franklin, *The Militant South,* 33–62.

and Russell were to a certain degree colored by bias, especially an antislavery bias. For this reason the comic poetic description of "The Fine Arkansas Gentleman" by a converted southerner named Albert Pike is especially valuable. It is one of a precious few antebellum works in which an inhabitant of the Old Southwest takes a genial, comic, and irreverent look at the region's dominant planter class. Though Pike was descended from old Yankee stock, he enthusiastically transferred his allegiance to the South after settling in Little Rock as a young man. He would later serve in the Confederate army as a brigadier general. Given his loyalty to his adopted region, there is no doubt that his portrait of "The Fine Arkansas Gentleman" is drawn with affection as well as with humor.

Pike's poem opens with a gently satiric description of the not-so-noble protagonist:

> Now all good fellows, listen, and a story I will tell
> Of a mighty clever gentleman who lives extremely well
> In the western part of Arkansas, close to the Indian line,
> Where he gets drunk once a week on whiskey, and immediately
> sobers himself completely on the very best of wine;
> A fine Arkansas gentleman,
> Close to the Choctaw line!

The Arkansas gentleman lives on a "mighty fine estate" of five or six thousand acres "that will be / worth a great deal some day or other." He owns four or five dozen slaves, and more pigs, horses, and cows than he can count. In a good year he raises several hundred bales of cotton. Each fall he floats downriver with his bales to the great city of New Orleans. Here, after a visit of several weeks, the Arkansas gentleman succeeds in selling his cotton and squandering all his profits. He returns to his plantation with nothing to show for his labors

> barring two or three
> headaches, an invincible thirst, and an extremely general
> and promiscuous acquaintance in the aforesaid New Orleans.[21]

Pike's good-natured satire presents his readers with one of the earliest southern fictional "good old boys." The Arkansas gentleman is

---

21. Albert Pike, "The Fine Arkansas Gentleman," in Pike, *Lyrics and Love Songs* (Little Rock, Ark., 1916), 223–27.

certainly far removed from the exquisitely cultivated and highly refined Cavaliers one encounters in conventional antebellum plantation fiction. But there seems no denying the substantial element of
verisimilitude in the sketch. Indeed the poem lends credence to
Olmsted's observation that he frequently encountered, behind a
planter's self-assured and self-confident facade, "the coarseness and
low tastes of the uncivilized boor."[22]

Yet in emphasizing the rawness of society in the Old Southwest
one must not go overboard. No one, not even Olmsted, denied that
the region contained a significant number of large plantations. Despite the sparse furnishings and meager libraries one often encountered behind them, the immense columned facades were capable of
impressing even the most skeptical Yankee visitor. If the Southwest
had simply been a land of small farms, assessing the quality of its culture would have been an easy matter for outside observers. Instead
cultivated northerners like Olmsted were perplexed by the lurid contrasts between opulence and coarseness that they encountered.
Equally perplexing was the southern planter's confounding mixture
of "frankness and reserve, recklessness and self-restraint, extrava-
gance and penuriousness." And behind the obvious boorishness of
this self-proclaimed gentleman, Olmsted was forced to admit that
there abided qualities authentically aristocratic. The same man who
uttered the opinions of a crude ignoramus was often capable of dem-
onstrating "the self-possession, confidence, and the use of expressions of deference, of the well-equipped gentleman."[23]

Pondering the congeries of conflicting characteristics that Olmsted
observed among the planter aristocracy of the Old Southwest, one is
reminded of the complex character of Andrew Jackson, who seems to
stand as both epitome and archetype of this new class of men. One is
also reminded of the reflections of historian Eaton. The Greek revival
mansions and the slave quarters that lay behind them represented the
maturing of a plantation culture modeled on the older culture of the
coastal South. But it was, Eaton points out, "a recent maturity . . . that
beneath the surface contained elements of violence and crudity."[24]

22. Olmsted, *The Cotton Kingdom*, 216.
23. *Ibid.*
24. Clement Eaton, *The Growth of Southern Civilization, 1790–1860* (New York,
1961), 124.

★ ★ ★

When physician Henry Clay Lewis arrived in the Louisiana delta during the 1830s he took up residence in a settlement that boasted only one frame dwelling. The remainder of the buildings were constructed of logs. Lewis knew that though a city doctor might live "at the top of the pot," a swamp doctor like himself perched precariously "at the rim of the skillet." In this backwoods region the only use of "courtly expression" was to induce "some bellicose 'squatter' to pay his bill in something besides hot curses and cold lead." Yet even though the great majority of Lewis' patients were dirt farmers, few of them would have been willing to define themselves as simple yeomen. "Every farmer," Lewis observed with irony, considered himself "a planter, from the 'thousand baler' to the rough, unshaved, unkempt squatter, who raises just sufficient corn and cotton to furnish a cloak for stealing the year's supply."[25]

The firsthand social observations of Lewis highlight the essential paradox of antebellum society in the Old Southwest. Though the region was largely composed of small farms, though the great majority of its inhabitants owned no slaves, though its culture was in many ways crude and frontierlike, the social and economic ideal that most southwesterners held before themselves was the plantation ideal. As Ingraham observed, the "plantation well stocked with hands" had become the "*ne plus ultra* of every man's ambition who resides at the South" (II, 84). Ingraham noted that large numbers of men, even ministers, abandoned their professions as soon as they accumulated a sum of money in order to buy land and slaves and to set themselves up as planters.

The seductive appeal of the plantation ideal is satirized in Gayarré's *School for Politics.* This novel includes a character named Beckendorf, a German immigrant who has amassed a quick fortune in Louisiana making beer and operating taverns. As soon as Beckendorf gains his wealth, however, he begins to scheme to go into politics, hoping eventually to gain a diplomatic appointment. Instead of "remaining a useful and honest laborer," the author observes he "apes

25. Henry Clay Lewis, *Odd Leaves from the Life of a Louisiana Swamp Doctor* (1843; rpr. Upper Saddle River, N.J., 1969), 24, 22, 87.

the white-kid-glove gentleman." Beckendorf also insists on his son's becoming a planter. His ambition is to make his heir an instant aristocrat "in a country where the bare conception of their being an aristocracy of any kind, in the true sense of the word, is ludicrously absurd" (46, 54).

One hundred years later in *The Mind of the South*, W. J. Cash continued to ponder the region's gigantic social paradox. The essential southerner, "the man at the Center" as Cash termed him, was a back-country pioneer farmer from whom the vast majority of present-day southerners could trace their ancestry. "This simple, rustic figure," he wrote, was "the true center from which the Old South proceeded— the frame about which the conditions of the plantation threw up the whole structure of the Southern mind." As Cash discerned, yeoman and Cavalier ideals had blended irresistibly in the mind of the Old Southwest, producing a strange and grotesque synthesis. "In the romantic simplicity of their thought-processes," he observed, "[southerners] seem to have believed for conscious purposes that in acquiring land and Negroes they did somehow automatically become aristocrats."[26] Every farmer was a Cavalier-manqué and every slave-owning planter a de facto aristocrat. This was an article of faith in the Old Southwest. No wonder Olmsted noticed in southerners a shocking mixture of the genuinely coarse and the authentically gallant.

The superimposition of a Cavalier upon a yeoman ethos is nowhere more obviously demonstrated than in the widespread embracing of the code duello. Henry Stanley, the famous African explorer, was surprised to discover the antebellum farmers of the Arkansas plains and even store clerks strictly upholding the aristocratic code of personal honor. He noted, for example, that a Jew of German extraction, who was the proprietor of a country store in the village of Cypress Bend, owned and proudly displayed a fine and costly pair of dueling pistols. Subscribing to the concept of personal honor was a way of identifying oneself with the gentlemanly tradition, and buying and carrying about a pistol was a relatively cheap way of asserting one's social validity. John Elliott Cairnes, traveling by steamboat down the Mississippi, had his attention directed by a certain "Colonel B" to "a crowd of men of all ranks clustered around a cabin stove." "Now," the

26. Wilbur Joseph Cash, *The Mind of the South* (New York, 1941), 31, 63.

colonel observed, "there is probably not a man in all that crowd who is not armed; I myself have a pistol in my state-room."[27]

Even though the Cavalier ideal exerted a powerful appeal on the minds of nearly all southerners, one must wonder how the nonslave-holding majority could have so identified themselves with the slave-holding minority that they would have been willing to sacrifice their property and their lives to defend the plantation system. Was it simply blind emotionalism that led enough small farmers, in the words of Elizabeth Fox-Genovese and Eugene Genovese, to hurl themselves "into a prolonged bloodbath to enable a proudly proclaimed slave republic to sustain itself for four ghastly years"? The Genoveses offer a more pragmatic and a more satisfactory explanation for the seemingly quixotic behavior of the southern yeoman in the Civil War. They believe that the common opposition of planter and yeoman to the powerful forces of Yankee merchant capitalism cemented most strongly the bond between the two groups. The influence of merchant capital seemed destined to undermine the rural, self-sufficient way of life of both classes. The small farmer of the Alabama hill country might quietly despise the pretensions of the black belt planter, but he would have agreed with his aristocratic neighbor that local autonomy was to be defended and that the intrusion of northern economic interests was to be resisted.[28]

In addition to sharing the planters' aversion to outside economic forces, yeomen were often dependent on the large planters for ginning and selling their relatively few bales of cotton. The planters, for their part, were willing to extract their profits from the sweat of their slaves rather than from the sweat of their small-farm neighbors. "So long as the yeomen accepted the existing master-slave relation as either something to aspire to or something peripheral to their own lives," observe the Genoveses, "they were led step by step into willing acceptance of a subordinate position in society."[29]

27. Eaton, *The Growth of Southern Civilization*, 2; John Elliott Cairnes, *The Slave Power: Its Character, Career and Probable Designs* (2d ed.; 1863; rpr. New York, 1968), 186.

28. Elizabeth Fox-Genovese and Eugene D. Genovese, *Fruits of Merchant Capital: Slavery and Bourgeois Property in the Rise and Expansion of Capitalism* (New York, 1983), 249, 255–56.

29. *Ibid.*, 263.

Viewed from a contemporary historical perspective the subordination of yeoman to planter would not necessarily have been difficult or demeaning. Standing alongside the plantation master and helping him defend his interests was easier when the small farmer felt he was defending his own interests as well, when the planter was a personal acquaintance, a neighbor who lived just down the road, or when the farmer's family was linked—as was not infrequently the case—by ties of kinship with the planter's family. When one adds to this occasional bond of kinship what James McPherson describes as the more enduring "bond of race," the loyalty of the southern yeoman to the established slavocracy seems less emotionally quixotic.[30] Common economic interests combined with a common faith in white supremacy to assure that the large majority of yeomen in the Old Southwest would remain loyal to the recently established planter aristocracy and would subscribe with varying degrees of fervor to the Cavalier ethos that underlay this aristocracy.

★   ★   ★

Nineteenth-century descriptions and modern historical studies combine to show that during the antebellum period the Old Southwest was essentially a rough, rural culture once removed from the frontier. Though it was a society composed largely of small farmers, it paradoxically exhibited both a strong propensity toward frontier egalitarianism and a fatal fascination for the lifestyle of the planter-aristocrat. No travel narrative or history illumines this paradox more fully than William Faulkner's epic story of the Deep South, *Absalom, Absalom!*

The triumph of Cavalier over yeoman ideals is dramatically embodied in the history of Faulkner's central character, Thomas Sutpen. Sutpen is a product of the western Virginia mountains, where there are no black slaves or large plantations, and where "nobody had any more . . . than you did because everybody had just what he was strong enough or energetic enough to take and keep, and only . . . a crazy man would go to the trouble to take or even want more than he could eat or swap for powder and whiskey." From this archetypically American landscape of rough equality the young Sutpen returns with his

---

30. McPherson, *Ordeal by Fire*, 33. See also James Oakes, *Slavery and Freedom: An Interpretation of the Old South* (New York, 1990), 129–32.

family "to the coast from which the first Sutpen had come (when the ship from the Old Bailey reached Jamestown probably), tumbled head over heels back to Tidewater by sheer altitude, elevation and gravity, as if whatever slight hold the family had on the mountain had broken." Here, in "the slack lowlands about the mouth of the James River," the young boy encounters a strange and initially perplexing new country, "all divided and fixed and neat with a people living on it all divided and fixed and neat because of what color their skins happened to be and what they happened to own, and where a certain few men not only had the power of life and death and barter and sale over others, but they had living human men to perform the endless repetitive personal offices, such as pouring the very whiskey from the jug and putting the glass into a man's hand." Here in Tidewater Virginia, Sutpen loses his innocence the day he stands before the white door of a plantation mansion and is confronted by a "monkey nigger barring [the entrance] and looking down at him in his patched made-over jeans clothes," commanding him never to present himself at the front door again. From that day he understands that the social code embodied by the plantation master is bigger than he, that "to combat them you have got to have what they have that made them do what the man did."[31]

Cleanth Brooks has correctly perceived that Sutpen is not a true representative of the Cavalier tradition. He is, rather, "fixated on the planter as an abstraction . . . not as a role actually lived, savored, and enjoyed. He has pursued an ideal of gracious ease and leisure with an almost breathless ferocity."[32] One of the most striking ironies of *Absalom, Absalom!* is that a man who embodies many of the character traits of both the stalwart yeoman and the rapacious Yankee carries a Cavalier vision of Tidewater Virginia to Mississippi, where he wrests a plantation from the wilderness and sets out, calculatingly, ruthlessly, and ultimately unsuccessfully, to establish a Sutpen dynasty like those of the Virginia aristocracy. In Sutpen, Faulkner brilliantly illustrates the strange process through which the Cavalier ideal was translated from the coastal South and imposed on a raw southwest-

31. William Faulkner, *Absalom, Absalom!* (1936; rpr. New York, 1951), 221, 222–23, 232, 238.

32. Cleanth Brooks, *William Faulkner: Toward Yoknapatawpha and Beyond* (New Haven, 1978), 293.

ern social structure just emerging from the frontier, a society that one would have thought thoroughly impervious to aristocratic ideals.

Faulkner's fictional masterpiece dramatizes the fact that by the mid–nineteenth century there were at least two Southwests. One was a region of small farms dominated by the reality of its yeoman traditions. The other was a land of large plantations dominated by the ideology of aristocracy and the mythic figure of the Cavalier. When the mass of southern yeomen took arms against the Union, they were in a sense warring against myths and political concepts that had been an essential part of their own inheritance, an inheritance most memorably articulated by the great southern advocate of the yeoman, Jefferson. But this repudiation of the Southwest's Jeffersonian heritage did not occur precipitately in 1861. The abandoning of the yeoman in favor of the Cavalier ideal is revealed in the region's literature decades before the coming of the Civil War. From 1830 to 1860 the Old Southwest's writers helped to convince southerners that they were a gallant and genteel race that lived according to a Cavalier code of conduct, a code that made it impossible to abide in unity with the rapacious and ill-bred Yankees living north of the Mason-Dixon Line and north of the Ohio River. The Southwest's road to rebellion would be a fictional as well as a political journey.

Three

The Old Southwest and the Virginia Syndrome

In the 1950s William Faulkner stood before students and faculty of the University of Virginia in the attitude of a semibarbaric colonial emissary to an imperial court. "Compared to you," he humbly confessed to his audience, "my country—Mississippi, Alabama, Arkansas—is still frontier. Yet even in our wilderness we look back to that motherstock. . . . There is no family in our wilderness but has that old aunt or grandmother to tell the children as soon as they can hear and understand: your blood is Virginia blood too . . . so that Virginia is a living place to that child long before he ever hears (or cares) about New York or for that matter America." Faulkner's reverent reflections on the potent and enduring appeal of Virginia blood to the imagination of his region suggests that the Old Dominion might plausibly lay claim not only to its metaphorical role of "Mother of Presidents" but also to its metaphorical function as "Mother of the Deep South." In a story entitled "Pillar of Fire," Shelby Foote analyzes with less piety and more irony than Faulkner the veneration of all things Virginian by the recently established aristocracy of the antebellum Southwest. When these newly rich planters built their fine houses, he observes, they named them "Westoak Hall and Waverly and Briartree, . . . names in imitation of those in the tidewater counties of Virginia, though in fact the Virginians were few among them. . . . For the most part they were not younger sons of established families, sent forth with the parental blessing and gold in their saddlebags. Many of them did not know their grandfathers' names, and some of them had never known their fathers."[1]

The observations of these two modern Mississippi writers concerning the nourishing cultural relationship between Mother Virginia and the new states of the interior South suggest an answer to an interesting question that inevitably poses itself when one considers the cultural development of the Old Southwest. If history tells us that this region was in reality a rough and raw society that could not be described as furnishing a favorable environment for the spontaneous growth of aristocratic concepts, whence did the inhabitants of these newly settled states borrow their notions of social hierarchy? A reading of both antebellum and postbellum literature from the Southwest clearly indicates that aristocratic attitudes were not native to the region but were transplanted from the societies of the seaboard South, just as Faulkner and Foote have suggested. It also shows that the chivalric ethos was overwhelmingly associated not with the slave-owning regions of the Carolinas and Georgia but with the more venerable and imaginatively evocative culture of the Old Dominion.

As early as the 1830s the Southwest had adopted Virginia as the model for its evolving social structure. Ingraham noted in his descriptive narrative, *The Southwest, by a Yankee*, that Mississippi claimed Virginia as her "mother country" (II, 192). Because southwesterners believed that the Old Dominion boasted "a nobler ancestry from England's halls than any other" state, planters with social aspirations were inclined to defer to those who claimed to be FFVs, even if their outward material circumstances seemed to belie their assertions of social superiority. "A Virginia gentleman (poor and living on starved lands though he may be) is," Ingraham pronounced, "*the* gentleman of the age!"[2]

Susan Dabney Smedes's memoirs provide ample evidence that those Virginians who immigrated to the Old Southwest took seriously their self-appointed task of representing the quintessence of so-

1. Frederick L. Gwynn and Joseph L. Blotner, eds., *Faulkner in the University: Class Conferences at the University of Virginia, 1957–1958* (Charlottesville, 1959), 212; Shelby Foote, "Pillar of Fire," in *A Treasury of Civil War Stories*, ed. Martin H. Greenberg and Bill Pronzini (New York, 1985), 385.

2. Joseph Holt Ingraham, *The Sunny South; or, The Southerner at Home* (Philadelphia, 1860), 523.

cial refinement in their new homeland. Although historian Fletcher Green contends that the Dabney family "could boast of little or no social prominence in England," Smedes provided in the introduction to her *Memorials of a Southern Planter* an exhaustive genealogy that auspiciously linked the Dabneys to "the old Huguenot name and family of d'Aubigne," thereby grafting onto the stout ancestral tree of the English gentry a more exotic French line of descent. After providing this grandiose account of her English ancestors, she followed with a complex and exhaustive rendering of the progress of generations of Dabneys in Virginia that only a Virginian or the spiritual heir of a Virginian could relish.[3]

Though Smedes was born and raised in Mississippi and had only occasionally visited her family's original Tidewater home, she had been properly taught by her parents to view their native state as a kind of Eden. There at Elmington, the Dabneys' Gloucester County plantation, her mother and father had lived during the Jeffersonian sunset of Virginia's eighteenth-century golden age. Along the shores of the Chesapeake her family had established itself in a land "settled by the best class of English people" (21), noble planters who had over generations perfected the art of living "the ideal life of a Virginia gentleman" (19). Alas, financial exigency had brought the expulsion of the Dabneys from this felicitous social order.

Having settled in Mississippi, how were these outcasts from Virginia's Tidewater Eden to survive in the rough-and-ready social atmosphere of the Old Southwest? By sticking together as best they could. Smedes observed that the only acceptable social connections for her family were to be found in the nearby town of Raymond. Here other Dabneys had settled, as well as "several other Virginia families who moved to the far South at this time. . . . They formed," Smedes recalled, "an agreeable and cultivated society" (79).

And what of the Dabneys' relations with non-Virginians living in Mississippi? Smedes's narrative suggests that those genealogically deprived unfortunates hardly figured in the social scheme of her family and of their Virginia neighbors. The compact society of Raymond, Mississippi, represented for Smedes and her relatives an island of

3. Fletcher M. Green, Introduction to Smedes, *Memorials of a Southern Planter*, xxix; Smedes, *Memorials of a Southern Planter*, lxi, hereinafter cited in the text by page number only.

Tidewater cultivation amidst a sea of frontier ruffians. We know from Smedes's remarks elsewhere in her narrative that many of the Dabneys' less socially privileged neighbors bore resentment toward them. But apparently those Mississippians who entertained social ambitions of their own suppressed whatever resentments they might have felt toward these snobbish expatriates from the Old Dominion and sought to enter the charmed circle of this society-in-exile, or at least to imitate its hauteur. After all, as Ingraham observed, Virginia was Mississippi's "mother country."

Occasionally a southwestern writer took an irreverent jab at the self-intoxicated attitude of Virginia settlers. In *Odd Leaves from the Life of a Louisiana Swamp Doctor*, Lewis offers his readers the character of "Major Billy Subsequent—First Family Virginia," who, we are told, never allowed himself or anyone in his family to contract "a plebeian or unfashionable disease." Billy is a man remarkable both for the exquisite nature of his illnesses and the skeletal looks of his horses. When his son comes down with an embarrassingly simple "chill and fever," Billy dies of shame. One Virginian, however, earns the swamp doctor's praise. Major Smith is celebrated "for being the first one of the race to acknowledge that he was not an F.F.V., which confession, showing his integrity of character, proved to me that he really was one of the very first of the land."[4]

Satire of a darker variety is directed toward Virginia in Thorpe's *The Master's House*. In this novel, slave trader Dixon rails against the hypocrisy of fastidious Virginians who are too sensitive to part with their body servants but who are willing enough to use them as collateral security for loans that they have scant hope of repaying. One Old Dominion squire has the audacity to offer to sell his slaves to Dixon if he "can manage to get them into [his] possession, without giving their owners the pain of going through the separation" (270). "This fellow," Dixon observes with bitter irony, "wants me to buy his live stock, and then kidnap it into the bargain" (271).

In his novel Thorpe introduces his readers to a Virginia character named Colonel Lee. Convinced of the superiority of all aspects of his native state's culture, Lee fulminates during a dinner party conversation against northern institutions of higher learning and touts the

4. Lewis, *Odd Leaves from the Life of a Louisiana Swamp Doctor*, 159, 162, 178.

merits of "Virginia University," which he celebrates as "the fountain of chivalry, of profound scholarship, and statesmanship." The university's refined pursuits include cockfights in the college chapel, during one of which, Lee notes approvingly, "one of the professors lost to [a student] nearly a half gallon of brandy, besides a box of the best Spanish cigars" (154). Lee specializes in encouraging and helping to arrange duels, which he considers especially elegant and aristocratic work. After the disastrous conclusion of a duel in which he has played a crucial role, the community discovers that this "high-toned, chivalrous representative of one of the first families of Virginia" is in fact the son of a tavern keeper whose knowledge of good horses and of good society "was what he picked up as a stable boy or in listening to conversations at the *table d'hôte*" (384). Disgraced by the revelation of his humble origins, Lee slinks west to Texas, where, Thorpe observes, he can "do over again the 'first family humbug,' and look down upon honest people" (384).

Humorous and biting though they may be, the satires of Lewis and Thorpe constituted exceptions to the fictional rule in the Old Southwest. Most writers adopted a properly respectful tone when introducing Virginians into their stories. In Gayarré's *The School for Politics*, Randolph, one of the novel's few men of principle, is determined "to remain neutral, and to be passive" (26) amidst the rampant corruption of Louisiana politics. He assumes the properly lofty attitude of an Old Dominion aristocrat. "I will not meddle with the dirty trash" (26), he superciliously declares.

The Southwest's writers were indebted to the Old Dominion, not only for their aristocratic characters, but also for their settings. Romantic fiction of the antebellum period supports Henry Nash Smith's observation that when literary plantations were placed in the Southwest "they [were] unhistorically depicted as duplicates of the Virginia and Carolina estates on which the convention was first based." A story entitled "Western Scenery—the Legend of Indian Creek" demonstrates this process of fictional transmigration. Though it is set near Louisville in 1800, during the early days of Kentucky's settlement, it describes in loving detail an "elegant residence" whose architecture reflects the "style of an Old English country residence" and whose owner is "an emigrant from the Old Dominion." At the turn of the nineteenth century Kentucky was in fact less than two decades removed from virgin, Indian-haunted wilderness. Yet the story's antebellum author plays fast and loose with history, transporting his plantation setting directly from Virginia to the banks of the Ohio. The fictional plantation house, "seen from the gate at the end of the long and ascending avenue," resembles very much a palace, rising above its "faultless lawn." The narrator, drawing from the Greek revival style that would sweep the South some years after 1800, bestows on his imitation Virginia estate a crowning architectural touch, a massive porch with "fluted pillars" encircled by vines and roses. The river that flows past this plantation mansion may in reality be the Ohio, but in the narrator's fancy it seems to possess all the romantic allure of the storied James and Rappahannock.[5]

The Virginia mystique thus strongly appealed to the writers of the antebellum Southwest, and it continued to exert its fictional appeal on the region after the Civil War. It was as if the Southwest's writers, in celebrating the plantation society that had been swept away by force of arms, found it imperative to continue deferring in their fiction to the state that represented for them the source of these peerless, though now extinct, social values. Virginius Dabney was one postbellum writer who evoked most reverently the splendors of antebellum Virginia.

Brother of Susan Dabney Smedes, Dabney moved to Mississippi with his family in 1835, before he was one year old. Many years after the Civil War, during which he had served in the Confederate army, Dabney undertook, like his sister, to write an encomium celebrating the plantation society that had shaped his character. Unlike his sister, who chose the form of the memoir, Dabney chose the romantic novel to celebrate the Old South of memory. But in writing his novel he did not select Mississippi, the state in which he had been raised, as the setting for his narrative. Instead he chose Virginia, the state of his birth. The Old Dominion was apparently a more appropriate locale for Dabney's story. After all, as he noted in his novel, Virginia was "almost the only one of the United States where anything like a fair type of the mother society has survived."[6]

5. Smith, *Virgin Land*, 151; "Western Scenery—The Legend of Indian Creek," *Southwestern Monthly*, I (1852), 195.

6. Virginius Dabney, *The Story of Don Miff, As Told by His Friend, John Bouche Whacker: A Symphony of Life* (2d ed.; Philadelphia, 1886), 217.

In *The Story of Don Miff*, Dabney limns a Virginia plantation culture that combines an "eminently aristocratic" tone with an "unshackled" and "unconventional" social atmosphere to produce an effortlessly gracious and pliant aristocracy that is superior to any in the world, even to English aristocracy.[7] Dabney's fictional Elmington Hall is no doubt inspired by Elmington, the ancestral seat of the Dabney family. In *Don Miff* the gentlemen of Elmington Hall spend most of their time hunting. When not engaged in blood sport, however, they divert themselves with more civilized pursuits, such as reading the French novels that liberally sprinkle the shelves of the mansion's substantial library. The lord of the manor is not only an expert hunter and horseman, but he is also an accomplished student of the violin, which he practices in a specially designed music room. *Don Miff* creates a Virginia aristocracy from which any self-respecting Mississippian would be more than proud to claim descent.

As before the Civil War, the interior South's postbellum writers shared the conviction that the next-best alternative to a Virginia locale was a Kentucky or Tennessee or Alabama locale that reproduced as nearly as possible the Virginia original. In *The Choir Invisible*, James Lane Allen romantically evokes a Lexington, Kentucky, of 1795, a charming village replete with "inns and taverns in the style of those of county England or of Virginia in the reign of George the third."[8] In Allen's novel the Kentucky frontier is already receiving the civilizing influences of the aristocratic tradition, and the bearers of these values are, not surprisingly, Virginians.

The most prominent Virginian in Allen's novel is Mrs. Falconer, a lady who hails from a James River "manor-house in the style of the grand places of the English gentry from which her father was descended" (194). In Lexington, Mrs. Falconer sells much of her land grant, and with the money procured from the sale builds in the Kentucky wilderness a smaller copy of a "seaboard aristocratic Virginia country place," complete with "Corinthian columns" and a "large library" (335). She plants her garden with "the same old familiar [roses] that had grown on her father's lawn" (336), and she is among the first to import slaves into the new territory to tend her Virginia garden.

7. *Ibid.*

8. James Lane Allen, *The Choir Invisible* (1897; rpr. London, 1925), 12, hereinafter cited in the text by page number only.

At the end of her many civilizing labors Mrs. Falconer can look at what she has built and muse with satisfaction, "But was not Kentucky turning into Virginia?" (338). This is a transformation of which both Mrs. Falconer and Allen strongly approve. If, as Allen rather improbably contends, Lexington is a wilderness settlement that nonetheless boasts "a society that would have been brilliant in the capitals of the East" (341), Kentucky clearly has Virginians like Mrs. Falconer to thank for carrying the seeds of civilization across the Appalachians and planting and nourishing them. Allen's novel is fascinating, not for its melodramatic, star-crossed–lovers plot but for its vision of Kentucky in the midst of a miraculous metamorphosis from wilderness into a replica of the Old Dominion.

As the nineteenth century turned into the twentieth, writers of the interior South continued to view the antebellum splendors of their region as fine copies of Virginia originals. In *A Gentleman of the South*, William Garrott Brown introduces his readers to two aristocratic Alabama families, the Underwoods and the Seldens. But he is careful to point out that both of these fine families lived originally on adjoining estates in the Old Dominion, emigrating to Alabama together and building two "outposts of civilization" in a rugged new land. The hallway of the Cedars, the white-pillared Selden mansion, is lined with portraits of ancestors, just as a Virginia plantation hall would be. The Selden children bear properly Virginian names, like Beverley, Fitzhugh, and Henry. In fact, the narrator informs us, Henry bears a striking resemblance to a Virginian to whom he is related in spirit if not by blood—Robert E. Lee. The beautiful Eleanor Selden lives much of the time with her Virginia relatives and possesses a beauty characteristic of "the type of English women, indefinably changed and softened with their Virginian environment." Reading Brown's novel, one is sometimes forced to remind oneself that it is the creation of an Alabama writer, not of a Virginian.[9]

★ ★ ★

The Southwest's writers probably would not have drawn so readily on the Old Dominion as the source of their fictional inspiration had

9. William Garrott Brown, *A Gentleman of the South: A Memory of the Black Belt, from the Manuscript Memoirs of the Late Colonel Stanton Elmore* (New York, 1903), 39, 83–84.

they not shared Ingraham's conviction that it boasted a nobler ancestry than any other state. This was a notion shared by historians as well as fiction writers. In his 1902 work entitled *The Lower South in American History*, Brown asserted that Oliver Cromwell's victories over the Cavalier forces of Charles II had driven "many of the gentry to Virginia," thereby marking the colony's early history with the strongly aristocratic cast that it had retained to the present day. This was a historical proposition given most convincing expression by Philip Alexander Bruce in his *Social Life of Virginia in the Seventeenth Century* (1907). By the middle and later decades of this century, however, Bruce's Cavalier thesis was under widespread attack. Carl Bridenbaugh, in *Myths and Realities: Societies of the Colonial South* (1952), convincingly argued that the Chesapeake plantation society of Virginia, Maryland, and northeastern North Carolina had been the product of what might best be termed a middle-class, bourgeois aristocracy, not an authentically Cavalier aristocracy.[10]

Fischer's *Albion's Seed* marks in a fascinating way a return to what most historians would consider the more romantic historiography of the nineteenth and early twentieth centuries. In a passage that one might easily imagine coming from Bruce's work, Fischer asserts that "nearly all of Virginia's ruling families were founded by younger sons of eminent English families."[11] He further argues that these wellborn men came largely from the south of England and that they consequently sought to reproduce the social pattern of the rural gentry that prevailed in that region. Thus in a deeply ironic way historical opinions about the precise nature of Virginia origins seem in the 1990s to have come full circle.

No doubt historians a hundred years hence will be arguing over the true extent of the Old Dominion's aristocratic inheritance. What one can assert with more confidence is that regardless of the exact English social class from which Virginia's landed gentry came, people like the Dabneys soon came to view themselves as inheritors of a Cavalier tradition. And, as Fischer makes clear, they bequeathed to the new nation a set of attitudes that can collectively be termed a

10. Brown, *The Lower South in American History*, 10. For a full survey of historical evaluations of Virginia's settlement, see Watson, *The Cavalier in Virginia Fiction*, 33–58.

11. Fischer, *Albion's Seed*, 214.

Cavalier folkway. Central to the Cavalier folkway of Tidewater Virginia was the notion of "hegemonic liberty"—the idea that liberty does not belong to all men equally and that the higher one's social status the more liberty one has a right to possess. Like the seventeenth- and eighteenth-century gentry of the south of England, the Virginia gentry saw the world as "a hierarchy in which people were ranked according to many degrees of unfreedom, and they received their rank by the operation of fortune."[12]

Clearly this Cavalier folkway was deeply at odds with the most fundamentally American ideas of freedom. And Fischer shows how it quickly came into conflict with the backcountry folkway. Interior sections of America settled by men from the north of Britain developed the profoundly different notion of "natural freedom"—a state that every man desires and must possess, regardless of his social origin. The backcountry folkway supported the idea of minimal government and allowed scant leeway for dissent or for the complexities of social compromise. It tended to make the brutally simple link between social status and power, and between power and the accumulation of wealth.[13] In short, the backcountry folkway embodied all the qualities so successfully championed by that great and charismatic Scotch-Irish leader, Andrew Jackson.

The relation of Virginia's Cavalier folkway to the cultural development of the Old Southwest is therefore bewilderingly complex and paradoxical. The natural development of southwestern culture was along the lines of the backcountry folkway. Few who arrived in the region carried with them the kinds of hierarchical notions that characterized the founders of Tidewater Virginia's landed gentry. Early accounts of the Old Southwest reveal an addiction to individual freedom in the most harsh and violent tradition of the backcountry. When the region turned to Virginia as a pattern for its social organization, it was, without realizing the full cultural implications, seeking to superimpose a cultural pattern fundamentally and even grotesquely at odds with the backcountry pattern natural to it.

Faulkner may have mused on the Virginia mystique with misty-eyed sentiment before his Charlottesville audience. But in novels

12. *Ibid.*, 412.
13. *Ibid.*, 777–82.

such as *Absalom, Absalom!* he saw with complete clarity the sometimes humorous, sometimes tragically grotesque effects of the
Southwest's addiction to this mystique. The Virginia syndrome
would not produce the harmonious social order that the Southwest
imagined it saw in the Old Dominion and that it so desperately desired for itself. The region's writers could fashion fantastic Tidewater
replicas and pretend they had been transposed to the new land west of
the Appalachians. But the Dabneys perhaps knew best of all that pre-
tending would never make the Old Southwest another Virginia.

Four

Southwest Humor, Plantation Fiction, and the Generic Cordon Sanitaire

As they turned insistently toward Virginia for their fictional inspiration, the writers of the Old Southwest's plantation romances implicitly chose to ignore a humorous narrative tradition that was thoroughly indigenous to their region. While romancers were creating
plantations inhabited by idealized aristocratic characters, writers of
southwest humor, in stories that anticipated many of the approaches
of the postbellum realistic movement, were portraying the varied life
of the backwoodsman—from hunts, dances, and camp meetings to
drinking bouts, gambling encounters, and outrageous frontier
pranks. Most significantly these writers were rendering the life of the
southwestern frontier in the fresh and metaphorically vivid language
of the yeoman. When newly elected militia captain Simon Suggs
made this wonderful pronouncement—"Let who will run, gentlemen, Simon Suggs will allers be found sticking thar, like a tick under
a cow's belly"—he was in a sense proclaiming a fictional declaration
of independence from the stylistic constraints of formal Old World
English and articulating a new style of fiction writing in America that
would come to full fruition in the works of writers like Mark Twain,
Faulkner, and John Steinbeck.[1]

It has often been acknowledged that southwest humor writing
clearly and significantly influenced later American fiction, but the
influence of this writing on antebellum southern literature is consid-

---

1. Johnson Jones Hooper, "Simon Becomes Captain," in *Humor of the Old Southwest*, ed. Hennig Cohen and William B. Dillingham (Boston, 1964), 230.

erably harder to detect. What was the relation between this backwoods tradition and a contemporaneously developing plantation tradition that articulated an aristocratic mythic pattern for the Old Southwest? If the region was indeed in the process of abandoning its Jeffersonian yeoman inheritance in favor of a Cavalier ethos, how can one explain the simultaneous flourishing of a literary tradition that, on its face, would seem to have nothing in common with the plantation tradition and, indeed, would seem to stand in hostile opposition to it?

One important observation about southwest humor that helps clarify its relation to plantation fiction has been made by Walter Blair, who points out that these exuberant depictions of the life of the southern plain folk were never judged by the literary establishment to be properly or seriously belletristic. The primary outlet for these tales—in addition to newspapers like the New Orleans *Picayune* and the St. Louis *Reveille*—was a New York weekly edited by William T. Porter called the *Spirit of the Times* (1831–1861). This periodical styled itself as a "Chronicle of the Turf, Agriculture, Field Sports, Literature, and the Stage." Providing a quirky mix of the contents of magazines as varied as today's *Argosy, Field and Stream,* and *Esquire,* the *Spirit of the Times* was characterized through all its varied contributions by "a racy masculine flavor."[2]

The association of southwest humor writing with sporting magazines thus determined the marginal role it would play on the contemporary cultural scene. A story that appeared in Porter's weekly would have had about as much chance of being taken seriously by nineteenth-century literati as an essay by Roy Blount would have today of being published in the *Yale Review.* Judged by the standards of nineteenth-century literary tastes, southwest humorists were simply not considered legitimate writers. Though the subject matter and language of their humorous tales might be construed as undermining the Deep South's view of itself as a highly cultivated replica of the Old Dominion, the very fact that they were relegated to the pages of sporting magazines made them essentially harmless and irrelevant. The view of the Southwest that would achieve widest literary currency would be one acceptable to the fictional palate of the nation's serious,

2. Walter Blair, *Native American Humor, 1800–1900* (New York, 1937), 82.

genteel, middle-class readers; and this view was most successfully and most widely purveyed by writers of plantation romances. The Southwest's humor writers could indulge in entertaining readers with portraits of boisterous southern bumpkins as long as the readers of these sketches were safely drawn from a masculine literary nether-world.

If the hairy-chested reader of southwest humor was inclined to forget—amidst the riot of colorful southern dialect and violent, bawdy, and burlesque action—that the region was, after all, governed by fundamentally aristocratic principles, a properly genteel frame-work narrator was usually present at the end of the story to remind him of this fact. As Hennig Cohen and William Dillingham have observed, the writers of these humor sketches were as aware as other southerners that their region was subject to the increasingly unsympathetic judgment of northern readers. They wanted to demonstrate in these tales their pride in the colorful and vivid plain folk of their region. But they also wanted the reader to recognize that they themselves were gentlemen. Therefore they usually adopted the detached authorial perspective of a framework narrator who speaks in the measured tones of the southern aristocrat, highlighting the contrast between that aristocrat's formal style and the colorful but crude dialect of the story's plain characters. "The Southwest humorist wanted to laugh at the earthy life around him and to enjoy it," Cohen and Dillingham write, "but he did not want to be identified with it. Like the romantics, he recognized the existence of the more humble aspects of life; but he had no desire to cast his lot with the yokels."[3]

The distancing provided by an aristocratic framework narrative was reinforced by the distinctly conservative, Whiggish political tone with which these narrators frequently invested their stories. Kenneth Lynn points out that the framework device provided a kind of "cordon sanitaire" point of view that enabled the genteel story-teller, as the embodiment of social harmony and order, to contain and control the boisterous frontier life that he described with such zest. Cohen and Dillingham similarly contend that the humorists' "amused observations on the outspoken, crude, and often illiterate democratic man reveal a persistent if sometimes only-half-conscious

3. Cohen and Dillingham, eds., *Humor of the Old Southwest*, xvi.

feeling that while these ring-tailed roarers had their virtues, they could not be trusted to run the country."[4]

The Whiggish sentiments that one often encounters in southwest humor sketches are nowhere more obviously displayed than in Augustus Baldwin Longstreet's "Darby, the Politician." In this tale Darby Anvil, a prosperous blacksmith of western Georgia, determines to run for office in spite of the attempts of several lawyers to dissuade him. "This is a free country, in which every man has a right to do as he pleases," he proclaims, "and 'cording to their chat nobody ha'nt got no right to be candidates but lawyers. If that's the chat, I don't know what our Rev'lution was for, and I fit in it too." Darby's reflections on the unfairness of lawyers' dominating the nation's political processes still touch a responsive chord in many an American breast, and the reader is indeed inclined to be pleased when the plainspoken protagonist wins his election. But, as it turns out, Darby is no James Stewart; and Longstreet is emphatically not a nineteenth-century version of Frank Capra. Darby ultimately reveals himself to be not a noble Jeffersonian blacksmith-turned-leader but rather a stupid know-nothing and do-nothing who becomes so fatally attracted to politics that he ignores his business and allows it to go to wrack and ruin. Unfortunately the damage is not limited to Darby's blacksmith shop or to his constituency. "Encouraged by his success," Longstreet's supercilious narrator observes, "worthless candidates sprung up in every county. If their presumption was rebuked, they silenced the reprover and repressed their own shame with 'I know that I am better qualified than Darby Anvil.'"[5]

Though it is set in interior Georgia, Longstreet's story could just as easily be placed in Alabama, in Mississippi, or in any other part of the Old Southwest. It describes a roughhewn society that is not governed by the right people (lawyers and planters) because apparently there are not enough of these right people to impose their will on the masses. Longstreet's Whiggish evaluation of the southwest yeoman is thoroughly unflattering; for make no mistake, Darby is a yeoman.

4. Kenneth S. Lynn, *Mark Twain and Southwestern Humor* (Boston, 1959), 68; Cohen and Dillingham, eds., *Humor of the Old Southwest,* xxiii–xxiv.

5. Augustus Baldwin Longstreet, "Darby, the Politician," in Longstreet, *Stories with a Moral, Humorous and Descriptive of Southern Life a Century Ago,* ed. Fitz R. Longstreet (Philadelphia, 1912), 69, 86.

He is a successful blacksmith who earns a good living from the sweat of his brow, not a shiftless redneck. Yet in this story Longstreet comes perilously close to equating yeoman with redneck. Darby is a conspicuously ignorant man who destructively derides men of intelligence and sophistication, and corrupts Jeffersonian principles to justify the elevation into the political sphere of the relentlessly quotidian rather than of the naturally talented. One feels after reading "Darby, the Politician" that the only yeoman Longstreet would fully respect would be the yeoman who held a proper veneration for his betters, like those docile Virginia farmers who knew their social place and whom Smedes sentimentally evoked in her *Memorials of a Southern Planter*.

The insistently conservative tone of "Darby, the Politician" by no means characterizes all southwest humor sketches, but one encounters it frequently enough. Joseph Glover Baldwin shared Longstreet's distrust of Jeffersonian idealism. In *The Flush Times of Alabama and Mississippi* he satirized a political system in which voters and officeholders alike rudely burlesqued Jefferson's concept of an informed electorate made up of civic-minded freeholders. He observed that justices of the peace, sheriffs, and clerks lived in "as unsophisticated ignorance of [legal] conventionalities as would be desired by J. J. Rousseau" and that these estimable officials were elected by "people who neither knew nor cared whether they were qualified or not" (56).

Longstreet and Baldwin are certainly more conservative in their fictional posture than other southwest humorists. Perhaps for this reason not all critics have been comfortable with the blanket characterization of this writing as Whiggish. Clement Eaton believes that these tales have provided valuable insight into the manners and mores of the rural southern middle class. And Merrill Maguire Skaggs has argued that there are numerous strong representations of plain folk in southwest humor stories. "While the participants in all these activities described by Southwestern humorists are often crude, rough, vulgar, and callous," she concludes, "they nevertheless assume their own worth, their equality with others."[6] Reading a reasonably generous selection of these tales, however, leads one to won-

6. Clement Eaton, *The Mind of the Old South* (Baton Rouge, 1964), 101–18; Merrill Maguire Skaggs, *The Folk of Southern Fiction* (Athens, Ga., 1972), 20, 35.

der just how much real equality the often-present Cavalier frame-work narrator is willing to allow the yeoman characters whom he presents to his readers.

Harden Taliaferro's "Ham Rachel" is a good exemplar of the notion that one treads on shifty, soft, and uncertain fictional terrain when he considers narrative tone in southwest humor writing. Skaggs uses this story to argue her case for the sympathetic treatment of yeomen by the region's humorists, but a careful reading suggests that "sympathetic" is only one of a number of different adjectives that could be profitably applied to describe the story's tone.

At the opening of "Ham Rachel" the narrator announces with humorous portentousness that it was his " 'manifest destiny' to spend a night in Barbour County [Alabama] in 1845." Though Taliaferro's story is set at the "very good-looking house" of a planter, its primary focus falls not on the owner but rather on the man who escorts the drunken master home from town and remains to dominate the dinner table conversation—a yeoman named Ham Rachel. The narrator is so intent on maintaining a safe social distance between himself and this garrulous and insistently familiar farmer that even the normally impervious Ham detects his standoffishness. "You're too durned stiff and pertic'ler," he frankly admonishes him. "Ham Rachel loves fur a man to be as plain as an old shoe, and as thick as cow-peas in thar hull." The narrator's polite disdain, however, cannot deeply or permanently offend the inveterately friendly and confident title character. After a night spent enduring Ham's stentorian snoring, the narrator is condemned to ride with the loquacious yeoman as far as his farm, listening all the while to a ceaseless "diarrhea of words." To prove there are no hard feelings between them, Ham invites the narrator to stay with him for a week. He guarantees that he will enjoy himself: "You may sing, pray, dance, drink, or do any thing else at Ham Rachel's." The narrator carefully responds, "Your generosity is great; but my business is quite pressing, and I must be going."[7]

At the conclusion of "Ham Rachel" many readers will feel that Taliaferro's rather stiff and formal narrator could only have been improved by a week's stay on Ham's farm. Indeed, the more we question

7. Harden E. Taliaferro, "Ham Rachel, of Alabama," in *Humor of the Old South-west*, ed. Cohen and Dillingham, 304, 306, 309.

the narrator's stiffness and consequently the reliability of his judgment, the more we may be inclined to view him, not Ham, as the ultimate object of the story's irony. Skaggs is accurate to a point when she describes the attitude toward the yeoman character as sympathetic. However, there remain the questions of just how much Taliaferro consciously intended to direct his irony away from Ham and toward his gentlemanly narrator, and of just how much of this complex irony-within-irony either the author or his nineteenth-century readers would have been aware.

Taliaferro would have possessed a truly sophisticated and radical literary imagination had he been bold enough in his story to suggest that the real idiot of the piece is its aristocratic narrator. But Taliaferro's text indicates that he is not willing to go so far. Ham is a colorful, hospitable, unpretentious man, and his lack of pretension certainly foils the narrator's rather unpleasant streak of snobbishness. But in other respects he seems to be the legitimate object of that narrator's amused condescension. He is portrayed unambiguously as an inadequately bred loudmouth who does not know when to shut up—at the dinner table or anywhere else—and who afflicts the narrator as thoroughly with his diarrhea of talking as he torments him during the night with his loud and insistent snoring. Taliaferro's yeoman snores; but one imagines his gentleman narrator would certainly not, at least not in the indecorous fashion of the coarse title character. Neither does he have the talent to describe adequately Ham's performance. As he archly observes, "no renowned artist, graphic pen, nor gifted music composer" could do justice to the sounds generated that evening. In this passage the lightly condescending tone directed by a southern gentleman toward a specimen of the plain folk is not qualified by the author's deeper underlying irony. At crucial points in his story Taliaferro deems it appropriate to draw a clear social line between the yeoman and his aristocratic narrator.

In "Ham Rachel," Taliaferro was unwilling to subject the conventional southern notion of the superiority of Cavalier to yeoman to a complex irony that would have been insurrectionary in its social implications. In fact contemporary readers may see in the story irony that the author never consciously intended and that his lowbrow readers could not have imagined. Though Ham is a generally sympathetic character, there remains a palpably patronizing element in the story's tone. At a crucial point author and narrator speak as one; both, in the words of Cohen and Dillingham, "liked the folk," but both ultimately realized the necessity of maintaining "a proper distance."[8]

Stories like "Ham Rachel" show why southwesterners concerned about their region's image in the outside world need not have worried about the humorous frontier sketch. The tales were safely relegated to the pages of newspapers and lowly sporting magazines. And even had they by some odd mischance found their way into publications like the *North American Review*, exponents of the plantation tradition need not have been unduly discomfited. Though they described the rough and violent texture of life in the Southwest and though they were dominated by plain-speaking yeoman types, these works were not hostile to the plantation tradition. Indeed, the narrators who usually shaped and framed the stories were clearly inheritors of the Cavalier ethos. These aristocratic observers guaranteed that even the most sympathetic treatment of a yeoman character would retain a just-detected edge of condescension, assuring both northern and southern readers that in the Old Southwest the yeoman remained in his proper social place. The hierarchical plantation system might come under assault in the egalitarian social atmosphere of the interior South, but most southwest humor sketches left the reader with the distinct impression that traditional order ultimately prevailed.

Yet what about those humorists—George Washington Harris chief among them—who abandoned the narrative framework device altogether and allowed their stories to be told directly by characters as potent in their rascality as Sut Lovingood? In examining Harris' work Edmund Wilson detected something remotely subversive in it, and he speculated that in these comic and often grotesque stories of Tennessee mountain life Harris had felt the need "to counterbalance those idylls of the old regime by Kennedy, Caruthers and Cooke and the chivalrous idealism of Sidney Lanier."[9] But how could Harris have intended to subvert the idealized moonlight-and-magnolia plantation South when he never took the pains to make one reference to that romantic tradition, in either a serious or an ironic vein, in any of his Sut Lovingood stories? What strikes the reader about Harris' work

8. Cohen and Dillingham, eds., *Humor of the Old Southwest*, xxiii.

9. Edmund Wilson, *Patriotic Gore: Studies in the Literature of the American Civil War* (New York, 1962), 517.

is the absolute separation it seems to endorse between plantation fiction and southwest humor writing. Harris could have chosen to direct Sut's corrosive and sometimes bitter irony toward plantation masters and their belles, but he was content to choose prim and proper farm women and pious Methodist circuit riders as the objects of Sut's comic revenge.

In studying Harris, one realizes that southwest humorists not only imposed the technical cordon sanitaire of an aristocratic narrative framework but they also observed and respected a broader generic cordon between their humorous stories and the plantation tradition. The plantation was simply off limits as the satiric object of the ribaldly comic voices of southwest humor writing. If, as Wilson speculates, Harris sought to diminish and undermine the idyllic literary plantation South, it was certainly an unconscious intention on the author's part. For consciously Harris was a fervent supporter of slavery and of secession who moved from his native Knoxville to Nashville after the beginning of the Civil War because he had no desire to live among the Unionists he so detested.[10] He may not have shared the Whiggish temperament of Longstreet or Baldwin, but, like nearly all southwest humorists, he did share their essentially conventional idea of a south founded on the plantation system and on the institution of slavery.

★ ★ ★

From Longstreet to Harris, humor writers of the Old Southwest either implicitly accepted the concept of an aristocratic southern social order by deftly manipulating a Cavalier narrative voice or they implicitly gave allegiance to the plantation South by respecting a generic cordon sanitaire between their writing and the romantic plantation novel. In light of this nearly total separation of genres, Randall Stewart's observation that the Tidewater and frontier traditions of southern literature "have maintained a good deal of separateness from each other" seems, if anything, an understatement, at least as far as pre–Civil War fiction is concerned.[11]

Of all the antebellum Southwest's humorists, only one made a se-

10. Milton Rickels, *George Washington Harris* (New York, 1965), 15–16, 30.
11. Randall Stewart, "Tidewater and Frontier," in *The Frontier Humorists: Critical Views*, ed. M. Thomas Inge (Hamden, Conn., 1975), 282.

rious attempt to breach the region's literary cordon. In *The Master's House*, published in 1854, Thorpe sought with some success to leaven the conventional plantation novel with the vigorous dialectal style, the violent action, and the social satire that were characteristic of the southwest humor tradition. Unlike other humorists, Thorpe—who achieved considerable success during his sixteen-year (1836–1852) residence in Louisiana as a writer of frontier sketches—was a born-and-bred Yankee from New England. This background probably explains why he was capable of writing a novel that incorporated the conventions of southwest humor writing to mount an effective fictional critique of slavery.

The protagonist of *The Master's House* is Graham Mildmay, son of a wealthy North Carolina planter. As his name implies, Mildmay is an enlightened southerner of moderate political opinions, a man who, as a result of his New England college education, combines "the cultivated manners and easy bearing" of a typical southern gentleman with a less typical industriousness and seriousness of purpose (17). After graduating as valedictorian of his class, Mildmay sells his father's worn-out acres in North Carolina and moves his possessions and his slaves to a new Louisiana plantation called Heritage Place, above New Orleans. Here he brings his northern bride, Annie, the sweetheart of his college days.

The Mildmays do not, alas, prosper in the exotic physical and cultural environment of the Deep South. Mildmay's sophistication and intelligence, his tolerant and mild administration of his slaves, and his conciliatory attitude toward the North cause many in the community to dismiss him as a milk-livered, overly refined gentleman not up to the martial standards of his class. The owner of an adjoining plantation, Mr. Moreton, voices the dominant opinions of the region's proud, narrow-minded, physically and intellectually assertive planters. He believes that slavery is an aristocratic institution, and he would dearly love to strip the political rights of nonslaveowners and poor whites if he could. And as for the South's Jeffersonian heritage? "The idea of man being free and equal is a humbug" (280), he declares.

Eventually, through a complex series of misunderstandings, Moreton challenges Mildmay to a duel. Mildmay opposes dueling in principle, but at the same time he feels bound to defend his name. In a hierarchically structured plantation society a gentleman's identity is

inseparable from his sense of honor, and his sense of honor is dependent on the judgment of the community. Like Bayard Sartoris, the
hero of Faulkner's *The Unvanquished*, Mildmay "cowered under the
idea of having these same people, for whom he really felt so little respect, condemn him, for doing what he knew to be right—to be just,—
to be Christian,—refuse to take part in a duel" (348). Unlike Sartoris,
Mildmay is denied the luxury of satisfying both his conscience and
his sense of honor. To the surprise of all, he bravely faces Moreton
and kills him.

For Mildmay the fatal duel is a catastrophe. He lives thereafter
with the sense that he has failed a moral test and that he has ruined
himself. Ironically the community approves his deed, completely re-
versing their heretofore unfavorable judgment of him. "What a
trump!" one gentleman declares. "He has, this morning, established
himself in society; every honor and office is henceforth open to him. I
wonder whether he will decide to go to Congress?" (365).

Mildmay is unable to use his duel as a springboard for political success because both he and his wife have been spiritually destroyed by
it. Perhaps it would be more accurate to say that they have been destroyed by a harsh, violent, essentially primitive society that has no
place for their intellectual sophistication and their impulse toward
compromise. As a Yankee, Annie cannot contend with the moral outrages she encounters in this heart of Deep South darkness. Neither
does Graham's broad-minded gentility adequately arm him to contend with the excesses of a newer, more brutal version of Tidewater
plantation culture. Annie dies, and at the novel's conclusion we see
Graham sitting alone on his plantation gallery. "As there is no twilight in a Southern sky," Thorpe tellingly writes, "the thick darkness
of a starless night enshrouded the form of Graham Mildmay" (391).

Though Thorpe undoubtedly sought to maintain his primary focus on Graham and Annie, as the novel progresses, more and more
fictional energy collects around the secondary character James
Dixon. Dixon is a Georgia-born slave trader whose contempt for
reform-minded Yankee abolitionists is matched in intensity only by
his hatred of blacks. He derives special delight in retrieving runaway
slaves, particularly those who have benefited from a life of freedom.
Dixon lures one such runaway—a man named Benson who looks
white and passes for white while living in Canada—across the border

to Detroit and captures him. Rather than submit to a return to slavery Benson hangs himself, and his white wife loses her mind as a result of the suicide. But Dixon spends little time considering the moral implications of his actions. After hearing of the wife's insanity, he concludes, "The idea of a white woman going crazy for a nigger, was working the sentimental with too much steam on, and I never thought about the subject afterwards" (108).

Dixon's observations of the most advantageous way of selling slaves reflects the dehumanization that Thorpe believed was inextricably bound to the South's peculiar institution. "Niggers is like pigs,—them that ain't worth much run ahead, and come into market before them that will bring the most money" (253). In fact *The Master's House* suggests that blacks are sometimes much worse off than pigs, particularly if they are "uppity" and run afoul of a brutal overseer like Mildmay's Toadvine. After catching a runaway slave named Jack, the drunken Toadvine ties a thick rope around his neck, runs him behind his horse until he falls in complete exhaustion, and then drags his body behind his horse until the rope nearly severs the dead slave's neck. The fact that Mildmay is an enlightened master who would never have knowingly hired a brutal overseer simply emphasizes the unavoidable and inevitable brutalities that attach themselves to the South's plantation slavocracy.

Characters like Dixon and Toadvine may be thoroughly repulsive to the reader, but there is no question that they achieve a kind of flesh-and-blood reality that Thorpe's paler and more conventional aristocratic characters lack. Through these morally callous plain folk, these corrupted yeomen, the author dramatizes the brutality of slavery; and he employs the powerful vernacular of the southwest humor tradition to articulate that brutality in a way that foreshadows the achievement of Twain.

Thorpe also uses his plain-talking secondary characters as part of a satiric attack on the sham ideals and the social pretensions of plantation society. Dixon eventually gives up slave trading, in part because he knows he can never achieve full social legitimacy pursuing a profession that planters paradoxically judge to be both necessary and slightly shameful. With the fortune he has amassed buying and selling slaves, he builds and impeccably furnishes a plantation mansion. Having acquired the appurtenances of a gentleman, he is accepted by the best society, which is willing to overlook his uncertain origin and to forget his former, morally suspect profession. Dixon becomes "Major Dixon." Thorpe writes, "As Major Dixon gradually developed himself, his equivocal . . . title of Major, warmed under the influence of popular favor, burst, like a well-perfected bud, into the full-blown luxuriance of 'General'; and so quietly had it been done, that no one could remember when the transition took place" (385). On the wall of his recently stocked library, General Dixon hangs a painting of himself. It is a portrait of a semiliterate former slave trader, holding a volume of Virgil in his hand (386).

As the structure of the preceding analysis may suggest, *The Master's House* is not a seamless narrative. It tends to split into two parts, the part that develops the story of the Mildmays and the part that details the adventures of Dixon. In the first part, the customary style and plotting devices of the plantation romance are utilized, while the second part frequently employs the colloquial style of southwest humor writing. Though he was a talented writer, Thorpe was too committed to the accepted techniques of romantic fiction to rise entirely above its conventions. He was able to feature the vigorous dialectal expressions and the harsh, even grotesque action associated with the southwest humor tradition only by setting aside a separate place for that tradition within his novel. Though he tried, not even in his most daring and provocative work could Thorpe entirely breach the generic cordon sanitaire that the Old Southwest's writers had imposed on themselves. The South would have to wait until after the Civil War to produce a writer with the emotional distance and the artistic genius to use the resources of the region's humor tradition to their fullest extent, to transform that tradition by making it a vehicle for penetrating and profound social irony.

Thorpe was no Twain. But his achievement in *The Master's House* should not be underestimated. Thorpe's novel deserves comparison with *Uncle Tom's Cabin;* and it is, in fact, more provocative in some respects than Harriet Beecher Stowe's novel in its analysis of the evils of slavery. Most significantly, its limited success in using the techniques of southwest humor writing to probe the deep social discordances that lay beneath the surface of southern life highlights the overall failure of this school of humor writing to use its considerable narrative and stylistic resources to oppose the region's headlong rush in its fiction toward the ideal characterization of the planter aristo-crat. By observing a fictional cordon sanitaire the Southwest's hu-morists conceded the field of legitimate fictional enterprise to the writers of conventional romances. Romantic writers, as we shall see in the following chapter, were more than willing to provide readers with an idealized fictional picture of the Southwest and of its noble planters.

Five

Sectional Paranoia, the Medieval Revival, and the Cavalier Mystique

In the summer of 1845 Fauquier White Sulphur Springs, a popular Virginia spa, hosted a "Tournament of Knights." The objective of the competing Cavaliers was to spear from the back of a galloping horse a small ring that dangled from a cord eight feet above the ground. The knight who successfully speared the ring presented it to his lady and crowned her the "Queen of Love and Beauty." Competitors included gentlemen with the assumed names of Brian de Bois-Guilbert, Wilfred of Ivanhoe, and the Knight of La Mancha. They were urged on by a crowd of genteel spectators, who shouted, "Love of ladies—glory to the brave!"[1]

The tournament at Fauquier White Sulphur Springs was typical of a number of such equestrian competitions that were being held throughout the South at that time, merely one symptom in antebellum Dixie of what might best be described as the Sir Walter Scott culture syndrome. Goaded by attacks from the North, accused of maintaining an inhuman and immoral social institution, southerners turned in their literature to Scott's romantic rendering, in ballad and novel, of medieval English and Scottish society. In these colorful period pieces the South found not only an escape from increasingly bitter sectional tensions but also an implicit justification of its own way of life. For in southern eyes Scott's courageous and honorable feudal lords and Scottish chiefs had been reborn in the nineteenth century in the person of the plantation aristocrat. The planter's slaves, like the

---

1. Osterweis, *Romanticism and Nationalism in the Old South*, 4.

feudal lord's medieval serfs, were necessary to nurture the flowering of the region's aristocratic society.

Twain, in his *Life on the Mississippi*, has probably given the most entertaining, if not the most accurate, estimate of Scott's profound influence on the southerner's self-image. "It was Sir Walter Scott," he wrote, "that made every gentleman in the South a major or a colonel, or a general or a judge, before the war; and it was he, also, that made these gentlemen value these bogus decorations. For it was he that created rank and caste, and pride and pleasure in them. Enough is laid on slavery, without fathering upon it these creations and contributions of Sir Walter."[2] Of course, Scott's enormous popularity in the South was as much a manifestation as a cause of Dixie's newly discovered reverence for the aristocratic ideal. But there can be no doubt that his novels and poems gave impetus to the creation of a southern myth expressive of cultural ideals that were radically opposed to corresponding democratic ideals being embraced in the North and West.

So pervasive was Scott's influence on the mind of the South that many of the region's writers sought determinedly, if rather bizarrely, to incorporate his word coinages into their vocabulary. Thus, in many formal essays "the Chivalry" came to stand for the southern planter, and northerners became barbarous "Saxons" and "Goths." Even in the roughest and most remote sections of the Old Southwest the cult of chivalry was grafted onto the original cultural stock of frontier folklore that had furnished the flamboyant and comic subject matter of southwest humor sketches. Scott's fictional characters, in the words of Rollin Osterweis, "supplied the names for steamboats, canal barges, and even stagecoaches . . . between New Orleans and Tennessee."[3]

Along with a fascination for Scott's characters and stories, citizens of the Old Southwest displayed a passion for the concept of knightly honor, which was an essential part of the texture of these historical romances. This addiction to personal honor permeated all levels of society in the region, as Thorpe's *The Master's House* makes abundantly clear. In this novel a plantation overseer—having been arrested and nearly hanged on the spot for the brutal murder of a run-

2. Samuel L. Clemens, *Life on the Mississippi* (1883; rpr. New York, 1927), 376.
3. Osterweis, *Romanticism and Nationalism in the Old South*, 46–48, 203.

away slave—is escorted to jail by a yeoman named Puckett. In the course of their journey together the two men discover that they like each other and that they share many attitudes. Most notably, they both believe that it is ludicrous to insist on punishing a white man for killing a slave. However, in spite of this personal rapport and fundamental agreement on the worthlessness of black slaves, Puckett cannot follow the instincts of his heart and allow the overseer to escape. "I *gave my word*," he stresses, "that I would take you to jail, and I must do it if I help you out agin [sic] at sundown." Not to fulfill his promise to deliver the overseer to jail would force this most unaristocratic of southerners to "forfeit his honor" (237).

It is highly unlikely that a yeoman such as Puckett would have been acquainted with the novels and poems of Scott. Indeed, he may well have been unable to read them. But if he had possessed the inclination and the means to read the Scottish romancer's work, he undoubtedly would have shared the enthusiasm of the region's more literate planters for the novelist's depiction of feudal honor, because he would have recognized that concept as a determining principle in his own code of conduct.

The effect of the Scott cultural syndrome can easily be detected in the plantation fiction of the Old Southwest. Ingraham's *The Sunny South; or, The Southerner at Home*, published on the eve of the Civil War, provides an excellent example of the numerous and subtle ways Dixie's writers drew on Scott's novels for their general inspiration as well as for their specific vocabulary. In contrast to the author's earlier and more realistic description of 1830s Louisiana and Mississippi, this romance provides a highly flattering view of plantation life as seen through the eyes of a Yankee governess. Ingraham seems determined to use the sympathetic first-person point of view of this young woman to establish the Southwest as the modern equivalent of aristocratic merry olde England. When Catherine Conyngham first glimpses the impressive "double storied portico" of the Tennessee plantation named Overton Park Lodge she imagines herself "approaching the mansion of some English Baronet."[4] Indeed, as she stresses more than once in letters to her northern friends, Tennessee

---

4. Ingraham, *The Sunny South; or, The Southerner at Home*, 26, hereinafter cited in the text by page number only.

"bears a striking resemblance to . . . the best part of England" (26–27). Having received the civilizing impress of the plantation, the original wilderness has been transformed into a countryside "whose broad patches of light and shade look like scenes in Claude Lorrain's pictures" and whose cultivated sward is "*so* green and soft" it might well represent "the work of trained English gardeners" (198).

Presiding over this verdant patch of England-in-Tennessee is the plantation master, Colonel Peyton. He is first viewed emblematically, seated on his fine horse like some feudal lord, "a rifle laid carelessly across his saddle, and two fine deer-dogs standing by his horse's forelegs and looking up wistfully into their master's face." With his "manly features and silver gray locks," with his "decided military air" (31), the magisterial colonel is the type of the patriarchal planter-aristocrat. He is a superior man of great personal power who demands instinctive recognition and obedience, whether from deer-dog, slave, or plantation belle. In short, he is the idealized English lord come via Tidewater Virginia to Tennessee.

Ingraham's text makes abundantly clear that submission to a plantation master like Peyton is more joyful than dutiful. For beneath his firm and manly exterior lies a heart softened and humanized by the influences of Christianity. Overton Park Lodge boasts a house of worship modeled on "an exquisite chapel which the colonel saw on the estate of the Earl of C——, when he was in England" (66). Within this architectural gem both master and slave are called to worship.

All of those who live under Peyton's control find his yoke an easy one. Contented slaves live in neat, whitewashed quarters. It is well that they are content, for the narrator assures us that their servitude is essential "to the happiness and comfort of the beautiful daughter or aristocratic lady of the planter" (118). Without slaves, how could the planter's highly bred daughter find time to read with a nearly faultless French accent Madame de Staël's *Corinne* to her father (123), or to play classical compositions on her harp or on her beautiful rosewood piano?

To make his fictional portrait of the sunny plantation Southland even more appealing, Ingraham invests his Tennessee landscape with a feudal ambiance that is directly derivative of Scott's novels. Indeed, in one description of the master's returning from a hunt with his retinue, Conyngham remarks that the scene reminds her of "a similar

description Scott has in one of his romances" (37). If Peyton's plantation seems to Conyngham's eyes the reproduction of a baronet's estate, Ashwood, the neighboring ancestral home of the Polk family, is
depicted as an even more impressive "princely domain" (112). The
governess concludes that "the lordly proprietors" of these Tennessee
plantations "live more like feudal nobles than simple farmers" (31).

  Princely domain, lordly proprietors, feudal nobles—this medieval-flavored diction employed by Ingraham was used in hundreds
of other novels and essays by the South's antebellum writers. Landon Carter, for example, penned this description of the Virginia
planter: "The barons of old were scarcely more despotic over their
immediate demesnes, than were the proprietors of these noble mansions, with their long train of servants and dependents; their dicta
were almost paramount to law throughout their extensive and
princely possessions."[5] Whether the plantation was set on the Rappahannock River or in the rolling hills of Tennessee, the intentions
of the South's writers were the same—to link southern society to
the magnificence of the Middle Ages as they had seen it depicted in
the novels of Scott.

  Amidst the medieval-tinged splendors of antebellum Tennessee
one might reasonably inquire as to the whereabouts of the descendants of the hardy pioneers who had blazed the trails across the Appalachians and settled the state. *The Sunny South* provides but a single
glimpse of people who might be described as yeomen. At a dance
given at a summer spa, brief mention is made of the presence of a
group of young men and women. The men are uniformly tall and the
women "handsome, but bold looking" (207), obviously lacking the
special aura, the delicate finish, that would mark them as plantation
belles. These robust country folk arrive at the resort for the day and
virtually take over the dancing hall. They seem to represent for the
narrator the equivalent of Scott's peasant or Highland characters. Indeed Conyngham compares their descent on the spa to "a foray of
Highlanders upon the lowlands" (207). In his novel, Ingraham depicts
Tennessee—the state that gave the nation Jackson, the man of the
people—as a land so dominated by an aristocratic planter class that

---

5. [St. Leger Landon Carter(?)], "Interesting Ruins on the Rappahannock," *Southern Literary Messenger*, I (August, 1834), 9–10.

its plainer citizens can serve the narrative only in the subordinate capacity of rough peasants or wild Highlanders.

★ ★ ★

The surge of interest in things medieval was not, of course, a fad that was unique to the American South. Mark Girouard has described the cult of antique chivalry among the nineteenth-century English aristocracy as a medieval revival that was used as a kind of talisman to ward off the unpleasant realities of rapid industrialization, democratic political reform, and the threat of extinction that these social changes posed for the old order. In a similar manner, medievalism served a talismanic purpose in antebellum southern society. It was an integral part of its justification of a social system that was being attacked in the North as outmoded and barbarous. As the nineteenth century advanced, the existence of slavery within a national culture that was profoundly democratic and increasingly industrialized in its orientation was viewed by more and more Americans as an intolerable condition. But by 1850 slavery had become a regional, not a national, phenomenon. Thus the burden of this intolerable condition lay on the South's back. Is it any wonder that southerners evinced a deep-seated desire, in the words of Clement Eaton, to "escape from reality" and that romanticism "attained a more luxuriant growth below the Potomac than elsewhere in America"?[6]

The essential hopelessness of trying to perpetuate slavery in an environment increasingly hostile to the institution was not the only unpleasant reality that southerners might have preferred to ignore. In addition to finding its interests opposed to those of the rest of the nation, the South also began to perceive itself as part of a Union tilting ever more strongly toward an industrial northern political agenda. As discussed earlier, the cultural and political isolation of the southern states was exacerbated by the eventual merging of midwestern with northern economic interests, a union ordained by such technological triumphs as the completion of the Erie Canal, tying the Great Lakes region with New York, and by the subsequent forging of numerous east-west rail links between the Midwest and the Northeast. As

6. Mark Girouard, *The Return to Camelot: Chivalry and the English Gentleman* (New Haven, 1981); Clement Eaton, *The Freedom-of-Thought Struggle in the Old South* (New York, 1964), 47.

Charles Sydnor notes, the South had begun to view itself as both a distinct and a beleaguered region by the 1830s. "Perhaps the chief product of the troublesome early 1830's," he writes, "was the strong charge of emotion added to matters that had hitherto been on a level of thought and calculation. In the previous decade, something of a Southern platform on national issues had evolved. Clashes over that platform convinced many Southerners that their interests were seldom respected by the rest of the nation and that the fabric of their way of life was being destroyed. A feeling of oppression, of defeat, and even of desperation was engendered."[7]

Southerners had valid reasons for feeling that their situation within the Union was growing more precarious and desperate. Statistics clearly indicate why the opinions of the region weighed less and less in the nation's councils. By 1850 only 378,204 of the 2,240,581 immigrants who had entered America were living in slave states. By 1855, with many of these new citizens voting, the northern states boasted 144 representatives in Congress, while slave states claimed only 90. Even more disturbing to southerners was the fact that slaveholding areas were not expanding but rather shrinking. How could the South hope to lay claim to new territories like Kansas when it was failing to maintain its claim on older slave states? Maryland, dominated by the burgeoning industrial city of Baltimore, was orienting itself more and more along northern lines; and Missouri, once firmly in the slave camp, was slipping away as well. William Freehling notes that by 1850 St. Louis, which in its early days had contained a large slave population, counted twenty times as many whites as blacks. The city's leading newspaper, the St. Louis *Democrat*, was regularly running editorials attacking slavery as a hindrance to Missouri's economic development.[8]

In response to the shrinking of their political influence and in reaction to attacks from the economically and politically ascendant North, residents of the slave states hunkered down into a defensive mental posture that tended to obscure the considerable cultural

7. Sydnor, *The Development of Southern Sectionalism*, 220.

8. Donald W. Zacharias, "The Know-Nothing Party and the Oratory of Nativism," in *Oratory in the Old South, 1818–1860*, ed. Waldo W. Braden (Baton Rouge, 1970), 220; William W. Freehling, *The Road to Disunion: Secessionists at Bay* (New York, 1990), 19–20.

differences between various areas of the South. Freehling has shown that in fact there were wide variations of attitudes within the region concerning slavery. As one traveled away from the Deep South and toward the Mason-Dixon Line, one encountered fewer intransigent opinions in favor of slavery and a greater willingness to compromise on the issue. But in spite of the substantial variety of southern opinion concerning slavery, attacks on the peculiar institution by Yankees—especially the common inference of the abolitionist argument that whites living in slave states were ethically inferior to northerners—had the ironic result of unifying southerners on the issue in a way that would have been otherwise impossible. "Defensive defiance," Freehling writes, "at least in black-belt districts, customarily gave proslavery zealots bountiful support. The further result, at least when Yankees were particularly holier-than-thou, was that even white-belt residents damned outsiders enough to create illusions that *a* South flourished."[9] What economics and geography could not do, intemperate denunciations of slavery accomplished. They created by 1850 a reasonably coherent southern consciousness that was unified in its opposition to what it considered Yankee meddling as well as to self-righteous abolitionist moral opprobrium.

During the early decades of the Republic the southern mind at its best had been epitomized by the subtle, humane, cosmopolitan liberalism of Jefferson. Even as late as the 1830s the newly settled regions of the Old Southwest had produced a national leader, Jackson, who embodied the surging, triumphantly expanding spirit of American democracy. By the 1850s, however, the vision of the South's political leaders had become sectional rather than national. "As the South declined in political power and as it experienced the growing force of the antislavery movement," Sydnor writes, "the mind of the South was transmuted into something very different from what it had been a generation earlier."[10] The defensive paranoia of this new mentality is brilliantly expressed in the bitter and pessimistic writings of Calhoun.

Calhoun's *Disquisition on Government* is a striking illustration of the degree to which the intellectual range of the South's political

9. Freehling, *The Road to Disunion*, 44.
10. Sydnor, *The Development of Southern Sectionalism*, 332.

leaders had contracted. Compared with the plenitude of Jefferson's vision, Calhoun's observations on the nature of man and on the workings of the political process seemed withered and shriveled. Calhoun rejected the Lockean-Jeffersonian idea of the social contract, which posited the notion that man voluntarily surrendered certain rights in order to form governments and that he possessed other rights that were natural and inalienable. Instead he argued that man was an inevitable product of his social milieu and that the only rights he could reasonably expect to possess were those rights bestowed on him by society. Jefferson had grounded his political theories in his underlying faith in the inherent goodness and wisdom of the common citizen. For Calhoun the distinguishing characteristic of an individual's temperament was his self-centeredness. "While man is created for the social state and is accordingly so formed as to feel what affects others as well as what affects himself," he observed, "he is, at the same time, so constituted as to feel more intensely what affects him directly than what affects him indirectly through others. . . . He is so constituted that direct or individual affections are stronger than his sympathetic or social feelings."[11]

Calhoun's Hobbesian understanding of man as an essentially self-centered and self-serving creature caused him to view majority rule as a dangerous condition in which the interests of an enlightened elite were placed "under the control of the more ignorant and dependent portions of the community." Though he was himself a product of the small landowning, Scotch-Irish, upcountry yeoman class, he professed the patrician idea that "inequality of condition" was "a necessary consequence of liberty . . . indispensable to progress." As for Jefferson's stirring assertion that "all men are created equal," it was for Calhoun an idea "destitute of all sound reason." Men were not born free in a state of nature, he argued, but were "born subject, not only to parental authority, but to the laws and institutions of the country where born."[12]

One can see how neatly Calhoun's conservative political theory served the interests of the southern slavocracy. For if a white man was born subject to parental authority, it was quite natural that a

11. John C. Calhoun, *A Disquisition on Government and Selections from the Discourse*, ed. C. Gordon Post (1853; rpr. New York, 1953), 4.

12. *Ibid.*, 35–36, 43, 44, 45.

slave was born subject to his master. But how could Calhoun's theories have appealed to the majority of southerners when historians tell us that they were as committed to the processes of popular democracy as Americans living in other sections of the nation? The regional defensiveness and the sectional paranoia that Sydnor has described help to explain the South's embracing of Calhoun's ideas. Southerners must have felt that in defending the interests of the minority, Calhoun was defending not only the prerogatives of a small plantation elite but also the rights of all southerners. For by the 1850s southerners saw themselves as an increasingly besieged minority, subject to the dictates of their ever more powerful northern neighbors.

As the writings of Calhoun indicate, the South was not able to maintain what Stephen Smith describes as a "regional vision based on the myths generated by Jefferson and Madison," because "there was no way to maintain the democratic theme of the independent yeoman farmer in the face of the reality of slavery and the counter vision of the abolitionist."[13] The institution of slavery and the plantation system that rested upon it could not be defended or intellectually nourished by drawing on the mythic figure of the stalwart and independent yeoman. If southerners were committed to slavery and to the corollary proposition of white supremacy—and the great majority of them were—they would have to appeal to a different figure. They would need to embody their cultural ideals in fictional characters such as Ingraham's Colonel Peyton, aristocratic Cavalier figures who represented the patriarchal benevolence of the plantation system. If the Southwest was in fact a rough land recently evolved from frontier conditions, it must in fiction be made into a replica of feudal England.

The medieval revival that swept the South from the 1830s to the coming of the Civil War thus must be understood not as an expression of cultural stability and harmony but rather as a fabrication by a culture that felt its very foundations being undermined. After 1830 northerners found themselves more and more inclined to agree with a writer in *Harper's Weekly* that southern civilization was like a mermaid—"lovely and languid above, but ending in bestial deformity."[14] In response to this progressively more malignant judgment,

13. Smith, *Myth, Media, and the Southern Mind,* 17.
14. Quoted in T. Harry Williams, "Romance and Realism in Southern Politics," in *Myth and Southern History,* ed. Gerster and Cords (Chicago, 1974), 115.

southerners retreated further into their medieval fantasy land of gallant knights and winsome ladies.

★   ★   ★

Given the South's attitude of defensiveness in the face of ever more frequently mounted attacks on slavery, given its feeling of beleaguerment and impending political subjugation, and given its consequent sectional paranoia, one can best understand the idealized fictional landscape of the antebellum southern novel as serving a fundamentally ideological function. The more plantation romances one reads, the more one understands that the writers of these works are not interested in plumbing the depths of the souls of their characters or in revealing the social tensions that underlie the surface of life in the South. The primary purpose of plantation fiction is to offer its readers a panegyric that defends and validates a southern culture assumed to be synonymous with a slave-owning plantation culture.

One way of explaining how ideology works is through what Clifford Geertz calls the "strain theory." According to this theory, ideology provides a "'symbolic outlet' for emotional disturbances generated by social disequilibrium."[15] The South's strong commitment to slavery in the face of its equally strong commitment to the political ideals embodied in the Declaration of Independence and the Constitution represents simply one of many severe conflicts within the southern psyche that continually threatened to destabilize its sense of cultural equilibrium.

And how could a regional ideology resolve the South's enormous cultural paradoxes? How could it eliminate the tension between Dixie's commitment to the ideas of freedom and slavery, of democracy and aristocracy? One way was to provide what ideology of any kind typically provides, what Geertz calls "morale explanations." Morale explanations sometimes seek to vindicate a culture in terms of higher values. A writer may assert, for example, that slavery is necessary in order to nourish the flowering of a civilization of the highest order, as Ingraham does in *The Sunny South*. Morale explanations also work by denying outright that social strains exist.[16] This is the

15. Clifford Geertz, *The Interpretation of Cultures* (New York, 1973), 204.
16. *Ibid.*, 204–205.

sort of glib ideological affirmation that the Southwest's novelists were particularly adept at making in their romances, as Ingraham's *The Quadroone; or, St. Michael's Day* amply demonstrates.

The setting of *The Quadroone* is the "ancient town" of New Orleans in 1769, three years after Louisiana has passed into Spanish hands.[17] In Ingraham's novel, Spanish lords and aristocratic French Creoles assume the role of southern Cavaliers, but they play their parts with the same fanatical devotion to honor and to the worship of the pure lady that is displayed by their Anglo-Saxon counterparts from the interior South. One Spanish nobleman, for example, is badly wounded in a duel. But when a lady who has visited him to offer her consolation rises to leave, the frail warrior rises as well, though naturally with great effort. In spite of tremendous pain the presence of such a "fair creature" inspires him to conquer "almost supernaturally . . . his physical weakness" (I, 91).

There is a seeming irony in the fact that the central characters of Ingraham's narrative are not aristocrats but a quadroon brother and sister named Renault and Azélie. Yet in spite of their mixed blood both brother and sister possess striking physical beauty as well as real nobility of character. Renault's spiritual strength and moral probity are especially notable because they stand in obvious contrast to the reckless, hot-blooded temperament of his legitimate white brother, Jules Caronde. Jules feels humiliated by Renault's presence in New Orleans and he hates his illegitimate half brother, a hatred that is only inflamed by Renault's obviously superior character. To make matters worse, Jules entertains incestuous designs on his half sister. Though Renault's status as a quadroon makes it impossible for him to defend his sister's virtue honorably through the code duello, he agrees with her that she would be better dead than defiled and dishonored by her wicked half brother.

Though shamelessly melodramatic and ridiculously overwrought, *The Quadroone* interests the reader initially because of its provocative reversal of traditional roles in the southern romance. Jules, the genetically authentic, pureblood aristocrat, is a thorough knave. Renault, his illegitimate half brother of mixed blood, is a spiri-

17. Joseph Holt Ingraham, *The Quadroone; or, St. Michael's Day* (2 vols.; New York, 1841), I, vii, hereinafter cited in the text by volume and page number only.

tually authentic nobleman; and his quadroon sister is as pure-minded, innocent, and refined as any lily-white plantation belle could hope to be. Is it possible that *The Quadroone* is engaging a subject that would be examined in the twentieth century by Faulkner in *Absalom, Absalom!*? Is Ingraham's reversal of roles part of an ironic deconstruction of the South's cherished myths of racial purity and white supremacy?

Alas, *The Quadroone* fails to develop the ironies implicit in the narrative's reversal of conventional character roles. In order to work these ironies out to their inevitable conclusions the author would be compelled to confront in his text the deep discordances in southern culture, and Ingraham is incapable of moving his novel to such a confrontation. The intractable problem presented by the social limbo into which Renault and Azélie have been cast by the abstract stigma of their blood turns out to be no problem at all. Renault is discovered to be the real Marquis de Caronde, switched at birth by his father's quadroon mistress for her illegitimate son, Jules. Azélie is no more racially tainted than her brother. She turns out to be the illegitimate daughter of a Spanish nobleman and a Moorish princess who had been secretly given to her quadroon foster mother for rearing.

Now the reader understands why Renault and Azélie are such sterling characters. They are not just, in Huck Finn's words, "white inside"; they are white through and through. And once Jules's quadroon inheritance is revealed, his thorough villainy, his hot-bloodedness, and his instinctive hatred and envy of his half brother are completely understandable as well. They are just the sorts of character traits one would expect to see in a mulatto. The reader also understands why the aristocratic Estelle, daughter of the Spanish governor, seemed certain that Renault would be "proved . . . one of [her] own race" (II, 163) and would be destined to have her hand in marriage. Being a lady of inherently noble sentiments, she recognized instinctively those corresponding qualities in Renault. Ingraham's novel has abandoned irony and complexity of character for a standard southern variation on an old maxim: It takes an aristocrat to know an aristocrat.[18]

If Ingraham was determined to resolve the racial problems of his

18. The element of recognition as part of the structural pattern of the southern heroic romance is analyzed by Michael Kreyling in *Figures of the Hero in Southern Narrative* (Baton Rouge, 1987).

hero and heroine by providing an arbitrary, rabbit-out-of-the-hat solution, why did he choose to deal with such a potentially explosive subject at all? A cynical reader might speculate that he chose the subjects of incest and miscegenation because he knew that these were precisely the kinds of sensational topics that would titillate potential buyers of his romance in both North and South. However, it is also tempting to consider whether Ingraham felt the urge to expose the dirty little secret hiding in the plantation closet, to probe the dehumanizing and destructive effects of the abstract idea of racial purity on his characters in the manner of George Washington Cable. If indeed Ingraham was possessed of such a subversive impulse, it was an impulse upon which he lacked the nerve to act. At its conclusion *The Quadroone*, in the typical manner of an ideological text, addresses one of the South's most profound social discordances by simply denying that the discordance exists through arbitrary plot resolutions and a conventionally romantic happy ending.

Novels like *The Sunny South* and *The Quadroone* were perfect fictional vehicles for southern ideology. To a region that felt itself to be incessantly harassed by condemnatory outside opinion they offered the consoling vision of an exalted and harmonious plantation culture. But they offered southerners something even more. In the midst of the rapidly spinning gyre of nineteenth-century events—a gyre that threatened to draw the plantation South into its vortex—heroic romances provided a natural paradigm of the timeless, a type of storytelling in which the larger-than-life figure of the Cavalier could deny change and repudiate history.[19]

There was, therefore, a perfect sympathy between the time-transcending paradigm of the plantation romance and the implicit need of southerners to believe that their culture could escape the imperatives of modernity. Though published after the Civil War in 1867, Elizabeth Whitfield Bellamy's *Four Oaks* demonstrates as thoroughly as any nineteenth-century plantation novel the way in which these romances sought to escape the historical flux. Set in 1850s Alabama in and around the town of Netherford, *Four Oaks* presents its readers with the Fanning, Poinsett, Fletcher, and Innibee families, all splendid examples of southern aristocracy. Netherford is not a dusty,

19. *Ibid.*, 20.

bedraggled Alabama town, but a replica of an English village, complete with a Gothic Episcopal church named St. Botolf's and atmospheric haunted houses like Four Oaks.

In a manner remotely reminiscent of Jane Austen, Bellamy develops a plot full of intricate flirtations and delicate sentiments expressed with equal delicacy. The few black characters presented in the narrative are servants who obligingly wait on refined southern ladies and high-toned southern gentlemen. These Cavaliers court their belles with great formality, read Shakespeare, play chess, hunt, and while away their summers at local springs and watering spots. The few yeomen that the reader encounters serve in the capacity of obliging peasants, rather like the wild Highlanders of Ingraham's *The Sunny South.*

One of the remarkable aspects of *Four Oaks* is that it could have been written as easily in 1857 as in 1867. Although the plantation society that Bellamy lovingly describes has been immolated in the conflagration of the Civil War, there is absolutely nothing in her novel to suggest that what she is writing is a valediction for a way of life that has been swept away by the tide of history. Through her idealized setting she is simply denying the traumas of the recently concluded war, much as Ingraham denied the problems of race in *The Quadroone.* As antebellum writers of plantation fiction had done, she provided southerners with a timeless retreat into which they could retire and within which they could ignore realities that they found too disturbing or too humiliating to acknowledge.

Six

Southern Women Novelists and the Looking Glass of Plantation Fiction

In *The Madwoman in the Attic: The Woman Writer and the Nineteenth-Century Literary Imagination,* Sandra Gilbert and Susan Gubar describe the development of female writers between 1800 and 1900 as an explosion out of the looking-glass world imposed upon them by male writers, an intellectual rebellion that led them to discover their own speech and to conduct their own "dance of authority." This movement of nineteenth-century women writers toward fictional autonomy is confirmed by Mary Poovey in her study of Mary Wollstonecraft, Mary Shelley, and Jane Austen, entitled *The Proper Lady and the Woman Writer.* In her analysis Poovey argues that early nineteenth-century English society embodied a deep discrepancy between the possible and the actual rewards of "the ideology of bourgeois individualism," a discrepancy that was intensely felt by women. Female writers consequently crafted responses to this ideology that were "unique and sometimes startling in their ingenuity and creativity."[1] For Poovey, as for Gilbert and Gubar, the nineteenth century marks the beginning of the estrangement of female authors from the values of a male-dominated bourgeois capitalist society.

And what of the South's nineteenth-century women writers? Did they share the tendency of their English and Yankee cohorts to question and to undermine the sexual status quo? Were they entirely com-

1. Sandra M. Gilbert and Susan Gubar, *The Madwoman in the Attic: The Woman Writer and the Nineteenth-Century Literary Imagination* (New Haven, 1979), 44; Mary Poovey, *The Proper Lady and the Woman Writer* (Chicago, 1984), 241, 242.

fortable within the patriarchal confines of the plantation tradition? And if not, were they willing to use their fiction to challenge the tradition? Such questions are pertinent because women writers were among the most successful and prolific creators of plantation fiction in the Old Southwest.

But first it would be useful to delineate the passive and highly restricted role assigned to southern women in a male-dominated plantation society. As Anne Firor Scott has observed in *The Southern Lady: From Pedestal to Politics*, properly bred belles were expected to be pure, submissive, modest, self-denying, and pious. Such traits validated their role as the symbolic repository of the region's most cherished ideals. Of course, the concept of the pure, submissive, and modest woman was, like the medieval-flavored chivalric ideal, widely subscribed to in England and in the northern states as well as in the South. But like medieval romanticism, the notion of the submissive woman was articulated with more frequency, intensity, and fervor in the South than in any other region of the nation; and Scott's analysis indicates why this was so. The plantation system and the institution of slavery fostered the development in the southern states of a particularly strong patriarchal family structure. "Women, along with children and slaves, were expected to recognize their proper and subordinate place and to be obedient to the head of the family," Scott writes. "Any tendency on the part of any of the members of the system to assert themselves against the master threatened the whole, and therefore slavery itself."[2]

The institution of slavery was thus inextricably linked to the South's view of women as pliant and submissive creatures. It was also linked to the region's obsession with the southern belle's sexual purity, for the miscegenation that inevitably resulted from the day-to-day contact between white masters and their black female chattel made it necessary for the region to trumpet ever more insistently the idea of racial purity, a purity symbolized by the untainted southern lady. W. J. Cash has observed that if miscegenation was to be denied on the one hand, southern women had to be compensated on the other: "The revolting suspicion in the male that he might be slipping

2. Anne Firor Scott, *The Southern Lady: From Pedestal to Politics, 1830–1930* (Chicago, 1970), 17.

into bestiality [must be] got rid of, by glorifying her; the Yankee must be answered by proclaiming from the housetops that Southern Virtue ... was superior, not alone to the North's but to any on earth, and adducing Southern Womanhood in proof."[3]

Even on the rare occasions when the Southwest's antebellum writers admitted to the existence of miscegenation, they used this admission in a paradoxical way to demonstrate how it guaranteed the purity of the white woman. In *Mississippi Scenes* Joseph Beckham Cobb followed this line of argument. Cobb believed that female slaves served as a kind of sexual safety valve, assuring, somewhat in the manner of Oriental concubines, the purity of white women of both high and low social orders. "The existence of a class of females who set little value on chastity, and afford easy gratification to the licentious desires of men who belong to a higher caste, in addition to the absence of all temptation," he contended, "accounts for this unparalleled purity and abstinence among lower classes of Southern females. As regards our higher and polished circles, I have yet to see or hear the first insinuation thrown out or the first charge brought. Their preeminence is conceded."[4]

A similarly exalted view of the southern lady was articulated by Virginian Nathaniel Beverley Tucker in his novel *The Partisan Leader*. For Tucker southern women walked traditionally "in the steps of their chaste mothers ... safe in that high sense of honor which protects at once from pollution and suspicion." Like Cobb, he believed that the southern lady represented a natural line beyond which the promiscuity of the lower orders—Tucker termed it "the gangrene of the social body"—could never pass.[5] Southern men from Virginia to Mississippi thus idealized their women and turned them into symbols of social virtue and racial purity.

The Cavalier's belle was a chaste vessel, and she was expected to meld her chastity with an attitude of exquisite submissiveness. Such submissiveness was intuitively understood to be essential to the perpetuation of the plantation slavocracy, as an antebellum southern

3. Cash, *The Mind of the South*, 86.
4. Joseph Beckham Cobb, *Mississippi Scenes; or, Sketches of Southern and Western Life and Adventure* (Philadelphia, 1851), 181.
5. Nathaniel Beverley Tucker, *The Partisan Leader: A Tale of the Future* (1836; rpr. Chapel Hill, 1971), 130.

magazine article entitled "Women's Rights" clearly indicates. For the writer of this article a southern lady's natural virtues consist of her "sensibility, modesty, and . . . personal timidity." As for her role in life, "love," he contends, "is her destiny, and the sum of her duties." Those women who would argue for equal rights with men are not women at all, but "men-women . . . wonderful quacks invariably" who simply cannot be taken seriously. In a final attempt to put women's rights within its proper context, the writer equates proponents of sexual equality with the most detested of agitators. "They are abolitionists; they would free the slaves of the South, only to enslave the Southerners themselves."[6] For this writer, freeing slaves and granting women new rights would have equally devastating consequences. Slaves would be liberated into a life of irresponsibility and ladies freed into a life without slaves, a life of drudgery. They would no longer have leisure to strum their harps or read French novels, like Ingraham's fictional ladies.

As the article "Women's Rights" suggests, southern men were inclined to condemn any movement advocating the rights of women, any attitude contradicting the idea that women ought to be pliant and submissive, any activity drawing a woman away from home and hearth, as antisouthern agitation that struck at the heart of the region's values. To a woman who insisted on asserting her rights and her identity and who refused to take her proper place within the patriarchal order Tucker contemptuously offered the suggestion that she "go North; write books; patronize abolition societies; or keep a boarding school. She is no longer fit to be the wife of a Virginia gentleman."[7] Southwestern planters would have enthusiastically seconded Tucker's sentiments, merely substituting *southern* for *Virginia.*

In Tidewater Virginia the relegation of the southern lady to the narrow compass of a pedestal might have seemed a not-entirely-illusory undertaking. After all, some of these women had been ensconced within their riverside mansions for generations. But the Old Southwest was a different matter. On the eve of the Civil War the region was a mere forty years removed from the frontier. How could it

---

6. G. M. Wharton, "Women's Rights," *Southwestern Monthly*, I (1852), 147, 149.
7. Tucker, *The Partisan Leader*, 123.

reconcile its vision of exquisite, pure, refined, and passive woman-hood with the memories of those mothers and grandmothers who had stoutly labored alongside their husbands to carve civilization out of a wilderness? And how could these women willingly submit themselves to the role of passive symbols of cultural purity?

Scott's work reveals that the private opinions of southern women concerning their place in the plantation patriarchy were varied and complex. Publicly, however, they consistently professed undiluted loyalty to their society and their contentment within its framework.[8] As noted previously, a sense of beleaguerment impelled southerners to put aside their differences, to submerge their individual doubts about issues like slavery, and to pretend that they stood together as one. Southern women were not exempted from this impulse to close ranks. Female writers used plantation fiction to defend the southern way of life, just as their male counterparts did. However, the novels of the region's male and female writers were not totally indistinguishable. Women writers occasionally and obliquely betrayed their unease about the role that the southern lady was expected to play in plantation society, but their attitude never was one of outright rebellion. Plantation romances by female authors possess their own particular fascination, because they testify both to the doubts that southern women tentatively entertained about their place in a patriarchal society and to the inexorable pressures toward social orthodoxy exerted by that society, pressures that ultimately forced these women to muffle and deny their provisional voices of dissent. The imperatives of southern ideology firmly entrapped the South's women writers within the looking glass of the idealized plantation patriarchy.

★   ★   ★

Of the numerous antebellum apologias for the southern way of life, none were more effective or more emotionally resonant than the novels of Caroline Lee Hentz. Like Ingraham, Hentz was a native of New England. In her midtwenties she moved to the South with her husband, and her remaining years were lived in border and southern states, primarily in Alabama. Here she and her spouse established

---

8. Scott, *The Southern Lady: From Pedestal to Politics,* 3–79.

and conducted a number of girls' schools. During the period in which she raised four children and helped her husband teach, Hentz also found time to write fiction, composing within one 7-year period an astonishing total of seventeen novels and short-story collections.[9] Like Ingraham, she embraced with genuine fervor the cause of her adopted region. Her novels were appealing projections of plantation life that emphasized its romantic allure and its perfection.

The Planter's Northern Bride (1854), as the preface to Hentz's most popular novel makes clear, was written with the specific purpose of correcting erroneous impressions of the South held by northerners, impressions gained from reading such pernicious works as Stowe's *Uncle Tom's Cabin*. Hentz counted herself among those loyal southerners who were devoted to their region because they knew it to be "the home of noble, generous hearts, of ingenuous and lofty minds. . . . We love the magnanimity and chivalry of its sons," she rhapsodized, "the pure and high-toned spirit that animates its daughters."[10] *The Planter's Northern Bride* is thus a paean to the chivalric and spiritually elevated qualities of the South's aristocracy as well as a vigorous defense of the institution of slavery on which the power of that aristocracy rests.

As Hentz's novel opens, the Cavalier hero, Russell Moreland, is in the midst of a tour of New England, accompanied by his mulatto body servant, Albert. While attending Sunday services in a rural village Russell hears the divinely pure voice of Eulalia Hastings and falls immediately in love with her. She fully reciprocates his love. Unfortunately her father is the town's leading abolitionist. Mr. Hastings has no intention of allowing his daughter to marry a planter, notwithstanding the devoted and solicitous courtship undertaken by her chivalric southern admirer. Confronted with a seemingly insurmountable obstacle to their love, both the delicate Eulalia and her equally sensitive suitor languish and waste away in the conventional manner of love-sick romantic characters. Eulalia's precipitous decline carries with it the threat of consumption, and her sickness forces her father

9. Ritchie D. Watson, Jr., "Caroline Lee Hentz," in *Southern Writers: A Biographical Dictionary*, ed. Robert Bain, Joseph M. Flora, and Louis D. Rubin, Jr. (Baton Rouge, 1979), 221–22.

10. Caroline Lee Hentz, *The Planter's Northern Bride* (1854; rpr. Chapel Hill, 1970), 578, hereinafter cited in the text by page number only.

to choose between his daughter's life and his antislavery principles. He finally accedes to Moreland's request for his daughter's hand and sends the happy girl forth "as a missionary" (152) to help reform the errant South. Little does he suspect that this beautiful northern emissary will quickly be converted to a southern point of view.

Even in the midst of the author's New England chapters, while she is resolving the complications of the couple's courtship, Hentz sets out to develop assiduously one of her novel's major themes—the paternalistic and inherently benign nature of southern slavery. In his debates with Eulalia's father, Moreland insists that the slave owner's primary duty is to love, nourish, and protect his slaves and to act as a guide "appointed to civilize and Christianize the sons and daughters of Africa" (108–109). Because Moreland assumes the role of a benevolent father figure, it is not surprising that Albert cannot be enticed away from him by the wiles of Yankee abolitionists. When Moreland courteously offers the services of his slave to help an understaffed innkeeper's wife, Albert complains to his master of being worked nearly to death. "It is well to have a taste of what the Northern bondwomen have to endure," the planter sagely observes, "so that you may be more contented with your own lot" (90–91). Neither Albert nor the reader should have trouble getting Moreland's point: southern chattel slavery promotes milder working conditions than New England wage slavery.

Hentz's portrait of the contented darky is placed within an even more completely idealized setting when Moreland and his bride arrive at his plantation and are greeted with the joyous shouts of his entire slave family. Succeeding chapters show why Moreland's slaves are overjoyed to see their master return. His plantation is a model of firm but not oppressive order. Eulalia discovers that his field hands are not burdened with soul-destroying labor. In fact, they have time to grow their own crops as well as the master's, and to sell their produce for pocket money. A simple chapel has been built to provide for the slaves' spiritual needs, and their basic material needs are supplied as well. In short, they bask in the protection and care of their kindly master.

How distressed Hentz would have been had she foreseen the verdict of modern historians, that slave owners "were hard, calculating businessmen who priced slaves, and their other assets, with as much shrewdness as could be expected of any northern capitalist."[11] Could Hentz return from the grave and answer such a charge, she would probably reply that history had been seduced by the distortions of the fanatical abolitionists. For by the 1850s, abolitionist attacks had prompted her and most of her fellow southerners to defend themselves by insisting that slavery was a perfectly humane institution.

A few southerners might have been willing to admit to the presence of a snake in the plantation garden. Cobb, for example, describes in his *Mississippi Scenes* a slave sale in which a debt-laden master is forced to part with his old nanny's single surviving son. The grief expressed by mother and son at their separation would convince the "hardiest skeptic," Cobb asserts, "that natural affections, though restrained and subdued, are not wholly extinct in the negro's bosom, because of his degraded lot."[12] However, admissions such as Cobb's that slavery might be a less than completely compassionate establishment are rarely to be found in southern writing. More common is the insistently rose-colored view of Hentz's fiction.

In her novel *Marcus Warland* Hentz presents a plantation master who would rather kill himself than see his slaves sold away from him, a master who risks his own life to save a slave from a burning house and later insists that the doctor tend to the slave's burns before he tends to his own. Is it any wonder that the dying slave begs to "kiss once more the dear hands that suffered for me"? The corpus of Hentz's plantation fiction supports her flattering assessment of slavery in *The Planter's Northern Bride*. If the slave is bound by chains, they are chains "kept moist and bright with the oil of kindness applied with a downy touch."[13]

The defense of slavery in *The Planter's Northern Bride* necessarily rests on the concept of an idealized Cavalier like Moreland, one who combines strength and firm manliness with courtesy, kindness, and noblesse oblige toward men of lower social rank. This hero's superior breeding is revealed early in the novel when an earnest but mannerless New England innkeeper insists that the planter's body servant sit

11. Stanley L. Engerman and Robert William Fogel, *Time on the Cross: The Economics of American Negro Slavery* (Boston, 1974), 73.

12. Cobb, *Mississippi Scenes*, 94.

13. Caroline Lee Hentz, *Marcus Warland; or, The Long Moss Spring* (1852; rpr. Philadelphia, 1854), 84, 59.

next to his master at the dining table. Russell betrays no anger or discomfort; he simply preserves his dignity by giving the servant his place and leaving the room. The slave later tells his master that dining with common Yankees was an unpleasant experience for him because, as he superciliously observes, "they are no gentlemen" (30).

Again and again *The Planter's Northern Bride* stresses its hero's chivalric temperament. In courting Eulalia, Moreland assumes the properly reverent attitude of the suppliant knight. Even the most trivial of his dealings with his wife are marked by a quality of worshipful adoration. In one scene he returns from the hunt, entering the plantation hall dressed in a green hunting outfit and holding before him a brace of partridges. "Here, Eulalia," he announces, "I lay my trophies at your feet" (215). It is understandable how Hentz's delicate and sensitive northern bride could turn her back on her emotionally pinched Yankee suitors and follow her Cavalier lover to the sunny Southland.

One of the structural patterns that Michael Kreyling identifies in the southern heroic romance is the combat between its idealized aristocratic hero and a northern villain who is associated with time-bound materialism.[14] In *The Planter's Northern Bride* this villain presents himself in the guise of a minister who secretly preaches insurrection to Moreland's slaves while availing himself of the planter's liberal hospitality. When Moreland discovers the disguised abolitionist's treachery, his sense of honor demands a formal confrontation. But though the Cavalier hero is skilled in the use of pistols, his adversary is not. In deference to his foe Moreland eschews firearms for more dangerous hand-to-hand combat. Moreland's decision highlights the essential cowardice of his abolitionist adversary and epitomizes what Hentz terms Moreland's "chivalry of . . . nature" (521).

In the manner of classic epic figures such as Aeneas, Moreland is a heroic figure who embodies the highest ideals of his race. He is the concrete symbol of a hierarchically structured plantation society; and his superior qualities of character, which represent the superiority of an entire class of southern planter-aristocrats, are instinctively acknowledged by members of the lower classes, both black and white. A northern servant in the Hastings house recognizes him instantly as "a real gentleman. . . . I'd as lieves wait upon him as not.

14. Kreyling, *Figures of the Hero in Southern Narrative*, 16–18.

He's as handsome as a pictur, and he don't look a bit proud neither, only sort of grand, as t'were" (68). Such admiring observations are echoed later by a slave named Kizzie. "He's a gentleman, a raal gentleman. Tain't no sham, nuther. It's sound, clean through. Black folks knows it as well as white folks" (230).

The instantaneous recognition accorded to Moreland by characters drawn from lower social orders is also, as Kreyling has observed, an essential structural element of the romantic narrative pattern that is inspired by a hierarchical social myth. "Individuals on the lower rungs of the social ladder need not consciously know much about the ideal by which they are nurtured," he explains, "but they must instinctively identify the hero who embodies that ideal and they must freely submit their single fates to him. Recognition and submission are never omitted from the heroic narrative structure."[15] Such submission is most fulsomely dramatized in Moreland's return to his plantation from the North, when his field hands swirl around him "eager to get within reach of his hand, the sound of his voice, the glance of his kind, protecting, yet commanding eyes" (331–32). At this point Hentz seems on the verge of translating her hero from an earthly father figure into a heavenly one.

And how does the southern yeoman fit into a novel dominated by the aristocratic profile of Moreland? Hentz provides but a single glimpse of these plain folk. On their wedding journey home from New England, Moreland and Eulalia spend a night in the piney woods, where they are taken in by a coarsely dressed farmer who lives in a log cabin and offers the hero and heroine a supper of bacon and greens. The farmer addresses Moreland as "squire," obviously an appellation of deference and respect. Though this yeoman avers that he would "change places with nobody" and that he "wouldn't give a snap for a fine house" (325), Moreland tells Eulalia that he "has already made money enough to purchase some negroes, who assist him in the field, he being chief workman, as well as overseer. His children, I doubt not, will be rich, and be associated with the magnates of the land" (327).

The piney woods scene shows how neatly Hentz has subordinated the yeoman and brought him into the Cavalier's orbit. The farmer is

15. *Ibid.*, 21.

stalwart and independent, but his independence is not construed as threatening the plantation hierarchy. He clearly defers to Moreland when he calls him "squire"; and although he affirms his own self-reliance, Hentz is careful to inform us that he has begun his ascent into the planter class, a social ascension from which his children will more fully benefit. *The Planter's Northern Bride* makes clear that the ideal that unifies the South and fires the ambitions of her most humble farmers is the plantation ideal.

Moreland's union with a northern bride is a happy and fulfilling one, crowned by the birth of a son and the family's triumphant return to New England. Russell Junior becomes an all-too-obvious symbol of "the reunion of these now too divided parties" (549), which Hentz seemed so sincerely to desire. But how could her vision of national unity have appealed in a profound way to northern readers when it was a union achieved on such blatantly southern terms? The idea of meaningful reconciliation might have carried some force if Hentz had developed qualities in Eulalia that were specifically northern. But a perceptive reader quickly discerns that, though the novel's heroine may be a Yankee in body, she is a southern belle in spirit. In her interactions with her lover and husband she is as completely submissive as the purest plantation maiden. And she carries within her the same finely developed senses of charity and noblesse oblige that characterize Moreland. When she leaves her New England home with her husband, the poor of the village wonder apprehensively, "What shall [we] do?" (158). They mourn Eulalia's departure much as loyally dependent slaves would mourn the departure of their mistress. Eulalia is not really a Yankee; she is a southern lady in disguise. And by turning her into a clone of the southern belle Hentz seems to imply that there are ultimately no northern values worthy of being united with the finest qualities of the southern aristocracy.

Hentz seems to have instinctively recognized that uniting her idealized southern male with an authentically northern female would have adulterated the timeless heroic culture he represents by bringing it into ruinous contact with the pragmatic, materialistic, and temporizing concerns of Yankee culture. The structural dynamic of her heroic narrative pattern demanded a heroine whom Kreyling has termed a "female cognate," a "mate with whom [the hero] can halt the metamorphosing nature of time. The nearer the hero is to his mate in type and blood, the likelier a successful denial of time."[16] Hentz could satisfy the structural imperatives of her novel only by making Eulalia a spiritually southern lady. This character transformation embodies the narrative's terrible irony. Though *The Planter's Northern Bride* was written to promote sectional conciliation, its underlying assumption is that the cultures of North and South are absolutely incompatible.

The development of character and theme in *The Planter's Northern Bride* illustrates Frederic Jameson's notion that "ideology is not something which informs or invests symbolic production; rather the aesthetic act is itself ideological, and the production of aesthetic or narrative form is to be seen as an ideological act in its own right, with the function of inventing imaginary or formal 'solutions' to unresolvable social contradictions."[17] It is the blatantly ideological nature of the author's heroic narrative structure that vitiates her text, trivializes her plot, and makes her formal solutions to the South's political and social dilemmas seem, from the perspective of the twentieth century, ludicrously inadequate. Still, the very ludicrousness of her solutions suggests how absolutely intractable were the social contradictions that the South's antebellum writers felt compelled to resolve in their fiction.

The Planter's Northern Bride is perfectly consonant with antebellum southern ideology. There is certainly nothing in the characterization of Eulalia that would suggest Hentz had reservations about the position of women within the plantation hierarchy. In other novels, however, she does feature, though in a conventionally melodramatic way, young women who resist the plantation society's demand that they passively yield to the strictures of its social orthodoxy. One of these novels is *Linda; or, The Young Pilot of the Belle Creole* (1850).

The heroine of Hentz's romance is Linda Walton, a sprightly belle who stands to inherit the Louisiana cotton plantation of her grandfather. Linda's antagonist is her wicked stepmother, who is determined that the young lady will marry her selfish, ambitious, and haughty son, Robert. Linda does not really like her stepbrother, and she likes him even less after she is saved from a runaway carriage about to

16. *Ibid.*, 20, 24.
17. Frederic Jameson, *The Political Unconscious: Narrative as a Socially Symbolic Act* (Ithaca, 1981), 79.

plunge over a cliff by a dashing young man named Roland. Roland's father was a planter who squandered his fortune and died penniless. Lacking land and money, the son hopes to become a riverboat pilot. Unfortunately, such limited social aspirations make him an unsuitable candidate for Linda's hand in marriage.

Linda develops two conflicts that implicitly call into question certain aspects of the South's social status quo. The major conflict pits the heroine against her dangerously overbearing stepmother. Linda opposes the wishes of this woman as well as the conventional expectations of plantation society by resisting the demand that she marry her well-established stepbrother and thereby join her land and fortune with his own. Against the claims of society she places her love for the penniless Roland. When her stepmother tries to force her to marry Robert, Linda runs away from home in desperation. Beneath the melodramatic excesses of this particular conflict Hentz seems to be disputing the accuracy of the myth of Dixie's worshipful adoration of its women. Instead of positioning her young belle securely on her pedestal, the author dramatizes the plight of a powerless girl trapped in the vise of social conformity.

A second conflict pits Linda's rich but selfish stepbrother against the poor but high-minded Roland, much in the way that Ingraham had opposed half brothers Jules and Renault in *The Quadroone*. Linda's preference for Roland is understandable, but Roland's lack of money and social position makes her preference problematic. As one of her school friends observes wistfully, "I only wish that he was a real gentleman, then you could marry him."[18]

As Hentz views it, however, the problem is not that Roland has failed to prove himself as a gentleman but that society's superficial qualifications of land and money make it impossible for him to be recognized for the authentically noble young man that he is. The author takes pains to let her readers know that Roland's deceased father was a planter, though one who foolishly wasted his fortune. It is clear that Roland has imbibed from an aristocratic spring, and he quickly demonstrates his chivalric nature when he saves Linda and then nobly refuses to accept a reward for his deed of courage. Most of all he is

---

18. Caroline Lee Hentz, *Linda; or, The Young Pilot of the Belle Creole* (1850; rpr. Philadelphia, 1889), 127, hereinafter cited in the text by page number only.

recognized in the traditional manner of the heroic narrative as a spiritual, if not a material, Cavalier. Hentz tells us in her initial description that, though Roland was not well dressed, "there was sufficient gentility in his bearing to give [Linda] the impression he was a gentleman's son" (65); and Linda herself calls him "one of nature's noblemen" (100). The narrator observes that this Cavalier, dressed in rags, "might have walked by the side of the proudest aristocrat of the land without being distinguished as one of lowlier station" (128). Since Roland is obviously a noble hero, Hentz seems to be questioning the stigma that a culture founded on the ownership of land and slaves places on men who possess neither of these assets.

The conflicts presented in Hentz's narrative thus indirectly raise objections to the plight of women and of the poor in southern society. But these objections can be fully registered only if the conflicts that generate them remain viable. Alas, the conflicts initially presented in *Linda* quickly evaporate in the sunny light of the author's happy ending. Hentz chooses not to resolve the social tensions of her narrative by condemning the standards that southern society employs to judge Roland. Instead she simply chooses to reward her hero with a fortune, a fortune conveniently bestowed by a childless planter whose life the ever helpful young pilot has saved in a steamboat explosion. Once the problem of Roland's suitability for marriage is solved by his acquiring of money and land, it is equally easy for Hentz to deal with the problem of her heroine's victimization by her cruel stepmother. Now that her beau has acquired social position, Linda's preference for him seems no longer rebellious or willful. All that is needed to provide a completely satisfactory ending is the born-again religious conversion of the haughty Robert. This formerly immature and tyrannical stepbrother becomes a minister, and he personally blesses the union of Linda and Roland at the novel's conclusion.

The frustrating pattern that underlies Ingraham's *The Quadroone* repeats itself in Hentz's *Linda*. In both novels a potentially interesting critique of the abstractions of the southern social code—the tragic stigma of race or poverty, the helpless position of the southern belle within a male-dominated hierarchy—is short-circuited by arbitrary "happy endings" that cannot begin to address the vexing social problems on which the novels initially seemed determined to focus. After reading these works one is left to wonder whether the aborted development of their conflicts reflects the authors' incompletely articulated reservations about southern society or whether it reflects their conscious refusal to dispose the social questions they initially dared to raise in their narratives. In any case their insistently felicitous endings demonstrate the determination of the South's antebellum writers to resolve the social contradictions of their culture, no matter how capriciously or unconvincingly.

Though Hentz could never bring herself to criticize directly and openly the plantation patriarchy, there is reason to suspect that she brooded to some extent over the southern lady's prescribed attitude of helpless passivity. For in a number of her novels she presents young women who, like Linda, are expected to toe the line and accept their places in the southern social scheme, who resist that society's demands, and who seem fated to be punished for their resistance. In *Eoline; or, Magnolia Vale* (1852) the title character refuses to marry the son of her father's best friend. As a result she is cast out of her plantation home by her proud, choleric squire of a father and forced to support herself teaching music at a seminary for young ladies.

In spite of her banishment, the reader eventually discovers that Eoline is a far cry from Henrik Ibsen's Nora and that Hentz is too much committed to the idea of the conventional southern lady ever to allow her heroine to slam the door decisively on her old life. Eoline finally agrees to meet the young Cavalier whom her father has chosen for her; and she discovers him to be a highly estimable gentleman who combines good looks, a manly temperament, and erudition (a law degree from the University of Göttingen) with the exalted sentiments of a knightly lover. "I love you," he professes to Eoline, "with a love purer, deeper, stronger than ever yet warmed the breast of man."[19]

Hentz begins by lionizing her heroine as a brave young lady who has turned her back on the demands of her father and resolutely set out to affront her destiny. Ultimately, however, the novel suggests that she is an earnest and aspiring, but misguided, girl who would have been better off following the wise dictates of her parent. Nevertheless Hentz remains willing to overlook Eoline's rather ridiculous

19. Caroline Lee Hentz, *Eoline; or, Magnolia Vale* (1852; rpr. Freeport, N.Y., 1971), 194, hereinafter cited in the text by page number only.

presumption of independence and freedom. For she is, after all, "fair as the magnolia of the South" (251), an obvious symbol of the highest and purest traits of southern womanhood. Under the ministrations of her Cavalier lover she must be brought to her senses; she must be led to accept her natural place in the southern system. When she recognizes her responsibility and accepts her noble suitor's love, her proper position in the plantation hierarchy is confirmed. The Cavalier can be wed to his southern-belle cognate and the "twin mansions" (251) of the two aristocratic households can be united as well.

Whatever doubts Hentz may have harbored concerning the severely restricted social role of the southern lady, she ultimately repressed them. She repressed her heroines as well, subjugating them to the bonds of masculine authority. It was, however, a happily willed fictional subjugation. No doubt Hentz convinced herself that the lady's chains were as moist and bright and were applied with as downy a touch as those that fettered the slaves of her plantation romances.

★   ★   ★

Sustained speculation by any southern writer concerning the expanded role of women in plantation society wilted in the face of the fierce determination of the region's self-styled planter-aristocrats to protect their privileged position from the attacks of an implacably hostile outside world. And this subordination of the idea of women's rights to the idea of a benevolent slave-owning patriarchy became more imperative as the region drew closer to and then entered the Civil War. Augusta Jane Evans' *Macaria; or, Altars of Sacrifice* (1863), published at the height of this conflict, illustrates the distortions imposed on the concept of the independent, free-thinking woman in the name of southern patriotism.

Though it boasts most of the familiar trappings of the southern romance, *Macaria* also presents two female characters who embody the possibility of self-fulfillment outside the conventional boundaries of plantation culture. In this respect it stands alone among novels of the period. Indeed, Evans' dramatization of her characters' capacity for intellectual and artistic independence is much more forceful than Hentz's uncertain and ambivalent attitude toward the quest for freedom of her fictional women. Representing the possibility of artistic fulfillment for southern womanhood is Electra Aubrey, a talented painter who has followed her muse to Tuscany. Irene Huntingdon is the novel's spokesperson for women's intellectual potential. She proclaims "the truth of female capacity to grapple with some of the most recondite problems of science"; and as proof of her assertion she writes brilliant scientific articles, which she publishes under the signature of "Sabaean."[20] Irene also places herself in opposition to her imperious father by preferring a rising young politician named Russell Aubrey, Electra's cousin, to the suit of her own cousin. When her father forbids her marriage to Russell, Irene throws herself into social work, ministering to the poor workers of "Factory Row" (292) in her unnamed southern hometown during a deadly typhoid epidemic.

In giving voice to women's desire for artistic and intellectual autonomy and in providing a field of action for women characters outside the assigned roles of plantation fiction, *Macaria* seems to be on the verge of breaking the masculine shackles of that tradition and of removing the southern lady at last from her fictional looking glass. Unfortunately, Evans' novel fails—as those of Hentz failed—to proclaim an unqualified declaration of independence for the southern lady, because the author feels compelled to use her would-be liberated characters to defend the very system that stands as an obvious impediment to their liberation.

Irene, the transcendental spokeswoman for spirituality and free inquiry, is at the same time a rabid supporter of secession. She sees her region's options as a clear choice between "political bondage—worse than Russian serfdom—or armed resistance." There is, she concludes, "no other alternative, turn it which way you will" (340). She also agrees with her high-minded Cavalier lover that abolitionism is a fanatical movement that has, with the election of Lincoln, become "triumphantly clad in robes of state—shameless . . . and . . . hideous" (337). Irene's artistic ally, Electra, is just as passionately devoted to the cause of the southern slavocracy. At the onset of hostilities she cuts short her sojourn in Florence and hurries home to her beloved Southland with crucial Confederate diplomatic dispatches secreted in her oil paintings.

20. Augusta Jane Evans, *Macaria; or, Altars of Sacrifice* (1864; rpr. New York, 1866), 194, 176, hereinafter cited in the text by page number only. A reprint of *Macaria* (Baton Rouge, 1992), edited by Drew Gilpin Faust, appeared subsequent to my completion of this work.

By the time Evans introduces readers to her novel's wartime action she has wrenchingly shifted fictional gears, turning her former spokeswomen for equal rights into clichéd female representatives of the South's sacred traditional values. The narrator assures us that the region that finds itself forced to take up arms enters the Civil War as a nation of "prayerful-hearted, brave-spirited women, and chivalric, high-souled, heroic men" (348). The erstwhile transcendental Irene has been transposed to her pedestal, where she is the proper object of her martial Cavalier's worship. In the manner of Richard Lovelace's poetic Cavalier, Russell makes clear that he is fighting for his lady as well as for the South. Indeed, the two are virtually synonymous in his mind. "With God's grace," he pledges in knightly fashion, "I will so spend the residue of my life as to merit your love, and hope of reunion beyond the grave" (372).

Irene, who has been portrayed earlier in the novel as the advocate of an active scientific skepticism, now devotes herself with mind and soul to the holy cause for which her aristocratic warrior is fighting. She believes that the successful conclusion of the Civil War will vouchsafe a new system dominated socially, economically, and politically by slave-owning planters. In rhetoric that echoes the reactionary tones of antebellum apologists such as Nathaniel Beverley Tucker she argues that an independent South must remain agrarian.[21] "If our existence as a republic depends upon the perpetuity of the institution of slavery," she argues, "then . . . the aim of our legislators should be to render us *par excellence* an agricultural people—and, with the exception of great national arsenals and workshops, to discourage home manufactories" (414). It is hard to imagine how any thoughtful southerner, much less a female character who has argued for the intellectual equality of the sexes and the virtues of rational inquiry, could seriously advocate an economic system that would relegate the South to the role of a third-world agrarian economy dependent on more technologically advanced societies for its essential manufactured goods. But these are the sorts of fictional gymnastics that all of the region's writers, women as well as men, seem to have been expected to perform in order to justify a future for the South's plantation culture and the peculiar institution so vital to its prosperity.

21. See Tucker, *The Partisan Leader*, 242, 247.

And who will be primarily responsible for maintaining the integrity of this new southern slave republic by assuring its firm moral foundation? The culture's "safeguards will be found," according to Irene, "in the mothers, wives, and sisters of our land" (416). Just as before the war, Evans' southern women seem destined to assume their traditional role as symbolic repositories of their culture's most exalted ideals. Of course, the author has not entirely forgotten the earlier pronouncements of her characters, and she seems unwilling to abandon entirely the possibility that they might achieve a new kind of freedom in the postwar South. After the conflict is over, Irene decides, she will help foster an independent national culture by establishing a school of design for women with Electra at its head. Practically, however, Irene and Electra's places in the new southern republic seemed destined to be scarcely less confining than their old roles in the antebellum patriarchy.

In *Macaria* Evans could not imagine a way of reconciling her idea of liberating the southern lady with her conviction that said lady must continue to buttress the plantation patriarchy and serve as its pure vessel, transmitting its cherished values intact from generation to generation. Her dilemma was that of a southern woman writer who, in the words of Anne Goodwyn Jones, "found herself split between an inner vision and a desire to conform."[22] Ultimately this conforming spirit led her to assign bizarrely antipodal roles to her novel's heroines.

Evans probably realized by 1863 that the brave new world of the postbellum slave republic envisioned by Irene and Electra was never to be, for her novel's conclusion suggests that the South's holy cause is destined to be lost on the battlefield. Her two heroines are serving in the hospitals of the besieged Confederate capital of Richmond. Russell has fallen at Malvern Hill, having "conscientiously tried to do [his] duty to [his] fellow-creatures, to [his] command, and [his] country" (455). Purified by the love of his philosopher-turned-belle, the vanquished Cavalier warrior ascends to heaven. Here, Evans assures us, his union with Irene, denied on earth, will be ultimately and triumphantly consummated. Through his death Russell becomes a

22. Anne Goodwyn Jones, *Tomorrow Is Another Day: The Woman Writer in the South, 1859–1936* (Baton Rouge, 1981), 91.

symbol of the South's chivalry and of its martyrdom, the first of a host of such martyred knights who would troop through Dixie's hallowed fictional halls in the decades following the war. Irene, like the multitude of fictional ladies who would come after her, presides with mute resignation "at the foot of the Red Dripping Altar of Patriotism, where lay, in hallowed Sacrifice, her noble, darling Dead" (458). Evans' intellectual adventurer has been grotesquely transformed into a black-draped saint of the Lost Cause.

★   ★   ★

Clifford Geertz has observed that "it is when neither a society's most general cultural orientations nor its most down-to-earth, 'pragmatic' ones suffice any longer to provide an adequate image of political process that ideologies begin to become crucial" as sources of social attitudes.[23] The antebellum South illustrates vividly this deep gulf between political process and cultural orientation. American ideals of freedom and equality could not serve as entirely suitable paradigms for a region committed to slavery and to the plantation system. Thus the South found it necessary to fashion a credo based on the concept of the lordly planter that would justify it to the nation and to the world at large. Southern writers were consequently impressed into the service of disseminating their region's aristocratic ideology, and no author, male or female, was exempted from service.

Though the Southwest's women writers might have been expected to assume their ideological burden with resignation and resentment, in fact they rose to the defense of Dixie's unique way of life with remarkable enthusiasm. Far from using a female perspective to criticize or deconstruct the plantation ideal, writers like Hentz and Evans trumpeted the virtues of the chivalric planter class as effectively as any of their male contemporaries. Their narratives, unlike those of southern male writers, do sometimes suggest that they harbor a modest but nonetheless detectable amount of resentment toward the very male-dominated social order that they celebrate so adroitly in their fiction. On occasion they even present characters who, in the words of Gilbert and Gubar, "act out the subversive impulses every woman inevitably feels when she contemplates the

---

23. Geertz, *The Interpretation of Cultures*, 219.

'deep-seated' evils of patriarchy." Yet compared with their literary peers in England and in the northern states their anger seems much more thoroughly repressed and their reservations about the circumscribed role of women in southern society much more hesitant and tentative. After all, their homeland had been placed, first intellectually and then militarily, under siege. They simply could not resist the enormous pressure to adapt their vision of the South to an ideological construct that apotheosized the patriarchal planter and enshrined his pure, passive, and submissive lady. If these women covertly sought, like the writers of Gilbert and Gubar's analysis, to destroy "all the patriarchal structures which . . . their submissive heroines seem to accept as inevitable," they did a nearly perfect job of concealing their subversive intentions.[24]

In the final analysis women writers of the Old Southwest chose not to blaze new fictional paths but to join forces with the region's male writers in celebrating an idealized plantation society. Not surprisingly, their fictional renderings found favor with southern readers, who felt, amidst sharp and often telling abolitionist attacks, a natural need to be flattered and who were hungry for approval, even if it was lavished on them by their region's own writers. More surprising was the receptivity of northern readers to these southern romances, a receptiveness that resulted in a strong national market for plantation fiction that flourished up to the very threshold of the Civil War. Paradoxically, plantation novels remained popular among northern readers even while those same readers were expressing progressively more negative opinions about the peculiar institution to which the fictional plantation was inextricably linked.

How can one explain the schizophrenic attitude of northern readers toward Dixie, their inclination to view the southerner as both an appealing exotic and a moral pariah? In his *Cavalier and Yankee*, William R. Taylor sheds light on the North's complex and ambivalent response to the South's aristocratic ethos. He points out that beginning in the 1830s and continuing through the 1850s a surge of interest in southern society and its noble slavocracy swept the nation. And he links the popularity of these romantic fictional projections of plantation life to the deep reservations that many northerners began to en-

24. Gilbert and Gubar, *The Madwoman in the Attic*, 77, 78.

tertain in the middle decades of the nineteenth century regarding the disturbing tendencies of their own go-getting, laissez-faire culture. The nation's unsettling social course was beginning to manifest itself, in the eyes of many Americans, in bewilderingly rapid change, pervasive social alienation, and moral anarchy. Northerners of conservative temperament increasingly came to believe that the original principles of the Republic had been abandoned and that this heedless forsaking of the past called into question both the beneficence of democratic institutions and the virtue of the natural yeoman. "Figures like Ishmael Bush, [James Fenimore] Cooper's brutal soulless squatter in *The Prairie*, underlined one of the threats these men saw in the process of westward settlement," Taylor writes. "If men were naturally self-centered and rapacious, bent on pursuing their own private ends, and nature was an amoral and neutral force, then what was there in the classless and open society of America to prevent its becoming a social jungle the equal of which the civilized world had never seen?"[25]

Taylor's observations help explain the intense pleasure with which many northerners responded to the literary plantation South. Here was a land founded on the principles of benign paternalism and aristocratic noblesse oblige, a land exempt from the exigencies of progress and change, a land where everyone recognized and accepted his place. How comforting this vision must have been to those Americans who had early established their fortunes and social prerogatives and were now scrambling to maintain them amidst the riot and flux of an expanding, increasingly industrialized and urbanized milieu. Plantation romances offered the consolation that somewhere within this vast American sea of classless modernism there remained islands of traditional order and graceful living where simpler old-fashioned virtues survived.

Northern writers, as well as northern readers, not infrequently lamented the grasping and unprincipled character of the stereotypical Yankee and gave their imaginative allegiance to his opposite—the chivalrous and noble southern Cavalier. Cooper and James Kirke Paulding were two of the most important northern writers of the an-

25. William R. Taylor, *Cavalier and Yankee: The Old South and American National Character* (New York, 1961), 98.

tebellum period to treat the southern gentleman with sympathy and admiration.[26] In *Notions of the Americans* (1828) Cooper opined that "in proportion to the population, there are more men who belong to what is termed the class of gentlemen, in the old southern states of America than in any other country of the world." More than two decades later, as sectional disagreements grew more pronounced, a writer for the New York *Daily Times* took southerners to task for closing their eyes "to every evil the removal of which will require self-denial, labor and skill." Yet even this more skeptical Yankee critic admitted with muted admiration that the character of the southern planter was more like that "of the 'old English gentleman' than any class to be found now, perhaps, even in England itself," echoing Cooper's earlier pronouncement. He also acknowledged that the southern gentleman's honesty and "unstudied dignity of character" and his "well-bred, manly courtesy" were "sadly rare at the North— much more rare at the North than at the South."[27]

The widespread popularity of the southern plantation romance was therefore largely the product of collusion between southern writers and northern readers. Southern writers needed to believe that their region was governed by the humane, paternalistic, and aristocratic principles of a plantation society; and many northern readers, for their own complex reasons, needed also to believe that this idealized southern landscape really existed. But the success of Dixie's novelists ultimately carried terrible implications for the nation. For though contemporary historians describe a diverse antebellum South dominated, as in other sections of America, by a broadly based middle class and resting, like the rest of the country, on equally broad democratic political foundations, sectional discourse between North and South was scarcely influenced by such realities as the United States drifted ever more steadily toward civil war. Americans of all sections responded much more readily to the aristocratic visions of novels like *The Planter's Northern Bride*, novels that suggested the South was fundamentally not like the rest of the nation, that it was different in an appealing and excitingly strange, but also inherently disturbing

26. For a detailed discussion of Cooper's and Paulding's use of Yankee and Cavalier types, see Taylor, *Cavalier and Yankee*, 95–109, 225–59.

27. *Ibid.*, 98; "The South: Slavery in Its Effects on Character, and the Social Relations of the Master Class," in *The Leaven of Democracy*, ed. Eaton, 481, 483, 484.

way. Antebellum southern fiction contributed significantly to the idea that Americans were divided into different races—a plebeian northern race and a patrician southern race.

Ironically, the exotic version of the South concocted by Dixie's writers was also central to the writings of the abolitionists whom southerners so detested. The dominant southern character for William Lloyd Garrison as well as for Hentz was the privileged planter. However, Garrison deftly transformed Hentz's paragon into an irresponsible tyrant, a heartless sadist, a woman beater and infant stealer, who refused to bring the word of God to those whom he held in bondage.[28] Romancers like Ingraham, Hentz, and Evans would have been shocked to learn that their idealized characters had provided fuel for abolitionist propagandists, but this was the indirect result of their fictional efforts. For it is easier for a propagandist to convert a stereotyped character into a villain than a complex and fully developed human being, even though the original purpose of the stereotype may have been to represent moral perfection. Ultimately, southern novels that had become vehicles for the region's strident ideology provoked an equally strident literary response from northern abolitionists.

★   ★   ★

Antebellum novels of the Old Southwest clearly illustrate the profound shift in mythic focus that occurred in the region between 1815 and 1860. The Jacksonian yeoman virtually disappeared from the pages of the plantation romance, and his place was assumed by the lordly Cavalier. These novels record the Southwest's effective abandonment of its frontier inheritance and its embracing of Tidewater Virginia as a cultural model. Though in reality southwesterners spoke with diverse accents, in the region's novels they spoke with one aristocratic voice. Women as well as men writers shared the conviction that the South's patriarchal society was unrivaled in its perfection. They were also convinced that the culture they celebrated in their fiction was profoundly different from that of the rest of the nation.

Drew Gilpin Faust has observed that in 1861, on the verge of the

---

28. Floan, *The South in Northern Eyes*, 7–8.

Civil War, southerners were "strikingly self-conscious about the need to undertake . . . introspection ['to explain themselves to themselves'] and to publicly define the foundation of their unity."[29] This cultural introspection and self-definition had been initiated by the Southwest's writers at least four decades prior to the coming of secession, though with less self-conscious intensity than that demonstrated in the months leading to the Civil War. In the 1840s and 1850s plantation novels of the Old Southwest were patiently building a case for the existence of a southern race of people and a southern nationality. By 1861 the region's writers could rightfully claim to have played a significant role in ushering southerners along the road to rebellion.

29. Drew Gilpin Faust, *The Creation of Confederate Nationalism: Ideology and Identity in the Civil War South* (Baton Rouge, 1988), 7.

Seven

The Cavalier Goes to War

On September 2, 1785, Thomas Jefferson wrote a letter to the Marquis de Chastellux that contained one of the earliest commentaries by an American on the differences between inhabitants of the North and the South. According to Jefferson, northerners could be described by the following key adjectives: "cool; sober; laborious; persevering; independent; jealous of their own liberties, and just to those of others; interested; chicaning; superstitious and hypocritical in their religion." The sage of Monticello observed that southerners were, by contrast, "fiery; Voluptuary; indolent; unsteady; independent; zealous for their own liberties, but trampling on those of others; generous; candid; without attachment or pretensions to any religion but that of the heart."[1]

Jefferson's description of the contrast between northern and southern character is, of course, a highly subjective one. A reader might well wonder, for example, how a region that ultimately constituted the heart of the Bible Belt could ever have been described as having no "attachment or pretensions to any religion." And northern contemporaries would probably have dismissed as uninformed prejudice Jefferson's blanket condemnation of their religious affections as "superstitious and hypocritical." In spite of its subjectivity, however, the letter to Chastellux indicates that even during the earliest days of the nation southerners perceived themselves as being significantly different from northerners. Indeed, many of Jefferson's observations—his perceptions that Yankees were industrious and hardwork-

1. Julian P. Boyd, ed., *The Papers of Thomas Jefferson* (24 vols.; Princeton, 1953), VIII, 468.

110

ing, but also grasping and devious, and that southerners were indolent, but also generous and forthright—would be echoed again and again in future commentaries on sectional character by southern writers, and by northern writers as well.

Yet if Jefferson's commentary reveals that Americans were conscious of differences between North and South even before the ratification of the constitution that created the United States, it also suggests that the recently established nation was far less polarized by these regional distinctions than it later would be. Jefferson's posture is neither so defensive nor so self-consciously regional as that of later southern commentators. When he is describing the northern character his tone is no more judgmental or hostile than is his attitude toward his fellow southerners. While Yankees are "chicaning" and tend toward overly fervent and hypocritical religious expression, they are also "sober," hard-working men who value freedom and are willing to respect the freedoms of others. And although southerners are a generous, open, and manly lot, they also tend to be lazy voluptuaries who are possessed of distinctly intolerant natures. Indeed, Jefferson seems to prefer the middle state of Pennsylvania, where, he observes, "the two characters seem to meet and blend and to form a people free from the extremes of both vice and virtue."[2]

Certainly in his letter to Chastellux, Jefferson views neither the northern nor the southern character as a repository of absolute virtue, and he does not believe that the differences between North and South are profound or unbridgeable ones. In fact he seems distinctly optimistic about the prospects of combining the best aspects of these regional temperaments, as he believes Pennsylvanians have done. His letter displays the liberal cosmopolitanism of the South's early political leadership, before increasingly acrimonious debate over slavery and the region's subsequent sense of beleaguerment stunted and constricted its intellectual and political vision. Had Jefferson lived into the middle decades of the nineteenth century he no doubt would have been disturbed by the inflammatory nature of North-South sectional discourse and shocked by what would become a commonly held opinion that northerners and southerners constituted completely different races of people.

2. *Ibid.*

Today many historians agree with Jefferson that the differences between the northern and southern mind were, from the beginning of the Republic, relative rather than absolute; and they go on to argue that even at the height of the controversy over slavery these differences remained relative ones. Edward Pessen contends that the attitudes that separated northerners from southerners in 1860 were more than counterbalanced by common beliefs and assumptions. "For all of their distinctiveness," he writes, "the Old South and North were complementary elements in an American society that was everywhere primarily rural, capitalistic, materialistic, and socially stratified, racially, ethnically, and religiously heterogeneous, and stridently chauvinistic and expansionist." David Potter similarly observes that in 1861 southern and northern Americans generally shared pride in the accomplishment of the Revolution, a suspicion and hostility toward Europe, an orthodox Protestant theology, a commitment to hard work and success, a belief in progress and in technological advances, and a profound faith in America's future destiny. "In spite of all the emotional fury," he contends, "there was probably more cultural homogeneity in American society on the eve of secession than there had been when the Union was formed, or than there would be a century later."[3]

If—as Jefferson early observed and contemporary historians have subsequently confirmed—white Americans were knit more tightly by common character traits than they were divided by conflicting sectional attitudes, how did they come to view themselves as products of cultures so diametrically opposed to each other that they might be considered members of separate races? For there is no question that by the beginning of the Civil War most northerners and southerners believed that the differences between them were deep and irreconcilable. William Taylor succinctly describes these stubbornly entrenched sectional attitudes:

> By 1860 most Americans had come to look upon their society and culture as divided between a North and a South, a democratic, commercial civilization and an aristocratic, agrarian one. Each section of the country, so it

---

3. Edward Pessen, "How Different from Each Other Were the Antebellum North and South?" *American Historical Review,* LXXXV (1980), 1149; David M. Potter, *The Impending Crisis, 1848–1861,* ed. Don E. Fehrenbacher (New York, 1976), 472.

was believed, possessed its own ethic, its own historical traditions and even, by common agreement, a distinctive racial heritage. Each was governed by different values and animated by a different spirit. . . . Under the stimulus of this divided heritage the North had developed a leveling, go-getting utilitarian society and the South had developed a society based on the values of the English country gentry.[4]

Taylor's description suggests the significant role that romantic plantation novels had played in formulating the popular conceptions of a plebeian, democratic North and a patrician, oligarchic South. In truth neither region had a monopoly on the go-getting, laissez-faire American spirit. Joseph Glover Baldwin's *The Flush Times of Alabama and Mississippi*, among other contemporary works, shows clearly that southerners were as liable to chicanery and opportunism as other Americans. But if southerners were to preserve slavery and the plantation system, they could not content themselves with being merely a variation on the common national type. They had to adapt, in the words of John McCardell, a "whole ideological configuration—a plantation economy, a style of life, and a pattern of race relations—which made [them] believe that they constituted a separate nation."[5] Southerners insisted on believing that their peculiar institution had nourished the development of a race of men free from the taint of Yankee rapaciousness. For if slavery had not produced a class of finely bred gentlemen and ladies—Hentz's magnanimous and chivalrous sons and pure, high-toned daughters—then what other justification could possibly serve to vindicate and sustain it?

The South needed to feel that it was different from the North, and southerners likewise found it necessary to define their difference from Yankees as a matter of superior aristocratic breeding. This need of the South to see itself as both different from and superior to the North prompted writers like Hentz to offer their readers idealized characters like Russell Moreland as fictional proof of the superiority of the southern planter-aristocrat. Such characters were adduced again and again in southern plantation fiction.

On the eve of the Civil War most southerners gave blind allegiance to the Cavalier myth that the region's fiction writers so skillfully

4. Taylor, *Cavalier and Yankee*, 25.
5. John McCardell, *The Idea of a Southern Nation: Southern Nationalists and Southern Nationalism, 1830–1860* (New York, 1979), 4.

fleshed out. The spiritually destructive and mentally debilitating results of such an allegiance are clearly evident in an article contrasting the northern and southern "races," written for the *Southern Literary Messenger* in 1860. The author of this essay contends that northerners are primarily descended from the Puritans, who "constituted, as a class, the common people of England . . . and were descended of the ancient Britons and Saxons." Consequently, the author maintains, northerners are people of rigorous intellects who have no notion of honor—fanatics, incapable of controlling their passions. "Being devotional, they push their piety to the extremes of fanaticism,—being contentious withal, they are led to attack the interests of others, merely because those interests do not comport with *their* ideas of right."[6]

In contrast to this land of inbred extremists, the writer describes a "Southron" race descending from the English Norman aristocracy and manifesting that culture's generous, honorable, aristocratic nature. The southern states, and most significantly Virginia, were settled, by and large, by Cavaliers "directly descended from the Norman Barons of William the Conqueror, a race distinguished, in its earliest history, for its warlike and fearless character, a race, in all time since, renowned for its gallantry, its chivalry, its gentleness and its intellect."[7] For the writer of this essay, southerners obviously represent a type of master race divinely ordained by heritage and blood lineage to rule and best qualified to control black slaves.

The racial theories given voice in the capital of the Old Dominion in 1860 were echoed in the Deep South one year later. A writer for *De Bow's Review* was convinced that the coming dismemberment of the Union was the result of a "deeply defined difference in race" between North and South. Saxon elements of England had migrated to New England, while the "chivalrous, impetuous, and ever noble and brave" inheritors of the Norman tradition had settled the South. This Norman culture had "attained its full development in the Cavaliers of Virginia and the Huguenots of South Carolina and Florida." The controversy over slavery, this essayist contended, had merely exacerbated the "gloomy and ascetic" tendencies of New England's Saxon

6. "The Difference of Race Between the Northern and Southern People," *Southern Literary Messenger*, XXX (1860), 404–405.

7. *Ibid.*, 407.

temperament and strengthened the commanding Norman spirit of the South.[8]

The *De Bow's Review* essay indicates that, just as the Old Southwest had been fond of imagining its plantation culture as a near replica of the Tidewater Virginia original, the region's writers were also quick to claim blood ties to the Old Dominion's FFVs, whose preeminent virtues were celebrated in novels by Virginia writers such as William Caruthers and John Cooke and in essays such as that written for the *Southern Literary Messenger*. Langdon Cheves, speaking at the 1850 Nashville Convention, prophesied that secession would enable the South to form a splendid empire "of the most homogenous population, all the same blood and lineage." This homogeneous southern population was drawn by both its Norman composition and the civilizing influences of its institution of slavery to a high degree of cultivation. In a magazine for southern women published in Nashville, Maria McIntosh defended slavery in part on the grounds that it afforded the planter "leisure for the cultivation of his mind, and the practice of all the gentle courtesies of life." In contrast with the "rude, laborious North," southerners had created a stable, aristocratic rural order in which changes in social status were "less frequent and violent . . . than in a commercial country."[9]

The association of the North with the adjectives *laborious* and *commercial* indicated another source of southern racial superiority—its supposed repudiation of the aggressive principles of laissez-faire capitalism. Indeed, it was precisely the southerner's exemption from the "spirit of trade" that constituted his genius. For "every virtue flounders," one southern magazine writer self-righteously opined, "in a deluge of barter." The lordly southern planter contrasted most favorably with his Yankee counterpart, who, the writer superciliously observed, "swaps horses until his last exchange, . . . too poor to swap, is sold for a jackknife."[10]

8. "Conflict of Northern and Southern Races," *De Bow's Review*, XXXI (October–November, 1861), 391, 393.

9. Quoted in Ralph T. Eubanks, "The Rhetoric of the Nullifiers," in *Oratory in the Old South*, ed. Braden, 20; Maria J. McIntosh, "The South," *Home Circle*, I (1855), 539.

10. J. N. Maffit, "The Almighty Dollar," *Southern Lady's Companion*, VI (June, 1852), 76.

Southerners not only convinced themselves that they were the descendants of Norman lords, but they convinced outside observers as well. English travelers were especially prone to see close ties between the South's social system and that of the English gentry. John Cairnes concluded that in the North one found "a government broadly democratic alike in form and spirit; in the South one democratic in form, but in spirit and essence a close oligarchy." These stark political differences, he believed, were related to the different social compositions of the two regions. Though both areas had been settled primarily by those of Anglo-Saxon stock, the northeastern colonies had attracted men "of the middle and lower classes" who were more independent in spirit and less inclined to want slaves. In contrast, the settlers of Maryland, Virginia, and the Carolinas were "for the most part composed of the sons of the gentry . . . Cavaliers and loyalists." They were men who, in Cairnes's view, possessed both greater capital and a greater inclination to use it to purchase slaves. Traveler James Stirling also observed that there was a "*bona-fide* Democracy in the North, founded on a material equality of condition; but the South," he contended, was "a downright oligarchy." Like Cairnes he concluded that the North was "essentially Puritan; the South, Cavalier."[11]

Yankees tended to share the opinion of foreign observers that southern planters were American versions of Old World aristocrats. But they often gave a negative twist to the idea of a planter aristocracy. Though one northern writer admitted that the typical plantation owner exhibited a number of admirable personal qualities—some, indeed, that were superior to corresponding aspects of the Yankee character—he believed this Cavalier type in its most conservative manifestation represented a danger to the Republic. These sensual, brave, reckless and violent men, he asserted, "hate and despise the Democrats of Europe as much as Francis Joseph himself. They glorify Napoleon, and they boast of the contempt with which they were able to treat the humbug Kossuth. . . . They call themselves Democrats, and sometimes Democratic Whigs. Call them what you will, they are a mischievous class,—the dangerous class at present of

11. Cairnes, *The Slave Power*, xvi, 33–34; James Stirling, *Letters from the Slave States* (1857; rpr. New York, 1969), 60.

the U.S. They are not the legitimate offspring of Democracy, thanks to God, but slavery under a Democracy."[12]

Though the notion that inhabitants of the South constituted a separate people was widely subscribed to both within and without the region, a few southerners seem to have recognized that Dixie's addiction to the myth of an aristocratic "Southron" race had blurred the yeoman's sense of class consciousness and led him to equate the planter's economic interests with his own. Hinton Helper was one of those who saw the predicament of the southern middle class with uncompromising clarity. Helper understood that the powerful attraction of the Cavalier ideal to the mind of the yeoman had induced him "to act in direct opposition to [his] dearest rights and interests." In Helper's opinion slavery was an economic, not a moral, tragedy. It was an institution that impeded the region's economic development and hindered the prosperity of the white worker by forcing him to compete with slave wages. "Non-slaveholders of the South!" Helper exhorted, "Farmers, mechanics and workingmen, we take this occasion to assure you that the slaveholders, the arrogant demagogues whom you have elected to offices of honor and profit, have hoodwinked you, trifled with you, and used you as mere tools for the consummation of their wicked designs."[13]

In attacking the hegemony of the planter class Helper was appealing to the southern yeoman to honor his own interests by imaginatively disentangling himself from the complex of myths associated with the Cavalier figure. But how could the average southerner be expected to repudiate the Cavalier ideal when he considered himself the authentic inheritor of an aristocratic ethos? Instead of turning on the slavocracy, rank-and-file southerners turned on Helper with fury. "By the election of 1860," observed George Frederickson, "a majority of Southerners . . . had accepted the view that the Republicans were abolitionists and that the election of a Republican President would be equivalent to the triumph of Hinton Rowan Helper."[14]

On the eve of the Civil War the South was a political anomaly. It

12. "The South: Slavery in Its Effects on Character, and the Social Relations of the Master Class," in *The Leaven of Democracy*, ed. Eaton, 485–86.

13. Hinton Rowan Helper, *The Impending Crisis of the South*, ed. George M. Frederickson (1857; rpr. Cambridge, Mass., 1968), 120.

14. *Ibid.*, xvi.

was a democratic society in which a dominant slave-owning class of planters assumed, in the words of Stephen V. Ash, "the right to command in a world of God-given inequality among men." The yeomen of the South accepted this Cavalier political philosophy because, as Ash maintains, they had thoroughly internalized the planter's paternalistic values. "When the Civil War . . . offered the white masses the same revolutionary opportunity it had offered blacks," he observes, "the whites declined to seize it."[15] After the election of Abraham Lincoln the majority of southern yeomen ignored the admonitions of Helper, embraced defiantly the Cavalier ideal, and followed the planter class resolutely into battle.

★   ★   ★

In his analysis of the state of southern consciousness in 1860, Clement Eaton examined the opinions of fifteen men. These men represented a fairly diverse cross section of the region's society. Included among them were political liberals as well as conservatives, and members of the merchant and professional classes as well as the planter class. In spite of considerable differences in outlook and opinion, Eaton discovered that this varied group of southerners was unified by two powerful emotions: a strong race feeling and an "exaggerated sense of honor, based on the cult of the gentleman."[16] Indeed, the concept of honor was an article of the Cavalier code most easily appropriated by southern men, regardless of their precise standing in Dixie's social hierarchy.

Bertram Wyatt-Brown has explained that the concept of honor, as opposed to the inner-directed notion of conscience, tightly binds an individual's sense of personal worth to the acceptance of his self-definition by the community at large. To possess honor, therefore, one must possess the respect of others. One might have expected that this rather primitive and feudal concept would have been embraced only by the South's wealthiest planters. But as Thorpe's *The Master's House* effectively dramatizes, the idea of personal honor was esteemed by white men of all classes. Though lacking the manners of gentlemen, southern yeomen considered the possession of honor to

15. Stephen V. Ash, *Middle Tennessee Society Transformed, 1860–1870: War and Peace in the Upper South* (Baton Rouge, 1988), 230, 232.

16. Eaton, *The Mind of the Old South,* 241–42.

be important because, as Wyatt-Brown observes, "they had access to the means for its assertion themselves—the possessing of slaves—and because all whites, non-slaveholders as well, held sway over all blacks. Southerners regardless of social position were united in the brotherhood of white-skinned honor."[17]

The class-transcending nature of southern honor helps to explain why in the state of Alabama secessionist sentiment was strongest not in areas dominated by the large plantation but rather in small farming communities. It also helps to explain why the South achieved an impressive public consensus respecting secession, in spite of considerable private misgivings among individual southerners concerning the wisdom of leaving the Union. As Wyatt-Brown explains, "it was a part of the honor code itself that community consensus forced dissenters to surrender to popular decision, even if the dissenters thought the policy foolish. Otherwise, he ran the risk of communal disloyalty." Lee was the most famous southerner (but by no means the only one) to justify his joining the southern rebellion in terms of maintaining his personal honor. His decision to join the Confederate Army was expressed simply: "I could have taken no other course without dishonor."[18]

Thus the Cavalier code did more than simply persuade southerners that they were members of a superior, aristocratic race. The concept of honor, which was an integral part of this code, eventually made secession seem obligatory because it was perceived as the South's only honorable course of action. For years proud southerners had endured the humiliation of knowing that many men in the outside world considered their culture to be barbaric and second-rate and that they judged the region's espousal of slavery to be proof of its moral turpitude. Now the election of Lincoln seemed to have set the nation on a course toward the eventual freeing of slaves. Such an emancipation represented a total and profound humiliation against which earlier humiliations paled. Seen through the southerner's eyes, the region could have remained in the Union only at the cost of the complete abnegation of its honor. This was for the South an unacceptable price.

Wyatt-Brown is careful to point out that northerners also believed

17. Bertram Wyatt-Brown, *Yankee Saints and Southern Sinners* (Baton Rouge, 1985), 186, 187.

18. *Ibid.*, 201, 205; Dixon Wecter, *The Hero in America: A Chronicle of Hero Worship* (New York, 1941), 281.

in the importance of personal honor. But, as with the concepts of chivalry and female purity, they embraced the idea with nowhere near the intensity of their brethren in the South. Being more industrialized and urbanized, more "bourgeois and highly institutionalized," the North had developed a society in which "the strength of other institutions lessened personal dependency upon family and community opinion."[19] Honor could never have been as absolutely central to the northern experience as it was to the mind of the Old South.

Ultimately, then, the Civil War was more than a conflict over slavery or states' rights. On a deeper, more visceral level it reflected a "discrepancy between one section devoted to conscience and to secular economic concerns and the other to honor and to persistent community sanctions that eventually compelled the slaveholding states to withdraw."[20] Had southerners not subscribed to a Cavalier code, had they not insisted on seeing themselves as gentlemen of honor, some sort of pragmatic accommodation regarding slavery might well have been forged with the North. But southerners were not pragmatic men when it came to the issues of slavery and secession. They were not calculating Yankees. They saw themselves instead as Cavaliers cast in the Norman mold. And, as Jefferson had accurately observed seventy-five years earlier, they were fiery Cavaliers at that.

John Quitman of Mississippi, a spokesman for secession in the 1850s, gave an early indication of the importance the concept of honor was to assume in Dixie's sectional debate with the North. "The South," he protested, "has long submitted to grievous wrongs. Dishonor, degradation, and ruin await her if she submits further."[21] Quitman's inflamed rhetoric is in the best tradition of the proud, choleric, aristocratic slavocracy. But ironically he was not the product of such a background. He had been born in New York, the son of a German Lutheran minister; and he had emigrated to Mississippi to practice law in 1821 at the age of twenty-three. Lutheran minister's son though he may have been, by the end of his life he had developed an appreciation of his region's honor worthy of the most impressively

19. Wyatt-Brown, *Yankee Saints and Southern Sinners*, 191.

20. Bertram Wyatt-Brown, *Southern Honor: Ethics and Behavior in the Old South* (New York, 1982), 20.

21. Quoted in H. Hardy Perritt, "The Fire Eaters," in *Oratory in the Old South*, ed. Braden, 241.

descended southern planter. Indeed, few who lived in the South for any length of time could resist embracing its Cavalier code, as the careers of Ingraham and Hentz have illustrated.

Concern for the South's honor remained paramount as the nation moved inexorably toward civil war. Writing to a sister who was visiting the North in the fall of 1860, South Carolinian Lewis Grimball predicted that the southern states would be forced to fight to protect "all that we hold dear—our Property—our Institutions—our Honor." Grimball's brother, William, expressed similar feeling to his sister, averring that only war would protect the family from "dishonor and death."[22]

After southern cannons were fired on Fort Sumter, both northerners and southerners rushed to enlist in their respective armies. But if Yankee recruits tended to see the cause for which they were fighting in moral terms—abolishing slavery and defending democracy—southern soldiers often saw the conflict as a matter of simple honor. "If we are conquered," one wrote, "we will be driven penniless and dishonored from the land of our birth." For this young southern warrior, as for most of his compatriots, death in battle was far preferable to seeing the South "dismantled of its glory and independence—for of its honor it cannot be deprived."[23]

Confederate Civil War verse clearly demonstrates that southerners continued to justify their struggle as an honorable combat, pitting an aristocratic "Southron" race against mercenary hordes of vandals from the North. In "The Cavalier's Glee" William Blackford proclaimed rapturously that the southern soldier's "path to honor" lay through glorious combat. Like the Cavalier lyricists of the seventeenth century, honor blended smoothly with chivalric love in Blackford's poem as a casus belli.

> The path to honor lies before us;
> Our hatred foemen gather fast!
> At home, bright eyes are sparkling for us,
> And will defend them to the last![24]

22. Randall C. Jimerson, *The Private Civil War: Popular Thought During the Sectional Conflict* (Baton Rouge, 1988), 10, 8.

23. James I. Robertson, Jr., *Soldiers Blue and Gray* (Columbia, S.C., 1988), 7.

24. William Blackford, "The Cavalier's Glee," in *South Songs: From the Lays of Later Days*, ed. Thomas Cooper De Leon (1866; rpr. Westport, Conn., 1977), 39.

Equally important to the southern war cause was the notion that the blood coursing through the veins of the South's gallant warriors was that of an aristocratic master race. In Joseph Brennan's "A Ballad for the Young South" such blood manifested itself in the southern soldier's "Norman grace and chivalry." An anonymous poem entitled "You Can Never Win Them Back" perhaps best expressed the region's sense of racial superiority and its contemptuous defiance of the lowly born Yankee:

> You have no such blood as theirs
>   For the shedding!
> In the veins of Cavalier
>   Was its heading:
> You have no such noble men
>   In your "abolition den,"
> To march through foe and fen—
>   Nothing dreading![25]

In searching for a symbol that best expressed the essence of the new southern nation, Arkansas poet Albert Pike found it in the flower of the magnolia:

> Ours, ours be the noble Magnolia
>   That only on Southern soil grows.
> The symbol of life everlasting;—
>   Dear to us as to England the Rose.

For Pike, the pure white flower of the magnolia was a "true Southern symbol" that captured the essence of the region's values. It was a "symbol of Honor and Right." It was the "type of Chivalry, loyalty, virtue."[26] The operative words in Pike's poetic amplification of the magnolia symbol—*honor* and *chivalry*—indicate the South's abiding concern for defending the one and preserving the other. After all, it was for these exalted values, not for slavery, that southerners were nobly fighting.

By 1861 the Old Southwest had fully joined with the coastal southern states in espousing the Cavalier ideology of a new southern na-

---

25. Joseph Brennan, "A Ballad for the Young South," in *South Songs*, ed. De Leon, 54; "You Can Never Win Them Back," in *South Songs*, ed. De Leon, 88–89.

26. Albert Pike, "The Magnolia," in Pike, *Lyrics and Love Songs*, 37–38.

tion. Even as they marched blindly toward disastrous defeat, many southerners were persuaded by their faith in the Cavalier myth that their cause would prevail. For, as one private from Georgia observed, how could a mercenary "race of clock makers and wood nutmeg venders" prevail in a contest of arms with the aristocratic South? How could a "degraded" northern race hope to defeat "a noble and respectable squad of Southerners"? To Lieutenant Henry Ewing of Tennessee the prospect of northern victory was equally inconceivable. "The scum of the North," he acidly observed, "*cannot* face the chivalric spirit of the South."[27] Dixie thus carried the Cavalier ideal into battle like an icon, convinced that it justified the righteousness of its cause and that it vouchsafed victory and vindication.

27. Jimerson, *The Private Civil War*, 127.

Eight

The Cavalier, the Lost Cause,
and the New South

The Civil War resulted not in vindication for the South's plantation culture but in its complete destruction. In the words of E. Merton Coulter, the war "freed the slaves, upset a social and an economic order, strengthened the powers of the national government, and riveted tighter upon the South a colonial status under which it had long suffered."[1] In material terms the region's defeat was equally devastating. Towns, cities, and plantations lay in smoldering ruins; railways and bridges were demolished; thousands of miles of fences were torn down; most livestock and cotton had been destroyed or seized by Federal forces. In short, the bulk of the Old South's wealth had simply vanished.

Ironically, one of the most effective and sympathetic descriptions of the desperate plight of the postbellum South was penned by a Yankee general who for decades would be associated in the southern mind with the most detestable excesses of Yankee savagery—Sherman. Though Sherman had contributed impressively to the destruction of the region, he bore no hard feelings toward his vanquished foe after the cessation of hostilities. Indeed, he movingly evoked Dixie's ruin for his fellow veterans in the following passage:

Look to the South, and you who went with me through that land can best say if they too have not been fearfully punished. Mourning in every house-

1. E. Merton Coulter, *The South During Reconstruction, 1865–1877* (Baton Rouge, 1947), 1, Vol. VIII of Wendell Holmes Stephenson and Coulter, eds., *A History of the South*, 10 vols.

hold, desolation written in broad characters across the whole face of their country, cities in ashes and fields laid waste, their commerce gone, their system of labor annihilated and destroyed. Ruin, poverty, and distress everywhere, and now pestilence adding to the very cap sheaf to their stack of misery; her proud men begging for pardon and appealing for permission to raise food for their children; her five million slaves free, and their value lost to their former masters forever.[2]

In the face of such widespread devastation the South set about restoring its economy, repairing its rent social fabric, and bridging the political gulf that lay between it and the rest of the nation. But would the region that eventually rejoined the Union be profoundly different from the region that had seceded from it in 1861? Would the South repudiate its past, cast aside its Cavalier mythic inheritance, and set out to forge an entirely new future? A close look at the postbellum South yields a negative answer to these questions. After roughly a decade of progressive but chaotic and often corrupt Reconstruction rule, Dixie reentered the Union on terms that were essentially its own, with its privileged white power structure resurrected and in control of most state governments. As C. Vann Woodward has explained, the Redeemers who restored the South's conservative white political dominance during the 1870s succeeded in uniting the remnants of the region's planter aristocracy with its newly ascendant business interests. Many Redeemers could boast of fine plantation manners and impressive pedigrees. But in casting votes for the full funding of state debts, for the granting of subsidies to railroads, for the securing of federal funds for internal improvements, or for the reducing of funds for newly established public education systems, these former planters were effectively merging their interests with those of a rising commercial class, thereby investing its political aims with "the prestige of aristocratic lineage and glorious war record."[3]

The new commercial-industrial political hegemony ushered in by Redeemers from Virginia to Louisiana was considerably different from the planter aristocracy that had dominated the antebellum South. But there were substantial continuities as well. Both hegemonies were white; both espoused deeply conservative concepts of gov-

2. Coulter, *The South During Reconstruction,* 2.
3. C. Vann Woodward, *Origins of the New South, 1877–1913* (Baton Rouge, 1951), 19, Vol. IX of Stephenson and Coulter, *A History of the South,* 10 vols.

ernment; both served the South's dominant economic interests; and both were determined to suppress and control the black population. In some respects the postbellum South had been significantly changed, but in other ways southern culture remained essentially unaltered.

One might not have expected the South's new ruling class to be terribly interested in maintaining the region's antebellum myth of Cavalier aristocracy. In fact, as the prominence of numerous old-guard planter-aristocrats in Redeemer political ranks suggests, New South leaders enthusiastically embraced a nostalgic view of Dixie's Edenic past. As Woodward succinctly and wittily observed, "One of the most significant inventions of the New South was the 'Old South.'"[4]

There were a number of advantages to be derived from celebrating an idealized plantation past. Waldo Braden has identified one of the least savory of these motives. As he points out, white supremacy was neither easily nor simply reestablished in the South. Redeemers were compelled to resort to vote buying, rigged elections, Klan harassment, and outright disenfranchisement of blacks in order to reestablish their political control. The Cavalier myth revived the postbellum South's flattering sense of itself as an island of cultivation and gentility amid a classless sea of modernity. The Old South ideal was useful in diverting Dixie's attention from the disgraceful expedients that were being employed under the table to restore the white man to what was deemed his rightful political place.[5]

The South thus refused to turn away from its old myths. As Stephen Smith has rather dolefully observed, the region "missed a perfect opportunity to refashion a new mythology and a world view consistent with the national dream of democracy, progress and success. Instead it turned inward and backward, determined to recreate a broken dream which would inevitably fall short in its attempt to organize and explain the events of the future." Southerners convinced themselves that the cause for which they had fought had not been cast into disrepute by defeat. Instead, as Father Ryan, a former chaplain in the Confederate army, rhapsodized in a poem entitled "March

4. *Ibid.*, 154–55.
5. Waldo W. Braden, "Repining over an Irrevocable Past," in *Oratory in the New South*, ed. Braden (Baton Rouge, 1979), 11–12.

of the Deathless Dead," Dixie's warriors had borne "the flag of a Nation's trust." And they had fallen "in a cause, though lost, still just."[6] The South's cause had been sanctified by defeat and transformed into a holy Lost Cause.

★ ★ ★

Southerners had left the Union convinced that they were members of a noble Norman race prepared to do battle with uncivilized hordes of Saxon-descended Yankees. The Lost Cause myth that dominated southern discourse after the Civil War continued to validate this sense of southern racial superiority. R. C. Cave, a Virginian who had fought under General A. P. Hill and who later became a minister in St. Louis, insisted as obdurately as his antebellum predecessors that the recently concluded hostilities had featured a contest between "two essentially different civilizations." Unlike the commercial North, Cave argued, the South, "led by the descendants of the Cavaliers," had inherited from its noble ancestors "a manly contempt for moral littleness, a high sense of honor, a lofty regard for plighted faith . . . and an unfaltering loyalty to constitutional government."[7]

Cave's rhetoric clearly demonstrates that, in spite of its military defeat, Dixie was unwilling to surrender the cherished conception of the South as a region inhabited by an aristocratic, honorable, and superior race of men. Moreover, his reference to the southerner's "loyalty to constitutional government" indicates a second, crucial article of faith embodied in the Lost Cause myth—the notion that southerners had been engaged not in rebellion but in a struggle to preserve the Constitution as they had understood it. J. H. McNeilly asserted in a speech titled "By Graves of Confederate Dead" that the South had been convinced by aggressive northern political policies that "the name of Union [was being] used to destroy their liberty under the Constitution." Thus southerners had been fighting for, not against, their nation's precious political document; and they had also struggled to preserve the concept of "a true Union." As Edward C. Walthall similarly explained, Dixie had not gone to war for slavery, for con-

6. Smith, *Myth, Media, and the Southern Mind,* 25; Father Ryan, "March of the Deathless Dead," in *Selected Poems of Father Ryan,* ed. Gordon Weaver (Jackson, Miss., 1973), 14.

7. R. C. Cave, "Honoring the Private Soldier," *Confederate Veteran,* II (1894), 162.

quest, or for ambition. Southerners had fought "'to save the Constitution,' as we read it, and to save ourselves, and to preserve our cherished form of government."[8]

There were obvious moral advantages to be gained by subscribing to the Lost Cause belief that the South had engaged in civil war to defend the Constitution and states' rights. As Howard Dorgan has observed, the effect of such an assertion was to pull attention away from the thorny question of slavery and to associate the Old South with a political principle rather than with a social practice that now seemed, even to many southerners, vaguely odious and embarrassing. More cynical bloody-shirt Republicans might hoot in derision and disbelief, but by the end of the nineteenth century the great majority of southerners would have heartily concurred with Alabama governor Thomas G. Jones that it was "just as absurd to say that the war was fought over the justice or morality of slavery, as it would be to declare that the conflict with the mother country was a dispute about tea thrown overboard in Boston Harbor."[9]

In addition to the states' rights argument, another essential element of the Lost Cause credo was the conviction that southerners in all sections of the region and from all walks of life had pledged their undiluted loyalty to the Confederacy. R. C. Cave boasted that "from stately mansion and humble cottage . . . with unanimity almost unparalleled, Southerners rallied for the defense of the land they loved."[10] Cave had apparently not visited large sections of western Virginia and North Carolina, as well as eastern sections of Tennessee, during the Civil War. If he had he might have been more circumspect in his claims for absolute southern unity; for he almost certainly would have encountered characters such as Bible Smith and Long Tom, eastern Tennessee Unionists who are vividly portrayed in James Roberts Gilmore's *Down in Tennessee and Back by Way of Richmond.*

8. J. H. McNeilly, "By Graves of Confederate Dead," *Confederate Veteran*, II (1894), 264; Edward C. Walthall, "The Confederate Dead of Mississippi," *Southern Historical Society Papers*, XVIII (1890), 300.

9. Howard Dorgan, "Rhetoric of the United Confederate Veterans: A Lost Cause Mythology in the Making," in *Oratory in the New South*, ed. Braden, 148–55; Thomas G. Jones, "To the Confederacy's Soldiers and Sailors," *Southern Historical Society Papers*, XXVI (1898), 192.

10. Cave, "Honoring the Private Soldier," 163.

In Gilmore's work Bible Smith and Long Tom are typical Tennessee yeomen who display—if postbellum southern rhetoric is to be believed—an untypical affection for the Union. Long Tom is a tall-tale–spinning mountaineer who can "outrun creation and give it two mile the start." Yet he uses his physical prowess to help a stranded Yankee captain get back to his lines. Bible Smith is a dedicated anti-Whig and Democrat who "goes fur the Decleration uv Independence . . . life, liberty, an' the pursoot uv whot ye loikes." Smith organizes a Home Guard of Unionists in his county, a company that brazenly carries off an 1862 Fourth of July celebration "at Richmond, Tennessee, under the very guns of a rebel regiment then forming in the town."[11]

In spite of their heroic exploits, there could obviously be no place in the Lost Cause myth for the likes of Long Tom and Bible Smith. To admit these characters into evidence would have meant repudiating the fond notion that all southerners, regardless of class, had supported the Confederacy with equal fervor. McNeilly spoke, no doubt, for the majority of southerners when he asserted that the war had vindicated the region's character by evincing its "noble manhood" and by producing warriors who had battled against "mere materialism in politics as in social life."[12] McNeilly believed that southern soldiers had sacrificed themselves for enduring values of the spirit. Unfortunately, the enduring values for which Long Tom and Bible Smith had fought were not the enduring values celebrated in the romantic war rhetoric of the postbellum South. Thus Long Tom, Bible Smith, and all southerners of similar pro-Union convictions had to be ignored and hidden in the closet along with the region's other skeletons. According to the Lost Cause myth, these independent, dissenting yeomen had never existed.

The unanimity of feeling the Lost Cause myth ascribed to the South's men was also attributed to her women. In 1899 *The Confederate Veteran* magazine lovingly described the dedication of a memorial erected in memory of the brave ladies of the Confederacy. The statue unveiled was a female figure sculpted in an attitude "calculated to impress the beholder with the sanctity of a pure woman's prayers." The viewer of this statue had no trouble determining what

11. James Roberts Gilmore, *Down in Tennessee and Back by Way of Richmond* (1864; rpr. Freeport, N.Y., 1971), 122, 149, 159.

12. McNeilly, "By Graves of Confederate Dead," 265.

this lady was praying for. The flag of the Confederacy lay draped about her knees; her hands were clasped, and her eyes were turned imploringly to heaven. Such a histrionic statue was a fitting representation of the southern woman who, according to Bradley T. Johnson, had "never flinched during that ordeal of temptation and of suffering, of fidelity and of fortitude." The South's staunch belles, he added, had "encouraged their fathers, husbands, and lovers. By them and through them the men were kept firm and straight."[13]

Even southern writers more attuned to New South ideas, such as Joel Chandler Harris, were convinced that the present superiority of the southern woman was the result of her inheritance from her plantation grandmothers, women who had possessed "the refinement that built up a rare civilization amid unpromising surroundings." In an elegiac exercise of Lost Cause nostalgia Harris celebrated the Old South's plantation life with the southern lady at the center, a life that had been "larger, ampler, and more perfect than that which exists in the Republic today." Thanks to this antebellum heritage he was confident that the South's ladies would continue to exert a "mellowing and restraining influence on the ripping and snorting age . . . the rattling and groaning age of electricity."[14]

Near the monument to the Confederacy's loyal ladies described in *The Confederate Veteran* was a companion monument to the "faithful slaves" who, according to the Lost Cause myth, had "toiled for the support of the Army with matchless Devotion, and with sterling Fidelity had guarded our defenseless Homes, women, and children during the struggle for the principles of our 'Confederate States of America.'" In order for the South to justify its cause it was necessary to believe that the plantation system had constituted a beneficent and mild, though perhaps anachronistic, patriarchy. Therefore, contented slaves and loyal and devoted ladies were viewed as twin pillars that had sustained the foundations of southern society while its men were away on the battlefield. As Thomas G. Jones proudly boasted, it was an "imperishable tribute" to the kindness of blacks "that

13. "Monuments at Fort Mill, S.C.," *Confederate Veteran*, VII (1899), 210; Bradley T. Johnson, "Monument to the Confederate Dead at Fredericksburg," *Southern Historical Society Papers*, XVIII (1890), 399.

14. Joel Chandler Harris, "The Women of the South," *Southern Historical Society Papers*, XVIII (1890), 279, 280, 281.

throughout a terrible civil war, in which hostile armies traversed a country filled with slaves, they never once rose anywhere in insurrection against their masters."[15]

The stalwart southern ladies and devoted slaves who had helped to sustain the Confederacy through four years of savage warfare constituted proof that the South's Lost Cause had been a noble one and that it had remained untainted by greed and corruption. From the southerner's point of view the region's character had not been judged deficient by its catastrophic military defeat. Rather, the trauma of war had vindicated a system that, in the crucible of battle, had produced examples of what McNeilly described as "noble manhood" and "gracious womanhood." Even though a new postbellum perspective had been forced upon them, southerners still insisted on interpreting their antebellum past in the same old clichéd way. They remained convinced that the Old South had been a noncommercial agrarian society governed by the humane, benign, and paternalistic principles of the plantation system. McNeilly admitted that pre–Civil War Dixie might seem quaint and antiquated when judged by a current age in which, he bitterly and ironically observed, "everything tends to be measured by money values . . . and self-sacrifice is considered Quixotism."[16] Yet McNeilly's defensive rhetoric as well as the more tempered nostalgia of writers like Harris indicates that southerners were determined not to allow their present submission to Yankee laissez-faire principles to qualify or spoil their reverence for their region's exalted past.

As Woodward has explained, the mind of the postbellum South was deeply and bizarrely divided. On the one hand, the region's political and economic leaders were pushing for rapid development and industrialization along northern lines. On the other, most southerners continued to despise a Yankee economic system that, as Bradley T. Johnson contended, was founded on the principle "that every man should be for himself and the devil could, would and should take the hindmost"—a system in which "supreme selfishness" seemed to be the "all-pervading sentiment and directing force." They might lobby in Washington for internal improvements and march obediently to

15. "Monuments at Fort Mill, S.C.," 210; Jones, "To the Confederacy's Soldiers and Sailors," 205.

16. McNeilly, "By Graves of Confederate Dead," 265.

meetings of their local chamber of commerce. But southerners remained convinced that their old civilization had been founded on the
ideals of "devotion to veracity and honor in man, chastity and fidelity
in woman." In their minds they might admit that such old values
were "primitive," but in their hearts they knew that these primitive,
outdated values were superior to the commercial values of the nation
at large that they had ostensibly embraced.[17] The Lost Cause myth
helped to confirm the South's unreconstructed attitudes—attitudes
that mixed confusingly and sometimes violently with the region's
New South mentality.

Far from allowing southerners to forget or conveniently push aside
memories of their vanquished warriors, the Lost Cause creed insisted
that the Confederate veteran be celebrated, apotheosized, and invested with the full trappings of chivalry. General Clement Evans,
dedicating a Confederate memorial in Macon, Georgia, in 1894, delivered an apostrophe to the rebel veteran's tattered but precious
"gray jacket." Unlike the northern uniform, which had been mass-
produced by wage slaves in the hellish textile mills of New England,
the southern soldier's clothing had been "woven in the loom at home,
cut and made by a mother's hand." Even though it was now tattered
by wear and shredded by bullets, it covered "the heart of a man as val-
iant as Rupert, as chivalrous as Saladin, as true to love of liberty as
Bruce."[18]

The names of Rupert, Saladin, and Bruce were not infrequently associated with the South's noble warriors; but by far the most popular
and repeated comparison employed by southern essayists and speech-
ifiers linked the gray-clad Confederate veteran to King Arthur and his
knights of the Round Table. As one essayist observed, the southern
race that had marched to war "like King Arthur and his greatest
knights . . . 'forebore its own advantage.' . . . It lived in an atmosphere
other than that of the mart." For Thomas G. Jones, Dixie's soldiers
had been Cavaliers within whose bosoms had been implanted "the
instinct that manhood required he should yield to other women, the
respect and deference he demanded for those about his hearthstone."

17. Woodward, *Origins of the New South,* 142–74; Johnson, "Monument to the
Confederate Dead at Fredericksburg," 400.
18. Clement A. Evans, "Honoring Our Dead at Macon," *Confederate Veteran,* III
(1895), 147.

The southern knight had imbibed from his culture a sense of natural hierarchy that guided at all times his dealings with "those he acknowledged as his 'betters,' and those who acknowledged him to be their superior." Is it any wonder that in such an ordered feudal atmosphere there had grown up among the Confederate troops "an instinctive order of knighthood"?[19]

Rather predictably, the destruction of the Confederacy was frequently likened in Lost Cause rhetoric to the defeat and death of Arthur, the disappearance of his magic sword, and the passing away of Camelot. "No 'arm clothed in white sasmite, mystic and wonderful' rises out of the earth to bear away our treasures from the sight of men," Jones sadly mused in a speech pregnant with Arthurian allusions that he delivered in Richmond in 1898. "But here, where the Confederacy was born," he continued, "we reverently dedicate . . . the priceless treasure of the life and character of the Confederate soldier." It may be, as Richmond author James Branch Cabell ironically observed, that the capital of the Confederacy was decidedly "not like Camelot." But one would have had a hard time convincing southerners who had been nourished and sustained by the Lost Cause myth.[20]

The South could also take solace in the knowledge that just as Camelot had had its King Arthur, Dixie had produced its own epitome of chivalric nobility—General Lee. This great military leader had risen to the defense of the Confederacy not because he supported slavery or advocated rebellion but because he felt his duty to his native state demanded his course of action. Lee's calm graciousness, his dignity of manner, and his sense of family and tradition combined with his self-denial, his abstinence, and his Christian piety to make him "the patriarch and oracle of the shattered South."[21] Even after the Civil War he continued to exhibit those aristocratic but humane qualities that set him off in vivid contrast to the political and social corruption of the Gilded Age. Refusing ten thousand dollars a year in return for the use

19. Joseph B. Cumming, "New Ideas, New Departures, New South," *Confederate Veteran*, II (1894), 361; Jones, "To the Confederate Soldiers and Sailors," 200, 202.

20. Jones, "To the Confederacy's Soldiers and Sailors," 208–209; James Branch Cabell, "Almost Touching the Confederacy," in Cabell, *Let Me Lie: Being in the Main an Ethnological Account of the Remarkable Commonwealth of Virginia and the Making of Its History* (New York, 1947), 147.

21. Wecter, *The Hero in America*, 281.

of his name as titular president of an insurance company, Lee instead accepted the presidency of an impoverished Virginia college, and he was among the first to apply to the federal government for a pardon.

It is difficult to overestimate the importance of Lee for the defeated South. Dixie might labor in poverty and humiliation, but as Douglas Freeman observed, southerners had one distinction: "Their stock had produced Lee; they had seen him, had known him, had obeyed his orders and, at his behest, had challenged Cemetery Ridge and had starved in the Petersburg trenches. Association with him was the glory of their generation." Perhaps most significantly, Lee's example gave southerners hope that the chivalric attitudes for which they believed they had fought had not been destroyed. In the words of Dixon Wecter, Lee "was the last and most perfect flower of that culture—which reclaimed her chivalry from bombast, and made into poetry the fact of her defeat."[22]

Lee's death relatively soon after the Civil War confirmed his sainthood. In tens of thousands of southern homes from Richmond to Vicksburg illustrations of the patriarchal, white-bearded Virginian reverently hung in a spot that became the house's "most hallowed place." More than that of any other southern leader, his image graced, in the words of Mark Neely, "the spot above or beside the family hearth once reserved for religious icons, and now increasingly the province of the heroes of contemporary culture." As before the Civil War, southwesterners would be proud to claim descent from Lee and other Virginians. Idealized images of the great leader of the Army of Northern Virginia, as well as of other generals, would confirm the Lost Cause ideal of a spiritual Confederacy, a "mystical entity within the political boundaries of the United States."[23]

★ ★ ★

On Sunday, May 30, 1886, before the first rays of sunlight had washed over Dixie's early-summer fields and forests, eight thousand laborers of the Louisville and Nashville Railroad set to work on the company's

---

22. Douglas Southall Freeman, *The South to Posterity: An Introduction to the Writings of Confederate History* (New York, 1951), 59; Wecter, *The Hero in America,* 284.

23. Mark E. Neely, Harold Holzer, and Gabor S. Boritt, *The Confederate Image: Prints of the Lost Cause* (Chapel Hill, 1987), 138, 150.

tracks. By the end of this long and grueling day they had shifted two thousand miles of rail three inches east in order to bring the L and N's gauge into conformity with the standard northern gauge. During the same hectic day the railroad company also succeeded in adjusting the wheels of its three hundred locomotives and its ten thousand pieces of rolling stock. As Woodward has tellingly remarked, "The strain and sweat of that desecrated Sabbath in 1886" fittingly symbolized "the South's desperate determination to conform. . . . For the South had come to believe—with at least part of its divided mind—in Progress."[24]

As Woodward's reference to the South's divided mind suggests, southerners were not consistent in their attitude toward the economic union with the North for which they were so fervently striving. Their reverence for the Lost Cause and for its idealized vision of the Old South resulted in a paradoxical attitude in which pride in the region's material progress was often mixed with bitter resignation over the surrender to alien northern values that this progress had exacted as its price. Joseph B. Cumming of Georgia expressed the South's most conservative and unreconstructed position concerning progress when he caustically insisted that there was, in reality, no New South, but only a South that had obediently "joined the procession," that had unprotestingly taken its place "in the uniformed ranks of the world generally."[25] The few authentic bits of culture of which the region could boast, he believed, were merely rather pathetic survivals of a dying plantation culture.

For Cumming, as for a significant number of southerners, there could be no real merging of New South with Old South, because the values of that older patriarchal civilization had no connection with those of the new commercial order. At the core of the Old South's Cavalier ethos, as Bradley T. Johnson observed, was a "respect for honor and veracity in man, love and purity in woman." These qualities, he believed, had enabled antebellum Dixie to withstand the social evils of "wealth and luxury, self-indulgence and selfishness" better than any other contemporary culture. But, he somewhat uneasily remarked, "whether they can always survive the progress of the civi-

24. Woodward, *Origins of the New South*, 124.
25. Cumming, "New Ideas, New Departures, New South," 362.

lization of industrialism no man can foresee." For the more conservative and pessimistic Cumming, however, the question of the survival
of traditional values had been effectively settled. "All hail! Thou
new!" he announced in an apostrophe filled with palpably bitter
irony. "We receive thee as our fate and fortune."[26]

A certain broad segment of southern opinion was therefore by no
means reconciled to the idea of a New South. Yet other southerners
who were committed to the restoration of the region's prosperity
were inclined to take a more sanguine view of its movement toward
commercial development and industrialization. They believed that
while the South ought never to repudiate its past, and indeed had
every reason to celebrate it, a respect for progress was necessary and
even beneficial.

The willingness of a broad majority of southerners to accommodate themselves to the imperatives of progress is evident even on the
pages of that most unreconstructed of publications, *Confederate Veteran*. A picture pregnant with unintended symbolism shows a monument to the South's faithful slaves being unveiled while in the background a freight train—rumbling, no doubt, on the now-standard
northern gauge—can be clearly seen. Prominent among the magazine's advertisers, along with monument makers and life insurance
companies, were business colleges and railroads. In 1896 the
northern-controlled Southern Railway boasted that it could trans-
port the region's honored Confederate veterans to their annual reunion in Richmond "over its *Own Line* . . . from all the eleven *Confederate States.*"[27] In the midst of an advertising appeal to Old South
chauvinism there is an unconscious celebration of the virtues of Yankee standardization and capitalist conglomeration.

In spite of a substantial residue of bitterness, resentment, and reaction against the North, most southerners experienced surprisingly little difficulty merging nostalgia for the antebellum past with enthusiasm for the commercial-industrial order of the future. This mixing of
old wine with new was especially evident in the rhetoric of New South
apostles. "Oftener than not," Woodward ironically notes, "archaic ro-

26. Johnson, "Monument to the Confederate Dead at Fredericksburg," 404; Cumming, "New Ideas, New Departures, New South," 362.

27. "Monuments at Fort Mill, S.C.," 210; Advertisement inside front cover, June
issue, *Confederate Veteran*, IV (1896).

manticism [and] idealizing of the past proceeded from the mouths of the most active propagandists for the new order. And this with no apparent sense of inconsistency, certainly none of duplicity."[28]

The rather glib synthesis of a Lost Cause mentality with more progressive attitudes is strikingly displayed in Henry Grady's important and influential essay entitled "The New South." From the perspective of 1886 it seemed to Grady that the region's military defeat could be understood as having had a partially beneficial impact on the Old Confederacy. It had settled once and for all the vexing questions of slavery and secession; and, Grady contended, it had resulted in an era of peace in which the South had achieved a greater prosperity and a "fuller independence" than that which had been sought by war.[29] Like most exponents of the New South creed, Grady was willing to accept the fact that slavery, if it was not an outright evil, was at least an impediment to southern economic development. Freed from the shackles of their peculiar institution, he was confident that southerners would now march forward toward a progressive and bright future.

Yet in spite of Grady's formal support for the idea of a new bourgeois-capitalist Dixie, a contemporary reader of his essay is bound to be amazed by the dominance within it of deeply conservative and nostalgic rhetoric, rhetoric that might just as easily have come from the pen of the most rabid Lost Cause acolyte. Though he was unwilling to defend slavery on economic grounds, Grady seemed perfectly willing to serve in other ways as its apologist. He pronounced the practical administration of the system to have been "nearly perfect among our forefathers," and he went on to add this benign assessment of the southern slave's lot in life: "It is doubtful if the world has seen a peasantry so happy and so well-to-do as the negro slaves in America" (108). The contented state of the black population had been confirmed, in his view, by the faithfulness it had exhibited during the Civil War. In a passage that might well have appeared in *Confederate Veteran* Grady asked his readers to remember "with what fidelity for four years [the slaves] guarded our defenseless women and children, whose husbands and fathers were fighting against his freedom" (9–10).

If many Lost Cause believers entertained reservations about Gra-

28. Woodward, *Origins of the New South*, 157.

29. Henry Grady, *The New South: Writings and Speeches of Henry Grady* (1890; rpr. Savannah, 1971), 8, hereinafter cited in the text by page number only.

dy's projection of the South's future, they could have had no such qualms about his understanding of her past. For Grady asserted that Dixie had "nothing to take back . . . nothing for which to apologize" in its history. The Civil War had found the region engaged in "revolution and not conspiracy" (11). The brave Confederate trooper had given his life for a noble cause. "Not for all the glories of New England, from Plymouth Rock all the way," Grady solemnly and defiantly pronounced, "would I exchange the heritage he left me in his soldier's death" (12). There was no need to defend an antebellum society that had been "feudal in its splendor" and "patriarchal in its simplicity," a culture nourished by graceful and gentle ladies and a simple Christian faith (110).

"The New South" illustrates how brilliantly Grady was able to appeal to the South's divided mind. To southerners weary of the region's impoverished and colonial present, he held out the promise of a prosperous future that would bring the Old Confederacy into economic concord with the rest of the nation. To those who were unwilling to relinquish what they considered Dixie's proud inheritance, he pulled out all the familiar stops of Lost Cause rhetoric. He implicitly assured the South that it could undertake its future without repudiating or having to come to terms with its past.

Though it is not surprising that Grady's rhetoric played well in Richmond, Charleston, and Vicksburg, one may wonder why it played equally well to northern audiences in New York and Chicago. There are, in fact, at least two ways of explaining this paradox. First, the North was inclined to adopt an increasingly forgiving attitude toward the southern states in the years following the Civil War. For their own complex reasons many northerners were not averse to hearing the South eulogize its antebellum plantation culture. Second, New South advocates like Grady courted audiences of Yankee businessmen with descriptions of a stable, traditional, agitation-free South—an environment perfectly suited for making money.

Northern industrialists had welcomed unrestricted immigration into the United States as a means of holding labor costs to an absolute minimum. At the same time many of these robber barons self-indulgently bemoaned their region's loss of cultural uniformity and damned its mongrelization by new influxes of "un-American" immigrants from southern and eastern Europe. Grady invited these disenchanted men to invest their money in a region free from the disorders of unrestricted "pell-mell" immigration (121), a region inhabited by a "homogeneous people" (120). The South was no longer a sectional pariah. In Grady's implicitly racist view it was the last redoubt of the simply, purely American character. "The spirit of Americanism," he assured northern audiences, burned bright in the region's Waspish love of liberty and democratic institutions. Alien attitudes and philosophies, "anarchy, socialism—that leveling spirit that defies government and denies God—[had] no hold in the South" (121).

And what of the South's own profound social discordance? What of the Negro? Grady soothed potential investors with the surety that relations between blacks and whites remained, as they always had, "close and cordial." Southerners were willing to grant former slaves their freedom and their franchise, he disingenuously claimed. And though he clearly implied that the South remained skeptical of the Negro's aptitude, he insisted that it was willing to stand back and see what this formerly servile race could accomplish with its newfound freedom (9–10).

If northerners were willing to indulge the South in its nostalgic assessment of its past, one can easily see how essays and speeches like "The New South" were calculated to warm the hearts of Yankee businessmen. Here was an orderly society with its roots still nourished by a patriarchal plantation culture, a place where people still recognized and accepted their social places and where alien, un-American ideas had not yet taken hold—a place ideally suited for the investments of entrepreneurs and robber barons. Paul Gaston has recently described in full detail how the idea of the South as a stable and unchanging land governed by the noble principles of a landed aristocracy—the South eulogized by Grady—ironically encouraged industrial development and the influx of northern capital. The trappings of the Old South were thus used to legitimize the bourgeois ventures of the New South. A new ruling class of merchants, industrialists, and planters, Gaston concludes, "supported by the New South creed, forged what it supposed was a mutually advantageous partnership with northern capitalists and fastened its control over the region's destiny in the 1880's."[30]

30. Paul M. Gaston, *The New South Creed: A Study in Southern Mythmaking* (New York, 1970), 219.

Ultimately spokesmen for the New South were not calling for a region that was socially, politically, or culturally new. They were really advocating a conservative restoration rather than a progressive renaissance. As Tennessee political leader Robert Love Taylor emphasized, the South would successfully compete with the North for "industrial supremacy"; but it would compete with most of its old values intact. In language charged with a mixture of Lost Cause passion and Christian fervor Taylor proclaimed: "There is no New South. It is the Old South resurrected from the dead with the prints of the nails still in its hands and the scar of the spear still in its side."[31] Or, as Grady somewhat less dramatically expressed the concept, the New South was "simply the Old South under new conditions" (107). The same chivalric blood that had valorously led the Confederacy during the Civil War would now come forward to address successfully the challenges of the future, a future symbolized by Grady's own burgeoning metropolis of Atlanta.

★   ★   ★

In 1899 Senator Thomas B. Turley delivered a speech in Shelbyville, Tennessee, dedicating the town's new Confederate memorial. Using standard Lost Cause vocabulary, he praised those soldiers who had answered the call "of nature, of honor, and of their country" and who had fought for "love of virtue and freedom." For Turley there was an acute and gratifying sense that the values for which the South had gone to war had been, by 1899, essentially redeemed. In Tennessee, he observed with obvious satisfaction, ex-Confederates controlled the local and state governments and sat in Washington as well. In confirmation of this sense of regional resurgence Turley pointed out that Dixie's soldiers had recently led the Union to victory in the Caribbean. On the verge of a new century, all Americans, not just southerners, could share a nation's pride in the South's great leaders. "From ocean to ocean," he boasted, "the memory of R. E. Lee is enshrined as the purest and greatest American since the days of Washington."[32]

By the end of the nineteenth century Dixie had completed its re-

31. Robert Love Taylor, *Lectures and Best Literary Productions of Bob Taylor* (Nashville, 1912), 171, 165.

32. Thomas B. Turley, "Confederate Monument, Shelbyville, Tenn.," *Confederate Veteran*, VII (1899), 498, 499.

union with the rest of the nation, a reunion confirmed by the region's enthusiastic participation in the Spanish-American War. But as Turley's speech clearly reveals, it was a reunion that had been fashioned according to the South's own special terms. Dixie was willing to accommodate itself as far as it was necessary to the demands of the present. But at the same time it insisted on adhering to the fundamental values and attitudes of its antebellum past. And this determination to hold on to the past was shared with nearly equal doggedness by both unreconstructed worshipers of the Lost Cause myth and advocates of the New South. The Cavalier figure had not died. He had, to borrow Taylor's metaphor, undergone a miraculous resurrection. The aristocratic ethos would be dexterously employed all over the region to justify the capitalist ventures of a new economic order as well as the reimposition of an old form of servitude on the region's black population.

Southerners were unwilling to consign their past and their noble cause to history's dustbin. Admittedly the cause had been lost. But even in its defeat they stubbornly believed that it had been vindicated. As Father Ryan poetically observed, the South adored its "Conquered Banner." That banner represented a cause "wreathed around with glory," one that would continue to "live in song and story." Dixie's postbellum writers seriously committed themselves to fulfilling Father Ryan's poetic prophesy that the fame of the Lost Cause, "Penned by poets and by sages / [Would] go sounding down the ages."[33]

33. Father Ryan, "The Conquered Banner," in *Selected Poems of Father Ryan*, ed. Weaver, 18.

Nine

The Cavalier's Literary Enshrinement

The mythic Cavalier had neither been destroyed by the Civil War nor cast out of the southern pantheon. He had, instead, been enshrined within the new myth of the Lost Cause. This cause, for which southerners believed their gallant, gray-clad knights had valiantly fought, would be celebrated during the concluding decades of the nineteenth century in hosts of stories, poems, novels, essays, and memoirs.

Though one may regret Dixie's stubborn refusal to repudiate the plantation ideal and to abandon its cherished illusion of being a highly aristocratic culture, one can hardly be surprised that the region, devastated and struggling to retain some shreds of its self-esteem, was unable to divorce itself from its antebellum mythic inheritance. It does seem decidedly strange, however, that Yankees did not strenuously and massively object to the tone of muted and not-so-muted apologia for the Old South adopted by southern writers as soon as the war was over. Indeed, not only were northern readers receptive to sympathetic portrayals of the South by its native authors, but writers from the North also demonstrated in a number of popular novels published as early as the late 1860s what Joyce Appleby has described as "an amazing readiness to let bygones be bygones." She writes, "Southern postwar characters are depicted as contrite, forgiving, and rededicated to the old Union." These early novels, Appleby believes, "supplied the Northern reader with a striking alternative to the angry political rhetoric emanating from Congress, the lecture platform, and the press."[1]

The sympathy offered by many northerners to their southern

1. Joyce Appleby, "Reconciliation and the Northern Novelist, 1865–1880," *Civil War History*, X (1964), 120, 129.

countrymen was not, of course, a uniquely postbellum phenomenon. Even during the acrimonious debates of the antebellum period, northern authors had expressed a substantial prosouthern literary sentiment. Dixie's admirers had included writers and artists as diverse as Cooper, Paulding, Stowe, Stephen C. Foster, and Daniel Emmett, the Yankee who had penned the lyrics to the South's unofficial anthem, "Dixie."[2]

Patrick Gerster and Nicholas Cords believe that part of the explanation for the North's abiding attraction to the South lies in its fixation on both the region's agrarian myth and its myth of plantation aristocracy. They also contend that the North has historically "conspired in southern mythmaking because of its guilt over slavery and its repressed attitudes on race relations."[3] Since most northerners realize—albeit imperfectly and reluctantly—that they are not entirely free of the taint of racism, they have always found it possible to brand southerners as bigots on one hand while extending to them a considerable degree of tacit support for that bigotry on the other.

As substantial as northern sympathy with southern cultural values may have been, it is evident that Yankees were also activated in the postbellum decades, as they had been during the antebellum period, by a strong sense of unease or disgust about their own culture. By the 1870s and 1880s a number of the nation's most distinguished literary figures were using southerners and southern attitudes as moral references by which the failures of American society might be better judged. In *The Burden of Southern History*, C. Vann Woodward details this use of southern characters in Herman Melville's philosophical poem *Clarel* (1876), in Henry Adams' *Democracy* (1880), and in Henry James's *The Bostonians* (1886). In each of these works, Woodward observes, "a Southerner, a veteran of the Confederate Army, is introduced in a sympathetic role. His importance varies with the work concerned, but in each of the three works the Southerner serves as the mouthpiece of the severest strictures upon American society or, by his actions or character, exposes the worst faults in that society."[4]

2. Patrick Gerster and Nicholas Cords, "The Northern Origins of Southern Mythology," *Journal of Southern History*, XLIII (1977), 568–71.

3. *Ibid.*, 574.

4. C. Vann Woodward, *The Burden of Southern History* (Rev. ed.; Baton Rouge, 1968), 110–11.

Not all northern writers were inclined to cede magnanimously the high moral ground of fiction to the recently vanquished foe. John William De Forest's *Miss Ravenel's Conversion from Secession to Loyalty,* published two years after Appomattox, avoids the blanket moralistic condemnation of bloody-shirt Republicanism; but the novel's ultimate judgment of the South's plantation culture remains firmly, though not hysterically, negative. De Forest delivers his fictional verdict through the character of Dr. Ravenel, a native-born southerner but a fervent Unionist, who at the beginning of hostilities flees his home in New Orleans to take refuge in the fictitious northern city of New Boston.

Being himself a southerner, Ravenel is capable of appreciating the planter's strengths—his social poise and fluency, his instinctive sense of good manners. But at the same time he recognizes clearly the anachronistic social and economic attitudes upon which the southern way of life is founded. His detached assessment of the collapse of Louisiana's sugar aristocracy might easily be applied to all of Dixie's great planters. He believes that the war is pushing these men inexorably toward extinction because, as he observes, "it was time. The world had got to be too intelligent for them. They could not live without retarding the progress of civilization. They wanted to keep up the social systems of the middle ages amidst railroads, steamboats, telegraphs, patent reapers, and under the noses of Humboldt, Leverrier, Lyell, and Agassiz. Of course they must go to the wall. . . . The grand jury of future centuries will bring in the verdict, 'Served them right!'"[5]

Ravenel's daughter, Lillie, initially shares neither her father's Unionist sympathies nor his detached attitudes toward the inevitable demise of the South's planter aristocracy. Her conversion from a secessionist to a loyalist point of view begins when the Ravenels return to Union-occupied New Orleans and encounter the implacable hatred of their former southern friends. The process is quickened when she falls in love with and marries a Union officer, a virile and martial Virginian named Colonel Carter.

By choosing to make Lillie's lover a Virginian bearing the distinguished name of Carter, De Forest complicates and qualifies his hero-

5. John William De Forest, *Miss Ravenel's Conversion from Secession to Loyalty* (1867; rpr. New York, 1939), 223, hereinafter cited in the text by page number only.

ine's conversion. For earlier in the novel she had been offered, but had rejected, the affections of another Union officer, Edward Colburne. Colburne, who is New England–born and –bred, is a thoroughly high-minded Puritan gentleman of whom Lillie's father distinctly approves. Though he does not possess the social panache and the masculine self-assurance of the Cavalier Carter, he is, in the words of Ravenel, "the most truly heroic, chivalrous gentleman that I know. . . . [O]ne of nature's noblemen" (189). Rather predictably, however, De Forest's imperfectly reformed southern belle prefers Carter to Colburne. Unlike her father, she does not detect the moral coarseness that lies under Carter's polished social veneer. Ravenel understands perfectly "from trifling circumstances, incidental remarks, general air and bearing" that the Virginian is "one of the class known in the world as 'men about town,' " and he realizes with equal clarity that such a man is "a natural product of that slave-holding system which he regard[s] as a compendium of injustice and wickedness" (179).

Lillie must learn from bitter experience what her father has suspected from the beginning. She has responded to Carter partly because of the strength of character that she associates with his Cavalier bearing. Yet Carter ultimately betrays his gentlemanly principles in order to rescue himself from debts accumulated as a consequence of his profligate lifestyle. Utilizing his military position as chief quartermaster of the Department of the Gulf, he sells ten government-owned steamboats for an average price of ten thousand dollars each and later buys them back at twenty-five thousand dollars each from the nominal purchaser, a "small and meager" southern gentleman of "composed and elegant manners" (374) who is more than willing to pocket a modest twenty-five-thousand-dollar fee and turn over the remainder of the spoils to the colonel.

Of course the properly bred Carter broods over what he calls his "only crime" and the "only ungentlemanly act of my life!" But De Forest is quick to provide an ironic editorial commentary on what he obviously views as Carter's crude southern moralizing. In De Forest's view Dixie's code of the gentleman, while adequate in acknowledging excesses of greed, is totally inadequate in addressing the sins of the flesh in which aristocrats like Carter habitually indulge, acquitting themselves with the notion that they are dissipating acceptably with gentlemanly circumspection and moderation. "Many people of high social position hold a similarly mixed moral creed," the New England author observed acidly. "They allow that a gentleman may be given to expensive immoralities, but not to money-getting ones; that he may indulge in wine, women, and play, but not in swindling" (380).

Ironically, the swindling that Carter considers such a violation of his code is never discovered; but his adulterous affair with the sensual and worldly Creole Mrs. Larue is accidentally revealed to Ravenel and, through him, to a devastated Lillie. Carter has considered this affair a relatively minor and unfortunate peccadillo, but it results in the potentially permanent alienation of his purehearted wife. De Forest resolves this marital dilemma by having Carter die bravely in battle. Though he obviously finds southern Cavaliers deficient in moral understanding, he seems willing to grant them a full measure of courage and manliness on the battlefield.

With Carter disposed of, De Forest allows Lillie to complete her full conversion to a northern point of view. She is free to accept the love of Colburne, the Puritan warrior whose devotion for her has remained pure and whose worthiness has been refined and strengthened in the crucible of battle. De Forest clearly intends for Colburne's personal vindication in love to parallel the North's cultural vindication on the field of combat. As the author's spokesman, Ravenel observes, "The victory of the North is at bottom the triumph of laboring men living by their own industry, over non-laboring men who wanted to live by the industry of others" (448).

Miss Ravenel's Conversion is the only substantial northern literary work of the postbellum period to award its moral palm not to the vanquished Cavalier but to the Yankee conqueror. The polish of Carter, it reminds us, is the polish of a morally flawed culture. It "is superficial and semi-barbarous, like that of the Poles and all other slaveholding oligarchies." Colburne represents for Ravenel the quintessence of an opposing democratic tradition. He stands for "equality" as well as for "honesty, sincerity, frankness, in word as well as deed." If Colburne is less self-assured and less socially adept than Carter, it is because of his Puritan commitment to "general hard work . . . in consequence of which there is less chance to cultivate the graces" (454). It is to Lillie's credit that in accepting Colburne's love she demonstrates her complete conversion, her full recognition of his plain Yankee virtues. De Forest clearly believes that these virtues will become the dominant virtues of the newly reunited nation.

Viewing *Miss Ravenel's Conversion* from a contemporary vantage point, one is struck by its relative balance of perspective and by the general absence within it of rancor and polemic. True, the novel does overstress what it considers to be deep and fundamental differences between northern and southern temperament. But compared with other observations on this subject emanating both above and below the Mason-Dixon Line before and after the Civil War, its author sustains a remarkably moderate tone. While it exhibits through Lillie a modest sympathy for the southern character, its moral judgment on the South's slavocracy remains firm and unwavering. In short, though southerners could not but have been offended by the portraits of Ravenel and Carter, *Miss Ravenel's Conversion* seems to have been tailor-made to appeal to a northern audience in 1867. Amazingly, however, De Forest's most impressive fictional achievement sold poorly, despite enthusiastic reviews; and it was virtually ignored through the later decades of the nineteenth century.[6]

To what can we ascribe the strange indifference of northerners to a novel of such obvious merit? Some critics cite the blunt realism of both its social and battlefield descriptions. Others point to the discomfort of genteel Victorian readers in the presence of the scarcely veiled eroticism of Carter's relationships with Lillie and Mrs. Larue. Still others argue that northern readers had grown weary of the subject of the Civil War. This last hypothesis, however, seems a particularly shaky one, since within a few years of the appearance of De Forest's novel these same readers would be avidly consuming the war stories of southern writers such as Thomas Nelson Page.

Paradoxical as it may seem, the failure of *Miss Ravenel's Conversion* can perhaps be linked most directly to its firm and rational indictment of the Old South as well as to its optimistic assessment of the nature of the victory that the North had achieved. Adams' *Democracy* and James's *The Bostonians* remind us that the North's most accomplished writers were far from confident about the moral tenor of the national culture that had emerged from the Civil War. Having destroyed the plantation South, the North was no longer sure

6. James F. Light, *John William De Forest* (New York, 1965), 87–88.

that Dixie's way of life had been a reflection of unmitigated evil or that postbellum northern culture was destined to embody fully the principles of freedom, justice, and equality for which the war had ostensibly been fought. It is quite likely that even as early as 1867, northern readers were no longer strongly drawn to fictional indictments of the Cavalier, no matter how measured those indictments might have been. Neither were they galvanized by fictional paeans to virtuous Yankees such as Colburne.

As they witnessed their nation careening recklessly through the Gilded Age, northern readers were less and less drawn to Unionist apologias such as *Miss Ravenel's Conversion*. They were more and more inclined to agree with censorious southern critics that the nation had given itself over to greed and materialism, thus vitiating the ideals for which the North had waged a holy war. Joseph Kirkland's *The Captain of Company K* captures most tellingly the postbellum North's underlying sense of cultural malaise. In this work the narrator gives full expression to America's cynicism and to its sense of self-betrayal, attitudes that had been absent from De Forest's more sanguine assessment of the Civil War's aftermath.

> The war is long past and gone—dead and buried and forgotten except for political purposes. We are now devoted to business and every thing is on a business basis. Greenbacks, worth forty per cent. before we won the fight, are now worth par, so *that* account is squared off. Eighty per cent. of the war debt is paid. Twenty per cent. of the war taxes are abolished; and if more are not done away with it is not because the United States Treasury needs the money, but because some favored citizens are not yet as rich as the United States Treasury, though they wish to become so. The nation is forty per cent. bigger than when the war closed, and a million per cent. more booming than any other nation ever was, ever dared to be, or ever will be. Fifty per cent. of the taxes collected are yearly paid out in pensions. Fifty per cent. of the dead are forgotten, and the other fifty per cent. are half forgotten; so that to the rest of the world (and to them) it is all the same, within twenty-five per cent. as if nobody had been killed at all.[7]

As Kirkland's bitter passage suggests, the North's cause had not been lost. It had been won and then inevitably betrayed by an explo-

7. Joseph Kirkland, *The Captain of Company K* (1891; rpr. Ridgewood, N.J., 1968), 346.

sion of prosperity and development that the Civil War itself had helped set into motion. Southerners might languish in poverty, but at least they were able to cling to myths that, because of the very fact of the region's defeat, had been exempted from what James Branch Cabell ironically described as "the wear and tear of existence." Southern writers could convince themselves, as an anonymous poet in the *Confederate Veteran* asserted, that their cause remained unsullied:

> Sorrow and pain and anger,
> Hatred and death are fled.
> It is only glory lingers
> With the great immortal dead.[8]

To a degree, northerners must have envied Dixie its precious Lost Cause. They must have understood on some level that it was a cause that, unlike their own, could never be betrayed. And since they themselves had destroyed this cause, they must also have realized that it was safe to indulge in the harmlessly nostalgic exercise of admiring the values for which the Old Confederacy had reputedly stood.

It is in this context that the remarks of Richard Watson Gilder concerning the reintegration of southern writing into the nation's literary mainstream can be understood. "It is well for the North, it is well for the nation," Gilder maintained, "to hear in poem and story all that the South burns to tell of her romance, her heroes, her landscapes; yes, of her lost cause, one of the greatest, most touching tragedies in the history of humanity."[9] Now that the Old South had been vanquished, it could be fictionally resurrected and even wept over by sensitive northern readers. Yankees were not merely going to allow Dixie's writers to indulge in literary fantasy; they were going to invite and encourage them to do so.

★   ★   ★

Southern writers were not reticent in answering the call of a sympathetic northern audience for nostalgic southern romance and lore.

---

8. Cabell, "Almost Touching the Confederacy," in *Let Me Lie*, 153–54; Cover of April issue, *Confederate Veteran*, XXXVI (1928).

9. Richard Watson Gilder, "The Nationalizing of Southern Literature: Part II—After the War," *Christian Advocate* (New York ed.), July 10, 1890, p. 442.

Two of the region's most popular forms of apologia were the personal reminiscence and the memoir. In his essay "The Old Plantation," Robert Love Taylor eulogized rural life in antebellum Tennessee as fondly as Thomas Nelson Page and George William Bagby celebrated the same lifestyle through their literary portraits of pre–Civil War Old Dominion.[10] Taylor heightened the allure of life on the plantation by contrasting it with an unnamed "city by the sea," probably New York. This urban milieu was a place of stark social contrasts where degrading poverty and festering slums existed alongside scenes of opulent wealth. It was also a place driven most profoundly by the spirit of heartless competition. In contrast to this ominous northern landscape Taylor depicted his plantation as a "paradise of . . . cotton and sugar cane, kept by the dusky Adams and Eves of toil. . . . [A]mid its magnolia-scented labyrinths of shade walked the chivalry and beauty of a lordly race."[11]

According to Taylor, the Cavaliers of antebellum Tennessee had lived in white-columned mansions "where life reached the high tide of baronial splendor." Around their mansions slaves had labored in the fields "without a single care to burden their hearts." These blissfully happy darkies "sang as they toiled from early morn till close of day" (153). Their simple but tidy quarters were "shrines of innocent pleasure" (153). Like fondly reared children they adored their benevolent master and mistress.

In Taylor's rose-colored view, Tennessee's planter aristocracy was fully deserving of the slaves' faithful adoration. For plantation matrons were invariably "perfect types of Caucasian beauty," and their mates were "as proud and courtly as ever shivered lances in the romantic day when knighthood was in flower" (156). Like most southern writers, Taylor could not resist investing his Tennessee Cavaliers with all the trappings of feudal splendor.

In her *Memorials of a Southern Planter*, Susan Dabney Smedes drew an equally flattering portrait of a Deep South planter—her fa-

10. See Thomas Nelson Page, "Social Life in Old Virginia Before the War" and "The Old South," in Page, *The Old South: Essays Social and Political* (New York, 1892); George William Bagby, *The Old Virginia Gentleman and Other Sketches*, ed. Thomas Nelson Page (New York, 1910).

11. Taylor, *Lectures and Best Literary Productions of Bob Taylor*, 152, hereinafter cited in the text by page number only.

ther, Thomas Dabney. As Smedes remembered her father, one of his most salient characteristics had been his Cavalier indifference to money. When one of his brothers had been threatened with bankruptcy, Dabney had sent him "a blank check, stating the amount he had in his bank (fifty thousand dollars or more, I think), and instructed [him] to draw upon it to the whole amount if necessary to prevent [his] name from going protest" (170). To a lordly Virginia-descended aristocrat, the preserving of the sacred Dabney name must have seemed a cause worth any price.

Though Smedes portrays her father as a firm Unionist, his rationale for standing with the Confederacy is as honorable in its own way as that of the sainted Lee. Initially determined to sell all his property and move to England before the winds of war are unleashed on Mississippi, Dabney is checked in this purpose when his wife quietly questions what will happen to the family's slaves if they are abandoned. Out of concern for those slaves he remains in Mississippi, and after the war he struggles to maintain his plantation. But he eventually loses possession of his lands, and as a result, spends his last years in Baltimore along with other impoverished natives of the Old Dominion.

If Smedes is to be believed, her father is amply rewarded for his devotion to his slaves. The author asks this question of Mammy Harriet, an old family retainer who continues to serve the Dabneys loyally after the war: "Will Papa be afraid to meet at God's judgment bar the face of any servant whom he ever owned? 'Oh, no, no, my good marster, no!'" Mammy makes this fervent reply while "tears [rain] down the venerable black face" (334). Like the fiction writers of the antebellum period, Smedes turns her father into a sanctified object of veneration to those from lower social orders.

In addition to the paeans of the region's memorialists, scores of southern poetasters added their voices to the chorus of praise for the Cavalier aristocrat, though the setting of their nostalgic lyrics was usually the battlefield rather than the plantation. Like their prose counterparts, they were fond of associating the South's aristocracy with heroic figures of the medieval and Renaissance periods. "The Hero Without a Name," in which W. S. Hawkins eulogizes a "paled-faced" Tennessee youth who died obscurely in a Yankee prison camp, concludes with this stanza:

> And I know I would rather wear to-day,
>   The crown that is his, with its fadeless bloom,
> Than Roderic's helm, so golden and gay,
>   Or Sidney's snow-white plume![12]

The association of the southern soldier with medieval knighthood was probably the most common motif in postbellum Civil War verse. Frank O. Ticknor celebrated "The Virginians of the Valley" as

> The Knightliest of the Knightly race
>   That, since the days of old,
> Have kept the lamp of chivalry
>   Alight in hearts of gold.[13]

In his "The Sword in the Sea" even a naval battle involving the Confederate ship *Alabama* was invested with courtly trappings and turned into a type of jousting contest.

> For here was Glory's tourney-field,
>   The tilt-yard of the sea;
> The battle-path of kingly wrath,
>   And kinglier courtesy. (29)

Southern poets like Ticknor were willing to go to absurd lengths to embellish their heroes with a medieval-tinged aristocratic sheen. Ticknor saw nothing incongruous in dubbing the homely Presbyterian mountaineer Stonewall Jackson the "Knight of the cloudless sun" (38). And he transformed Jefferson Davis—a man who had been pilloried in the northern press as a coward who had stooped to disguising himself in women's clothing—into a "gaunt" and "grizzled" King Arthur presiding over the dying embers of a ruined Camelot.

> Like moonlit mist on midnight snow,
> The sun of battle smoulders low!
> Alas, the King at Camelot! (53)

★ ★ ★

12. W. S. Hawkins, "The Hero Without a Name," in *South Songs*, ed. De Leon, 37.

13. Frank O. Ticknor, "The Virginians of the Valley," in *The Poems of Frank O. Ticknor*, ed. K. M. Rowland (Philadelphia, 1879), 22, poems hereinafter cited in the text by page number only.

Like their antebellum predecessors, the South's postbellum writers were compelled to come to terms with their region's unspoken imperative—that no southerner betray Dixie by questioning or repudiating its precious myths. Among more intelligent and thoughtful writers this external cultural pressure resulted in internal aesthetic tension as they struggled to reconcile loyalty to their region with the integrity of their artistic visions. This tension is revealed in two novels by writers who have been more commonly associated with a New South mentality: *The Cavalier*, by George Washington Cable, and *Tiger-Lilies*, by Sidney Lanier.

Cable published *The Cavalier* in 1901, more than twenty years after his critically acclaimed *The Grandissimes*. It is hard to imagine that a writer capable of conducting a penetrating critique of antebellum Creole society in his earlier novel would concoct such a blatantly romantic and clichéd treatment of the Civil War in his later work. Though it contains sympathetically drawn Yankee soldiers, *The Cavalier* is dominated, as its title implies, by dashingly aristocratic southerners such as Edgard Ferry-Durand, known more commonly as Ned Ferry, and Richard Smith, a young Confederate who serves somewhat in the capacity of squire to Ferry's knight.

The Cavalier focuses primarily on the rocky course of the love affair between Ferry and Charlotte Oliver. Although Charlotte is unhappily wed to an unprincipled and traitorous husband of Unionist sympathies, the genteel Ferry cannot consider courting her until her troublesome spouse is out of the way. Even after Ferry has disposed of Oliver, the lovers seem fated to remain star-crossed. Charlotte adores her Cavalier warrior as much as she detested her Yankee-loving late husband. But her delicate southern sense of honor and propriety make it impossible for her to marry the man who was responsible for his death. A substantial complication is rather mechanically resolved when it is revealed that another Cavalier, not Ferry, claims the privilege of having dispatched Oliver. This revelation assures a properly happy and tension-free conclusion.

Throughout *The Cavalier* Cable insistently stresses the chivalric qualities of his southern heroes, qualities that sometimes seem absurdly out of sync with the novel's action. In one scene Smith bravely risks his life to save Charlotte from a house about to be occupied by a detachment of northern troops. The two well-bred characters almost fall into Yankee hands, however, because they cannot decide who should run out of the front door first. Cable describes the two "pulling, pushing, and imploring each other in the name of honor, duty and heaven to let him—let her—go out first through the bright hall door."[14] A reader might feel more kindly disposed toward *The Cavalier* if he believed that its author was encouraging him to appreciate the ludicrousness of this scene. But given the novel's thoroughly romantic tone, one is hard put to know with what degree of irony Cable is inviting the reader to read the passage. Indeed, one cannot be sure how much the author himself is aware of his scene's irony.

When Cable's southern knights are not saving damsels in distress they are eulogizing them with properly florid rhetoric. This is how Smith addresses his lover, Camille Harper: "Oh, Camille, Camille! To this day I see you standing there in pink-edged white, pure, silent, motionless, a summer-evening cloud" (53). While it is tempting to conjecture that Cable's style may have been inspired in this passage by Edgar Allan Poe's "To Helen," the author's effect, unlike that of Poe, is cloying and artificial. Unfortunately it is an effect often produced in *The Cavalier* by the mixture of an overly lush style and an excessively reverent tone. For Cable is clearly intent on viewing his idealized Cavalier and belle through the rose-colored lens of memory where "they glow with nobility and loveliness yet, as they did in those young days when [Ferry's] sword led our dying fortunes, and [Charlotte] . . . followed them, binding the torn wound, and bathing the aching bruise and fevered head" (311).

How could a writer capable of creating lovers as complexly textured as Honoré Grandissime and Aurora Nancanou have descended late in his career to the clichéd characterizations of Ned Ferry and Charlotte Oliver? Thomas Richardson believes that the widely varying quality of Cable's fiction reflects the abiding antagonism within the author between past and present, New South and Old South, social reform and the romantic escape from social problems. Romances like *The Cavalier* represent, in Richardson's opinion, an attempt to "escape through the retrieval of an idyllic past,

14. George Washington Cable, *The Cavalier* (New York, 1901), 220, hereinafter cited in the text by page number only.

where the problems of racism are not present."[15] Not only was Cable unable to resist the Old South's siren song, but he also seems to have been more susceptible to its appeal after his self-imposed exile to the North. Though southern readers found much with which to object in the early stories of Cable's native Louisiana, they could only have been pleased by his fictional about-face in *The Cavalier*.

The same conflict between past and present, Old and New South underlies the writing of Lanier. Though he was not a native of the Old Southwest, Lanier chose the mountains of eastern Tennessee as the background for his romantic Civil War novel, *Tiger-Lilies* (1867). East Tennessee is a decidedly incongruous locale in which to place the idealized southern plantation. Yet Lanier's choice of setting indicates the extent to which postbellum southern writers embraced the proposition that all sections of Dixie had directly developed from the early plantation culture of the seaboard South.

Tiger-Lilies features the aristocratic Sterling family, lords of a mountaintop plantation named Thalburg Hall, a mansion graced with a "long, Doric-pillared colonnade."[16] As the name of the Sterling estate suggests, however, Lanier is not interested in developing garden-variety planter-aristocrats in his narrative. His characters represent instead a unique fictional type. They are southern transcendental aristocrats, melding the graceful manners of the southern Tidewater with the deep spirituality of Goethe's Germany.

Like most transcendental spirits, the male and female members of the Sterling family are devoted to music, especially to classical German compositions. In *Tiger-Lilies* southern gentlemen play violins and southern ladies sing Mendelssohn *Lieder* with exquisite voices (33). To the master of Thalburg, John Sterling, music is "a great, pure, unanalyzable yearning after God" (176). Such lofty spiritual inclinations have been passed on to his son, Philip, who is described as having "large, gray, poet's eyes, with a dream in each" (12).

15. Thomas J. Richardson, "Honoré Grandissime's Southern Dilemma: Introduction," in *The Grandissimes: Centennial Essays*, ed. Richardson (Jackson, Miss., 1981), 7–8.

16. Sidney Lanier, *"Tiger-Lilies" and Southern Prose*, ed. Garland Greever and Cecil Abernathy (Baltimore, 1945), 24, Vol. V of Charles R. Anderson, ed., *Centennial Edition of the Works of Sidney Lanier*, 10 vols. *Tiger-Lilies* hereinafter cited in the text by page number only.

Though he invests his Cavaliers with a spirituality derived from
Continental sources, Lanier also utilizes more conventional chivalric allusions to describe the landed gentry of eastern Tennessee. His
mountain aristocrats attend masked balls dressed up as medieval
knights and ladies. Above Philip's bed hang two swords, one a "naked
blade like Richard Coeur de Lion's," and the other "a delicate rapier
such as a gallant might wear at court" (53).

When the "blood-red flower of war" (93) intrudes into Lanier's idealized antebellum landscape, the novel's setting shifts to Virginia.
Most of its wartime action is indistinguishable from that described in
the standard romantic Civil War novels of southern writers such as
John Esten Cooke. For example, Philip vanquishes a band of black
Union soldiers as they are in the act of plundering a venerable Tidewater plantation mansion. Yet even in the midst of the exigencies of
war Lanier's southern soldiers manage to talk like transcendental poets. Viewing the lights of northern gunboats on the dark James River,
one Confederate observes that it "looks as if somebody had roused all
the *Ignes Fatui* in the world." His equally imaginative companion is
reminded of "a stately Polonaise, with flames for the dancers of it"
(128).

Tiger-Lilies is a rather grotesque hybrid, crossing the conventional
plantation novel, with its clichés of plot and character, with a philosophical narrative in which these aristocrats strive to make contact
with an elusive spiritual wholeness amidst the chaos of a brutally
physical world. But it contains, as well, a third element that is
strangely discordant with the work's dominant aristocratic-transcen-
dental thrust. In Civil War Virginia the voice of the lowborn Tennessee mountaineer startlingly intrudes into the story, bringing with it
the unpleasant odor of the South's dark social underside.

The yeoman class is represented in *Tiger-Lilies* by two brothers,
Cain and Gorm Smallin. Cain represents what Lanier probably considered an appropriately subservient yeoman mentality. He serves
Philip with loyalty and effectiveness, and he never questions the
rightness of the South's cause. By contrast, Gorm is the dark brother,
the villain, the traitor who deserts the southern cause and even
throws in his lot with the invading Yankees.

Cain, Lanier's high-minded mountaineer, is guided by the same
principles of honor as his aristocratic officers. He repudiates Gorm

because, as he phrases it, "you has stole our honest name . . . you has sneaked out f'om a fight that we was fightin; to keep what was our'n an' to pertect them that has been kind to us an' them that raised us" (121). Cain's repudiation of his brother expresses the devotion of the common southerner to the paternalistic planter class, a devotion that was assumed to have produced the unanimity of southern opinion celebrated in Lost Cause rhetoric.

Yet, to give Lanier his due, he does not restrict his point of view to Cain alone. He gives Gorm a voice as well; and it is a voice that is more eloquent than Lanier perhaps intended. Gorm challenges his brother to explain why he should feel loyalty to a class of large land-owners that has wrenched him from his peaceful pursuits and re-duced his family to starvation: "[w]hat did they drage me from hoam and fambly for? Which I haven't been married to her moar than a year and a rite young babi and they a starvin and me not thar" (114).

When Gorm deserts the army and returns to find his house burned, he reacts with the fury and the implacable sense of justice reminis-cent of Faulkner's epic poor-white demon Ab Snopes. If his house is fit to burn, so too is the mansion of John Sterling. "Hit's been a rich man's war an' a poor man's fight long enough. A eye fur a eye, an' a tooth fur a tooth, an' I say a house fur a house" (166). In a gruesome testament to southern underclass resentment, Gorm shoots both Mr. and Mrs. Sterling, drilling the plantation master with a bullet directly through his eye as he is in the midst of a prose rhapsody on the spirit-ual power of music. Then he burns Thalburg to the ground.

Soon after the destruction of Thalburg, Lanier returns his narra-tive to Richmond. Here in Capitol Square, as looters take the burning city, Philip embraces the high-minded lady who has followed his path and remained faithful to him through the years of dreadful conflict. Yet they embrace with the desperation of the lovers in Matthew Arnold's "Dover Beach." The barbaric armies of chaos have swept away Lanier's Old South. And at the conclusion of *Tiger-Lilies* it is difficult to imagine how the author's remaining transcendental Cava-liers can survive the age to come, the New South to which in other writings Lanier would give his enthusiastic allegiance.

Though by the conclusion of Lanier's novel the South's antebel-lum aristocracy has been destroyed, the author cannot resist punish-ing also his shadow yeoman, Gorm Smallin. The vicious traitor returns to Virginia and is blown apart by an artillery shell in the bombardment of Petersburg. Yet even though he is eliminated, Gorm's insidious memory haunts the novel's conclusion. For he is not only an individual; he is also the type of the brutal and animalistic southern underclass, the consummate redneck. His disturbing presence in Lanier's otherwise idealized fictional world confirms Mary Poovey's observation that fiction reproduces, knowingly or unknowingly, the tensions and contradictions between the ideal life of the imagination and the "diminished reality" of actual experience. These contradictions, Poovey contends, may reveal themselves "at the level of content or form; they may emerge in the discrepancy between the author's explicit aesthetic program and the emotional affect the text generates."[17] Gorm generates an emotional affect that undermines and calls into question the aesthetic program embodied in Lanier's lovingly rendered Thalburg Hall.

It is possible that Lanier came to realize that his characterization of Gorm implicitly called into question the myth of a benevolent plantation patriarchy resting on the foundations of a contented and loyal underclass. This realization probably prompted him to destroy the monster he had created. But he did not destroy him soon enough. The powerful presence of Gorm in *Tiger-Lilies* suggests obliquely the cancer at the core of the Old South's plantation culture. It also foreshadows an ominous new future for the South, a future that would be brilliantly revealed in Faulkner's saga of the Snopes family.

Lanier illustrates, perhaps more vividly than any other writer of the postbellum period, the divided mind of the New South so fully described by C. Vann Woodward. Lanier was enthralled by a romantic vision of the plantation South in *Tiger-Lilies* and deeply disturbed by the forces of brutality unleashed by the Civil War and typified by Gorm that had destroyed it. Yet this same writer turned his back on the plantation a decade later and confidently asserted: "The New South means small farming." In his essay "The New South," which contains no mention of or allusion to the Old South, he contended that small farms and diversified farming were the keys both to a secure future for the region and to an era of racial harmony. "In the identical aims of the small-farmer class," he predicted, "whatever now re-

17. Poovey, *The Proper Lady and the Woman Writer*, xiv.

mains of the color-line must surely disappear out of the Southern political situation."[18]

One wonders how Lanier had been able to reconcile the nostalgic voice of *Tiger-Lilies* with the progressive and sanguine voice of "The New South." The answer is probably that he was not concerned with reconciling these conflicting voices. Like most New South advocates, Lanier was willing to champion Dixie's future without confronting fully the burden of her past.

★ ★ ★

The enshrined figure of the Cavalier continued to be celebrated by the South's writers through the final decades of the nineteenth century and into the twentieth century. William Garrott Brown's novel, *A Gentleman of the South*, published in 1903, illustrates the potent appeal that the Cavalier continued to exercise over Dixie's imagination. Brown's work portrays an antebellum Alabama aristocracy of the highest order, worthy Southwest inheritors of a Tidewater plantation ethos.

The hero of *A Gentleman of the South*, Henry Selden, combines prepossessing looks with a composed and dignified bearing. To the author his strength of character justifies his being compared to the saintly Robert E. Lee.[19] Like Lee's, Selden's demeanor is imperturbable. Only once in the narrative does he lose his temper, when he sees his overseer beating a female slave "too weak from childbirth to take her place among the cotton pickers" (82).

Like all southern Cavaliers, Selden's manliness is unquestioned. The hunting trophies and swords that surround his huge fireplace presumably testify to his thoroughly masculine fiber. Yet he also displays a more refined and sensitive spirit. He possesses a "love of beauty," which "tends to separate him from his peers," men who are more drawn to "politics and government and war-making than to the study of the beautiful" (40–41). Like all self-respecting planter-aristocrats, he successfully stands for election and goes to Congress to defend his region's political interests; yet he enters politics with a

18. Sidney Lanier, "The New South," in Lanier, *"Tiger-Lilies" and Southern Prose*, 334, 344.

19. William Garrott Brown, *A Gentleman of the South*, 39, hereinafter cited in the text by page number only.

shudder of distaste. His sister sympathetically observes, "I know how hard it must be for you to give up your beautiful life here at The Cedars and go back into that vulgar world at Washington" (73). Brown's hero is thus a finely chiseled Cavalier in the tradition of Lanier's Philip Sterling or Mitchell's Ashley Wilkes.

The Cedars, the Selden plantation, was established by Selden's father on lands purchased from the Indians. But in Brown's novel this Indian-haunted wilderness has been quickly superseded by a replica of the Virginia hunt country. Historians and contemporary observers may tell us that black-belt Alabama was during the 1850s a raw society linked firmly with its early nineteenth-century frontier origins. But Brown insists that "the patriarchal mode of life which grew out of slavery [gave] the society of the South a dignity and an outward show of stability characteristic of ancient rather than extremely youthful communities" (79). The author's depiction of antebellum Alabama bears a stronger resemblance to medieval European society than it does to the society of the American frontier. The Cedars, Brown observes, was a seat "of nearly absolute power." He also contends that "hardly the castles of medieval Germany were remoter from the vast surges of modern life" than was the Selden domain (128–29). Though he writes from the perspective of a new century, Brown cannot resist imagining the Old South as antebellum authors before him had also imagined it—as a place isolated from the flux of history and from the imperatives of modernity.

The novel's feudal atmosphere is complemented by contented slaves who fully appreciate their master's kindly paternal oversight, and yeomen who accept Selden's authority as well as their own subservient role in plantation society. Brown is careful to note that it is the small farmers on the Whig committee who come to the Cedars to ask Henry to run for Congress. As one of them admiringly remarks, "Thee ain't nary a farmer within ten miles o' any one o' yo' plantations that you aint' he'ped out of some sort er werriment or yuther" (68). In Brown's novel the common folk of Alabama are depicted as fully cognizant of and grateful for the planter's sense of noblesse oblige.

Selden, the perfect embodiment of the southern Cavalier, is ironically undone by the finely wrought nature of his noble character. Though for years there has been bad blood between the Seldens and the neighboring Underwood family, dating back to a duel involving Selden's father, the son strives to bring peace between the two aristocratic families. He is additionally bound by a pledge he made to his dying mother never to imitate his father by fighting a duel. Unfortunately one hot-blooded Underwood will not be appeased by Selden's peaceful overtures; and he finally succeeds in goading the reluctant hero into fighting by attacking the very thing that no southern gentleman can live without—his honor. In a public confrontation Selden's enemy ridicules him as "a parlor knight . . . more skilled to rob a woman of her honor than to defend his own" (195). Forced into a duel he had promised never to fight, Selden resolves not to attack but only to defend himself. However, it is a hopeless strategy. He is mortally wounded in a contest of small swords.

For Brown the death of Selden prefigured and symbolized the fall of the Old South and the destruction of the Cedars, both of which were shortly to be accomplished by the Civil War. The antebellum world, whose highest values Selden embodied, was, as Brown nostalgically observed, "so different from the present and governed by such different laws." Indeed the author was convinced that many of his contemporary readers lacked the capacity to believe "that men should . . . have lived such lives, obeyed such codes, set themselves such standards" (15–16). So palpably did Brown yearn for the South's vanished past, so obviously did he disdain the diminishment of its present, that the death he visited upon his hero seems clearly to have been administered as an act of mercy. The author must have believed that killing Selden was preferable to condemning him to live into an age of alien and materialistic values.

It is remarkable that Brown's point of view in *A Gentleman of the South* is as fiercely nostalgic and as bitterly unreconstructed as the Lost Cause rhetoric of the 1860s, 1870s, and 1880s. His novel indicates, in fact, that neither the South nor its writers had by the end of the nineteenth century become reconciled to the loss of the precious plantation past. Entering into the new century, southerners remained deeply committed to their cherished myths. And this commitment was deepened and nourished by writers such as Brown. As Rollin Osterweis has observed, the survival of the Lost Cause myth into the second half of the twentieth century would be made possible in part by "a literary assertion of values that the defeated nation of

1865 intended forever to preserve against the onslaught of 'the commercial, industrial civilization of the erstwhile enemy, amoral and heartless.'"[20] Southern fiction would help to preserve the Lost Cause myth into the future, just as it had helped earlier to nourish the Cavalier myth upon which the Lost Cause myth had been established.

20. Osterweis, *Romanticism and Nationalism in the Old South*, 152.

Conclusion

The Cavalier Tradition and the
Orientalizing of Dixie

By the end of the postbellum period the Old Southwest had ceased to exist as a markedly distinct region. It certainly could no longer be considered a frontier society. Indeed, even during the antebellum period, as we have seen, it had been more and more prone to suppress its frontier heritage; and it had effectively abandoned the mythic ideal of the stalwart yeoman in its literature.

From 1815 to 1865 the Old Southwest experienced a profound mythic realignment. It turned away from the noble yeoman who had served as the hero of the nation's trans-Allegheny movement and whose potential had been consummately symbolized by the meteoric career of Andrew Jackson. Instead the figure to which it offered its imaginative allegiance was the aristocratic Cavalier who had been born and nurtured in the coastal South and who was most evocatively associated with Tidewater Virginia. By the 1860s and 1870s the Southwest had merged its sense of cultural identity with that of the seaboard South. Consequently the Lost Cause rhetoric of a Virginian like Thomas Nelson Page became indistinguishable from that of a Tennessean like Robert Love Taylor. In terms of its mythic traditions and the literary expression of those traditions, the Old Southwest had become by 1900 an integral part of what would be called the Solid South.

Looking at the Old Southwest's development from the perspective of the twentieth century, the region's cultural drift away from the states of the Midwest and toward the states of the coastal South seems inevitable. Wherever a plantation society was economically feasible, that society's aristocratic ethos overpowered social patterns commonly associated with the American frontier. As Jesse Hill Ford's *The Raider* brilliantly illustrates, the imaginative appeal of the white-columned portico and the lordly master surveying his slave domain was irresistible to southwesterners. And as Bertram Wyatt-Brown has shown, wherever there were substantial numbers of slaves, society was bound by the powerful brotherhood of white-skinned honor. Even if the Old Southwest had been able to seize the initiative and to form closer commercial links with the Midwest, it would have continued to gravitate toward the plantation cultures of Virginia and the Carolinas, on which it was determined to model its society, and it would have eventually found itself cut off from the cultural patterns of the states north of the Ohio and west of the Mississippi.

Although the Southwest's mythic realignment was inevitable, it carried ominous implications for the region's future. The Cavalier myth to which it so enthusiastically subscribed was an Old World myth based on notions of blood and inherited privilege that had been transported to the Old Dominion and nurtured and sustained there by the institution of slavery. An aristocratic myth of this particular type was profoundly and irreconcilably at odds with the dominant American myths of liberty, equality, and boundless opportunity—myths that coalesced naturally around the figure of the yeoman. The nation could not continue to prosper as a unified whole while it remained subject to the centrifugal cultural forces inherent in the Cavalier and yeoman ideals. In order for America to develop along the lines laid down by the Declaration of Independence, it would be necessary to vanquish or subordinate both the Cavalier concept and the region that subscribed to it. The Civil War accomplished this task most effectively and most terribly.

Though the Civil War destroyed the Old South, it did not succeed in eliminating the Cavalier from the nation's mythic fabric. It only succeeded in transforming him into the saintly champion of a sacred Lost Cause. Dixie continued to venerate the principles associated with its aristocratic ethos, and many of those principles remained hostile to prevailing American values. As the nineteenth century gave way to the twentieth, the mind of the South was deeply divided. Southerners professed loyalty to national myths while continuing to hold stubbornly to their own unique mythic past.

The literature of the Old Southwest played a crucial role in the region's progression toward an identification with a Tidewater social ideal. This role can be assessed from two perspectives. On one hand the writing of the period can be viewed as mirroring the region's inexorable shift away from a frontier cultural orientation to a regional plantation orientation. But this writing can also be understood as serving in an active, generative capacity, not simply reflecting, but also giving impetus to, the region's shift in cultural values. Unquestionably the romantic works of the Southwest's writers helped the newly settled residents of the region imagine themselves as products of a highly refined, aristocratic culture. And at a time when few people traveled extensively, these same works also played a crucial role in determining how northerners would understand the South. Indeed, it would not be an exaggeration to say that southwest fiction helped to nourish myths and sectional stereotypes and to create an emotional atmosphere that made the Civil War, if not inevitable, at least more likely.

To the extent that the Southwest's writers of plantation romances led their region down the fictional road to rebellion, they did the South a terrible disservice. In addition, these novels played a baleful role in fixing permanently in the mind of a northern audience the idea of Dixie as an exotic "other" culture. In understanding the pernicious effect of the antebellum plantation romance on the way the South was viewed by the outside world, Edward Said's observations in *Orientalism* seem particularly relevant.

Said's analysis of the phenomenon of Orientalism concludes that this intellectual cult has served as "a Western style for dominating, restructuring, and having authority over the Orient." "European culture," he provocatively observes, "gained in strength and identity by setting itself off against the Orient as a sort of surrogate and even underground self."[1] It is not farfetched to apply Said's assessment of Orientalism to an understanding of the historically paradoxical response of northerners to the South. Said has argued that the manner in which the West has viewed the Orient is, in itself, a demonstration of cultural imperialism; and one can detect a similar imperialism at work for over two hundred years in northern attempts to understand

---

1. Edward W. Said, *Orientalism* (New York, 1978), 3.

and interpret Dixie. Whether northerners have admired the region as a charming and quaint setting filled with the white-columned mansions of a landed aristocracy or whether they have excoriated it as a benighted land filled with ignorant and animalistic rednecks, the assumption of social superiority, or at least of technological supremacy, that has informed their interpretations has transformed the act of interpreting into a subtle exercise in cultural dominance.

If Said's Orient could be "orientalized," the nineteenth-century South could be southernized by the North because, like the Orient, "it *could be*—that is, submitted to being—made" southern. This southernizing of Dixie would continue into the twentieth century, and it is a process that would be partially apprehended by Patrick Gerster and Nicholas Cords. Northerners would always find it necessary to set the South apart, turning it into an exotic "other" culture, and making it— to borrow Said's vocabulary again—a "sort of surrogate" for the nation's "underground self," the shameful or disturbing or inconvenient self that America could only recognize by projecting onto the South.[2] Perhaps the most blatant and morally repugnant example of this projecting would be the nation's historical inclination to view racism as a southern problem rather than as an American problem.

And how were the Southwest's nineteenth-century writers guilty of abetting this uniquely American brand of Orientalism? By distorting their fictional landscapes, by celebrating their idealized Cavalier heroes and failing to consider the character of the independent yeoman, these authors encouraged the notion that Dixie was a region vastly different from others in America—a place where a planter aristocracy of Old World lineage ruled over happy slaves as well as masses of vaguely realized but equally subservient whites. Seeking to justify the South, the region's writers unwittingly helped to turn it into the "other"—an alien culture that could be manipulated according to the North's inclination and need, that could be transformed into a bucolic heaven or into a backward and uncivilized rural hell.

The failure of the Southwest's nineteenth-century writers to redeem Dixie in their fiction and their unwitting participation in the orientalizing of their region reflect the larger historic failure of south-

2. *Ibid.*, 6, 3. See also Gerster and Cords, "The Northern Origins of Southern Mythology," 567–82.

ern culture. For over one hundred years, both before and after the Civil War, southerners struggled to justify themselves to the rest of the nation. But they were never able to understand why they were being ostracized and punished for their stubborn allegiance to the Cavalier concept and to the plantation ideal. Nor did they realize that the ideal effusions of their writers could never garner the unqualified respect of northern readers, that the most rose-colored of plantation landscapes could never move the North to vouchsafe them the cultural and moral parity they so desired. Not until the twentieth century would southern Americans begin to assess more honestly in their literature the economic, social, and spiritual costs of their complex mythic inheritance.

Bibliography

Abernethy, Thomas Perkins. *The Formative Period in Alabama, 1815–1828.* Montgomery, Ala., 1922.

———. *From Frontier to Plantation in Tennessee.* 1923; rpr. University, Ala., 1967.

———. *The South in the New Nation, 1789–1819.* Baton Rouge, 1961. Vol. IV of Wendell Holmes Stephenson and E. Merton Coulter, eds., *A History of the South.* 10 vols.

Alden, John Richard. *The First South.* Baton Rouge, 1961.

Allen, James Lane. *The Choir Invisible.* 1897; rpr. London, 1925.

Appleby, Joyce. "Reconciliation and the Northern Novelist, 1865–1880." *Civil War History,* X (1964), 117–29.

Ash, Stephen V. *Middle Tennessee Society Transformed, 1860–1870: War and Peace in the Upper South.* Baton Rouge, 1988.

Bagby, George William. *The Old Virginia Gentleman and Other Sketches.* Edited by Thomas Nelson Page. New York, 1910.

Baldwin, Joseph Glover. *The Flush Times of Alabama and Mississippi: A Series of Sketches.* Americus, Ga., 1853.

Bellamy, Elizabeth Whitfield. *Four Oaks, a Novel.* 1867; rpr. New York, 1870.

Benton, Thomas Hart. *Speech of Mr. Benton, of Missouri, in Reply to Mr. Webster: The Resolution Offered by Mr. Foot, Relative to the Public Lands, Being Under Consideration.* Washington, 1830.

Blair, Walter. *Native American Humor, 1800–1900.* New York, 1937.

Boyd, Julian P., ed. *The Papers of Thomas Jefferson.* Vol. VIII of 24 vols. Princeton, 1953.

Braden, Waldo W. "Repining over an Irrevocable Past." In *Oratory in the New South,* edited by Braden. Baton Rouge, 1979.

———, ed. *Oratory in the Old South, 1828–1860.* Baton Rouge, 1970.

Bridenbaugh, Carl. *Myths and Realities: Societies of the Colonial South.* Baton Rouge, 1952.

Brooks, Cleanth. *William Faulkner: Toward Yoknapatawpha and Beyond.* New Haven, 1978.

Brown, William Garrott. *A Gentleman of the South: A Memory of the Black Belt, from the Manuscript Memoirs of the Late Colonel Stanton Elmore.* New York, 1903.

———. *The Lower South in American History.* 1902; rpr. New York, 1969.

Bruce, Philip Alexander. *Social Life of Virginia in the Seventeenth Century.* 1907; rpr. New York, 1964.

Cabell, James Branch. "Almost Touching the Confederacy." In Cabell, *Let Me Lie: Being in the Main an Ethnological Account of the Remarkable Commonwealth of Virginia and the Making of Its History.* New York, 1947.

Cable, George Washington. *The Cavalier.* New York, 1901.

———. *The Grandissimes.* 1880; rpr. New York, 1907.

Cairnes, John Elliott. *The Slave Power: Its Character, Career and Probable Designs.* 1863; rpr. New York, 1968.

Calhoun, John C. *A Disquisition on Government and Selections from the Discourse.* Edited by C. Gordon Post. 1853; rpr. New York, 1953.

[Carter, St. Leger Landon (?)]. "Interesting Ruins on the Rappahannock." *Southern Literary Messenger,* I (August, 1834), 9–10.

Cash, Wilbur Joseph. *The Mind of the South.* New York, 1941.

Cave, R. C. "Honoring the Private Soldier." *Confederate Veteran,* II (1894), 162–64.

Chevalier, Michael. *Society, Manners, and Politics in the United States: Letters on North America.* Edited by John William Ward. 1839; rpr. Garden City, N.Y., 1961.

Clark, Blanche H. *The Tennessee Yeomen, 1840–1860.* 1942; rpr. New York, 1971.

Clemens, Samuel L. *Life on the Mississippi.* 1883; rpr. New York, 1927.

Cobb, Joseph Beckham. *The Creole; or, The Siege of New Orleans.* Philadelphia, 1850.

———. *Mississippi Scenes; or, Sketches of Southern and Western Life and Adventure.* Philadelphia, 1851.

Cohen, Hennig, and William B. Dillingham, eds. *Humor of the Old Southwest.* Boston, 1964.

"Conflict of Northern and Southern Races." *De Bow's Review,* XXXI (October–November, 1861), 391–95.

Coulter, E. Merton. *The South During Reconstruction, 1865–1877.* Baton Rouge, 1947. Vol. VIII of Wendell Holmes Stephenson and E. Merton Coulter, eds., *A History of the South.* 10 vols.

Cumming, Joseph B. "New Ideas, New Departures, N—— South." *Confederate Veteran,* II (1894), 359–62.

Dabney, Virginius. *The Story of Don Miff, as Told by His Friend, John Bouche Whacker: A Symphony of Life.* 2d ed. Philadelphia, 1886.

Darnton, Robert. *The Great Cat Massacre and Other Episodes in French Cultural History.* New York, 1984.

De Forest, John William. *Miss Ravenel's Conversion from Secession to Loyalty.* 1867; rpr. New York, 1939.

De Leon, Thomas Cooper, ed. *South Songs: From the Lays of Later Days.* 1866; rpr. Westport, Conn., 1977.

"The Difference of Race Between the Northern and Southern People." *Southern Literary Messenger,* XXX (1860), 401–409.

Dorgan, Howard. "Rhetoric of the United Confederate Veterans: A Lost Cause Mythology in the Making." In *Oratory in the New South,* edited by Waldo W. Braden. Baton Rouge, 1979.

Eaton, Clement. *The Freedom-of-Thought Struggle in the Old South.* New York, 1964.

———. *The Growth of Southern Civilization, 1790–1860.* New York, 1961.

———. *A History of the Old South: The Emergence of a Reluctant Nation.* 3d ed. New York, 1975.

———, ed. *The Leaven of Democracy: The Growth of the Democratic Spirit in the Time of Jackson.* New York, 1963.

———. *The Mind of the Old South.* Baton Rouge, 1964.

Engerman, Stanley L., and Robert William Fogel. *Time on the Cross: The Economics of American Negro Slavery.* Boston, 1974.

Evans, Augusta Jane. *Macaria; or, Altars of Sacrifice.* 1864; rpr. New York, 1866.

Evans, Clement A. "Honoring Our Dead at Macon." *Confederate Veteran,* III (1895), 147.

Faulkner, William. *Absalom, Absalom!* 1936; rpr. New York, 1951.

Faust, Drew Gilpin. *The Creation of Confederate Nationalism: Ideology and Identity in the Civil War South.* Baton Rouge, 1988.

Fischer, David Hackett. *Albion's Seed: Four British Folkways in America.* New York, 1989.

Flint, Timothy. *A Condensed Geography and History of the Western States; or, The Mississippi Valley.* 2 vols. Cincinnati, 1828.

Floan, Howard Russell. *The South in Northern Eyes.* Austin, 1958.

Foote, Shelby. "Pillar of Fire." In *A Treasury of Civil War Stories,* edited by Martin H. Greenberg and Bill Pronzini. New York, 1985.

Ford, Jesse Hill. *The Raider.* Boston, 1975.

Fox-Genovese, Elizabeth, and Eugene D. Genovese. *Fruits of Merchant Capi-*

tal: Slavery and Bourgeois Property in the Rise and Expansion of Capitalism. New York, 1983.

Franklin, John Hope. *The Militant South, 1800–1861.* Cambridge, Mass., 1956.

Freehling, William W. *The Road to Disunion: Secessionists at Bay.* New York, 1990.

Freeman, Douglas Southall. *The South to Posterity: An Introduction to the Writings of Confederate History.* New York, 1951.

Gaston, Paul M. *The New South Creed: A Study in Southern Mythmaking.* New York, 1970.

Gayarré, Charles. *The School for Politics: A Dramatic Novel.* New York, 1854.

Geertz, Clifford. *The Interpretation of Cultures.* New York, 1973.

Genovese, Eugene D. *The Political Economy of Slavery: Studies in the Economy and Society of the Slave South.* New York, 1965.

———. *Roll, Jordan, Roll.* New York, 1972.

Gerster, Patrick, and Nicholas Cords, eds. *Myth and Southern History.* Chicago, 1974.

———. "The Northern Origins of Southern Mythology." *Journal of Southern History,* XLIII (1977), 567–82.

Gilbert, Sandra M., and Susan Gubar. *The Madwoman in the Attic: The Woman Writer and the Nineteenth-Century Literary Imagination.* New Haven, 1979.

Gilder, Richard Watson. "The Nationalizing of Southern Literature: Part II—After the War." *Christian Advocate,* New York edition, July 10, 1890, pp. 441–42.

Gilmore, James Roberts. *Down in Tennessee and Back by Way of Richmond.* 1864; rpr. Freeport, N.Y., 1971.

Girouard, Mark. *The Return to Camelot: Chivalry and the English Gentleman.* New Haven, 1981.

Grady, Henry. *The New South: Writings and Speeches of Henry Grady.* 1890; rpr. Savannah, 1971.

Green, Fletcher M. "Democracy in the Old South." *Journal of Southern History,* XII (1946), 3–23.

Greenblatt, Stephen. "Culture." In *Critical Terms for Literary Study,* edited by Frank Lentricchia and Thomas McLaughlin. Chicago, 1990.

Gwynn, Frederick L., and Joseph L. Blotner, eds. *Faulkner in the University: Class Conferences at the University of Virginia, 1957–1958.* Charlottesville, 1959.

Hamilton, Stanislaus M., ed. *The Writings of James Monroe.* 7 vols. 1898–1903; rpr. New York, 1969.

Harris, Joel Chandler. *On the Plantation.* 1892; rpr. Athens, Ga., 1980.

———. "The Women of the South." *Southern Historical Society Papers,* XVIII (1890), 277–81.

Helper, Hinton Rowan. *The Impending Crisis of the South.* Edited by George M. Frederickson. 1857; rpr. Cambridge, Mass., 1968.

Hentz, Caroline Lee. *Eoline; or, Magnolia Vale.* 1852; rpr. Freeport, N.Y., 1971.

———. *Linda; or, The Young Pilot of the Belle Creole.* 1850; rpr. Philadelphia, 1889.

———. *Marcus Warland; or, The Long Moss Spring.* 1852; rpr. Philadelphia, 1854.

———. *The Planter's Northern Bride.* 1854; rpr. Chapel Hill, 1970.

Hundley, Daniel R. *Social Relations in Our Southern States.* New York, 1860.

Ingraham, Joseph Holt. *The Quadroone; or, St. Michael's Day.* 2 vols. New York, 1841.

———. *The Southwest, by a Yankee.* 2 vols. 1835; rpr. New York, 1968.

———. *The Sunny South; or, The Southerner at Home.* Philadelphia, 1860.

Jameson, Frederic. *The Political Unconscious: Narrative as a Socially Symbolic Act.* Ithaca, 1981.

Jimerson, Randall C. *The Private Civil War: Popular Thought During the Sectional Conflict.* Baton Rouge, 1988.

Johnson, Bradley T. "Monument to the Confederate Dead at Fredericksburg." *Southern Historical Society Papers,* XVIII (1890), 397–406.

Jones, Anne Goodwyn. *Tomorrow Is Another Day: The Woman Writer in the South, 1859–1936.* Baton Rouge, 1981.

Jones, Thomas G. "To the Confederacy's Soldiers and Sailors." *Southern Historical Society Papers,* XXVI (1898), 186–209.

Kirkland, Joseph. *The Captain of Company K.* 1891; rpr. Ridgewood, N.J., 1968.

Kreyling, Michael. *Figures of the Hero in Southern Narrative.* Baton Rouge, 1987.

Lanier, Sidney. *"Tiger-Lilies" and Southern Prose.* Edited by Garland Greever and Cecil Abernathy. Baltimore, 1945. Vol. V of Charles R. Anderson, ed., *Centennial Edition of the Works of Sidney Lanier.* 10 vols.

Lewis, Henry Clay. *Odd Leaves from the Life of a Louisiana Swamp Doctor.* 1843; rpr. Upper Saddle River, N.J., 1969.

Light, James F. *John William De Forest.* New York, 1965.

Longstreet, Augustus Baldwin. *Georgia Scenes: Characters, Incidents, etc., in the First Half-Century of the Republic.* 1835; rpr. New York, 1897.

———. *Stories with a Moral, Humorous and Descriptive of Southern Life a Century Ago.* Edited by Fitz R. Longstreet. Philadelphia, 1912.

Lynn, Kenneth S. *Mark Twain and Southwestern Humor.* Boston, 1959.

McCardell, John. *The Idea of a Southern Nation: Southern Nationalists and Southern Nationalism, 1830–1860.* New York, 1979.

McIntosh, Maria J. "The South." *Home Circle,* I (1855), 537–39.

McNeilly, J. H. "By Graves of Confederate Dead." *Confederate Veteran,* II (1894), 264–66.

McPherson, James M. *Ordeal by Fire: The Civil War and Reconstruction.* New York, 1982.

Maffit, J. N. "The Almighty Dollar." *Southern Lady's Companion,* VI (June, 1852), 71–80.

Meek, Alexander Beaufort. *Romantic Passages in Southwestern History.* 2d ed. New York, 1857.

Mixon, Wayne. *Southern Writers and the New South Movement, 1865–1913.* Chapel Hill, 1980.

"Monuments at Fort Mill, S.C." *Confederate Veteran,* VII (1899), 209–11.

Neely, Mark E., Harold Holzer, and Gabor S. Boritt. *The Confederate Image: Prints of the Lost Cause.* Chapel Hill, 1987.

"New Orleans, Her Commerce and Her Duties." *De Bow's Review,* III (January, 1847), 39–48.

Nicholson, Meredith. *The Cavalier of Tennessee.* Indianapolis, 1928.

Oakes, James. *Slavery and Freedom: An Interpretation of the Old South.* New York, 1990.

Olmsted, Frederick Law. *The Cotton Kingdom: A Traveller's Observations on Cotton and Slavery in the American Slave States.* 1861; rpr. New York, 1953.

Osterweis, Rollin G. *The Myth of the Lost Cause, 1865–1900.* Hamden, Conn., 1973.

———. *Romanticism and Nationalism in the Old South.* New Haven, 1949.

Page, Thomas Nelson. *The Old South: Essays Social and Political.* New York, 1892.

Pessen, Edward. "How Different from Each Other Were the Antebellum North and South?" *American Historical Review,* LXXXV (1980), 1119–49.

Phillips, Ulrich Bonnell. *Life and Labor in the Old South.* Boston, 1929.

Pike, Albert. *Lyrics and Love Songs.* Little Rock, Ark., 1916.

———. *Prose Sketches and Poems Written in the Western Country.* Edited by David J. Weber. 1834; rpr. Albuquerque, 1967.

Pollard, Edward A. *The Lost Cause: A New Southern History of the War of the Confederates.* New York, 1866.

Poovey, Mary. *The Proper Lady and the Woman Writer.* Chicago, 1984.

Potter, David M. *The Impending Crisis, 1848–1861.* Edited by Don E. Fehrenbacher, New York, 1976.

"Progress of the Great West in Population, Agriculture, Arts and Commerce." *De Bow's Review,* IV (September, 1847), 31–85.

Remini, Robert V. *Andrew Jackson and the Course of American Democracy, 1833–1845.* New York, 1984.

———. *Andrew Jackson and the Course of American Empire, 1767–1821.* New York, 1977.

———. *Andrew Jackson and the Course of American Freedom, 1822–1832.* New York, 1981.

Richardson, Thomas J. "Honoré Grandissime's Southern Dilemma: Introduction." In *The Grandissimes: Centennial Essays,* edited by Richardson. Jackson, Miss., 1981.

Rickels, Milton. *George Washington Harris.* New York, 1965.

Robertson, James I., Jr. *Soldiers Blue and Gray.* Columbia, S.C., 1988.

Rowland, K. M., ed. *The Poems of Frank O. Ticknor.* Philadelphia, 1879.

Russell, William Howard. *My Diary North and South.* Edited by Fletcher Pratt. 1863; rpr. New York, 1954.

———. *Pictures of Southern Life, Social, Political, and Military.* New York, 1861.

Said, Edward. *Orientalism.* New York, 1978.

Scott, Anne Firor. *The Southern Lady: From Pedestal to Politics, 1830–1930.* Chicago, 1970.

Skaggs, Merrill Maguire. *The Folk of Southern Fiction.* Athens, Ga., 1972.

Smedes, Susan Dabney. *Memorials of a Southern Planter.* Edited by Fletcher M. Green. 1887; rpr. New York, 1965.

Smith, Henry Nash. *Virgin Land: The American West as Symbol and Myth.* 1950; rpr. Cambridge, Mass., 1982.

Smith, Stephen A. *Myth, Media, and the Southern Mind.* Fayetteville, Ark., 1985.

Stewart, Randall. "Tidewater and Frontier." In *The Frontier Humorists: Critical Views,* edited by M. Thomas Inge. Hamden, Conn., 1975.

Stirling, James. *Letters from the Slave States.* 1857; rpr. New York, 1969.

Sydnor, Charles S. *The Development of Southern Sectionalism, 1819–1848.* Baton Rouge, 1948. Vol. V of Wendell Holmes Stephenson and E. Merton Coulter, eds., *A History of the South.* 10 vols.

Tate, Allen. "A Southern Mode of the Imagination." In Tate, *Collected Essays.* Denver, 1959.

Taylor, Robert Love. *Lectures and Best Literary Productions of Bob Taylor.* Nashville, 1912.

Taylor, William R. *Cavalier and Yankee: The Old South and American National Character.* New York, 1961.

Thorpe, Thomas Bangs. *The Master's House: A Tale of Southern Life.* New York, 1854.

Tindall, George Brown. "Southern Mythology." In *The South and the Sectional Image: The Sectional Theme Since Reconstruction,* edited by Dewey W. Grantham. New York, 1962.

Tucker, Nathaniel Beverley. *The Partisan Leader: A Tale of the Future.* 1836; rpr. Chapel Hill, 1971.

Turley, Thomas B. "Confederate Monument, Shelbyville, Tenn." *Confederate Veteran,* VII (1899), 496–99.

Van Buren, A. De Puy. *Jottings of a Year's Sojourn in the South.* Battle Creek, Mich., 1859.

Walthall, Edward C. "The Confederate Dead of Mississippi." *Southern Historical Society Papers,* XVIII (1890), 298–312.

Ward, John William. *Andrew Jackson: Symbol for an Age.* New York, 1955.

Watson, Ritchie D., Jr. "Caroline Lee Hentz." In *Southern Writers: A Biographical Dictionary.* Edited by Robert Bain, Joseph M. Flora, and Louis D. Rubin, Jr. Baton Rouge, 1979.

———. *The Cavalier in Virginia Fiction.* Baton Rouge, 1985.

Weaver, Gordon, ed. *Selected Poems of Father Ryan.* Jackson, Miss., 1973.

Wecter, Dixon. *The Hero in America: A Chronicle of Hero Worship.* New York, 1941.

"Western Scenery—The Legend of Indian Creek." *Southwestern Monthly,* I (1852), 193–98.

Wharton, G. M. "Women's Rights." *Southwestern Monthly,* I (1852), 146–49.

Wigfall, Louis T. "Senate Speech." *Congressional Globe.* 36th Cong., 1st Sess., 1303–1304.

Wilson, Edmund. *Patriotic Gore: Studies in the Literature of the American Civil War.* New York, 1962.

Woodward, C. Vann. *The Burden of Southern History.* Rev. ed. Baton Rouge, 1968.

———. *Origins of the New South, 1877–1913.* Baton Rouge, 1951. Vol. IX of Wendell Holmes Stephenson and E. Merton Coulter, eds., *A History of the South.* 10 vols.

Wyatt-Brown, Bertram. *Southern Honor: Ethics and Behavior in the Old South.* New York, 1982.

———. *Yankee Saints and Southern Sinners.* Baton Rouge, 1985.

Young, Stark. *So Red the Rose.* New York, 1934.

Index